DEATH
IN
ST. GEORGE'S

DEATH
IN
ST. GEORGE'S

An Intrepid Traveler Mystery

M. A. MONNIN

LeVel
BEST BOOKS

First published by Level Best Books 2024

Copyright © 2024 by M. A. Monnin

M. A. Monnin asserts the moral right to be identified as the author of this work.

Author Photo Credit: Robert Monnin

First edition

ISBN: 978-1-68512-648-3

Cover art by Level Best Designs

This book was professionally typeset on Reedsy.
Find out more at reedsy.com

To Joy, with love

Praise for Death in St. George's

"Murder, romance, a splendid setting, engaging characters, buried treasure... M.A. Monnin's latest mystery has them all, and may just be her best and most engrossing novel yet."—Tom Mead, author of *Death and the Conjuror* and *The Murder Wheel*

"What a treat! Memorable characters, a subtropical setting, and intricate plotting. A binge-worthy read!"—Joan Long, Agatha Award-nominated author of *The Finalist*

"A charming mystery with twists I didn't see coming, Death in St. George's is a treasure in itself."—Jules Parker, Wild Rose Press author

"A contemporary cozy with the timeless charm of a classic whodunnit, *Death in St. George's* feels like a refreshing rum swizzle on a warm Bermuda evening. Archaeology and mystery buffs alike will root for Stephanie and Thomas as they unravel two intertwined mysteries—one archaeological, one modern."—Megaera Lorenz, author of *The Shabti*

"*Death in St. George's*, the third in M. A. Monnin's Intrepid Traveler Mystery series, will treat readers to the sensory pleasures of the subtropics while dipping their toes in danger. Monnin's writing is as crisp and sensual as fresh ironed linen. Readers are in for a delight and will hop on board wherever Stefanie travels.—Sara E. Johnson, author of the Alexa Glock Forensics Mysteries

Chapter One

"I don't believe you're the kind of woman who craves peace and quiet," Thomas said, holding Stefanie's hand in the back seat of the taxi.

His handsome face melted her heart yet again. She drank in the welcome sight of him, from the strong jaw beneath the stubble of a beard to his chestnut brown hair. The sun-bleached streaks she'd teased him about in Greece would return after a week in Bermuda, she'd bet.

Having arrived in Bermuda earlier in the day, she'd met him at the airport, and they were on the way to rent a car in the Town of St. George.

"A week alone sounds blissful to me," she countered. "No trying to discover who ran us off the road in Crete or chasing after Borgia Peacocks in Venice." And no former girlfriends, she thought. But she'd learned enough to not say that aloud. "No calls from René."

"René knows that I am not taking his calls for a full week," Thomas said.

René Renault, his boss, and therefore ultimately hers at Interpol's Cultural Heritage division, didn't willingly recognize personal time. Thomas, as the head of Interpol's Artifact Retrieval Team—ART for short—could dictate his own projects. So far their time together had been a non-stop whirlwind of undercover investigation in an effort to reclaim stolen objects that had been reported to Interpol. A little downtime was in order.

"We could lock our cell phones in our suitcases until next Monday," she suggested.

He smiled. "Is that really what you want?"

What she really wanted was to decide on their future living situation. There was no question that they would be together. But would she move in

1

with him at his place in Munich? Or keep her apartment in St. Louis and fly to Europe when she couldn't bear to be apart from him any longer? Asking so soon might go to his head, and she couldn't have that.

The taxi driver took a sharp curve a little too fast, then swung in to avoid a red scooter speeding from the opposite direction whose driver drove as though both lanes were his.

Stefanie shared a smile with Thomas as they listed from one side to the other with the motion of the taxi.

"I suppose we need the phones to look up places to explore," she said. "And I need photos for my travel blog."

That reminded her to take in the sights, something other than Thomas. She tore her gaze away from him, but kept her hand in his. The streets of St. George's were narrow, barely wide enough for two lanes, and in some places, not even wide enough for that. Low garden walls butted right up against the road. Sidewalks, where they existed at all, fit snugly between the road and the series of one- and two-storied houses.

Most of the houses were small and compact, as if hunkered down for impending storms.

"These buildings have been here since the 1690s or early 1700s," she said, charmed by their low profiles and the wooden shutters that adorned nearly every structure.

In no time at all, the taxi driver pulled up to the car rental.

As he paid the driver, Thomas's face blanked in disbelief at the tiny electric cars lined up for rent.

"The bigger cars must be in back," he said, taking his black leather bag, his only piece of luggage, out of the open Ford trunk.

The taxi driver grinned. "Not in Bermuda. It's the law. Tourists can only rent scooters or electric cars." Still grinning, he gave Thomas a business card. "Call me if you want me to take you anywhere."

When Thomas's gaze brightened on the row of scooters, Stefanie protested.

"No scooters," she insisted. "I've seen how people drive here. Driving on the left will be challenging enough."

"No problem," Thomas said. "I've driven in England."

He bypassed the Twizy models, which had a single seat in front and a single seat in back.

"I want you at my side," he said. "Not behind me."

"Or you behind me," she countered.

His mouth quirked up. "That would not happen."

Oh, how she missed the little games they played. It had only been a week since they'd parted at the Milan airport, but those seven days felt like a year.

After inspecting several small, square Italian Tazzaris, which had two front seats, Thomas grudgingly chose one in red.

"I didn't think I'd be driving a toy car," he said as they folded themselves into the Tazzari.

She laughed. "Admit it, you've always wanted a red Italian car." She buckled her seatbelt with difficulty due to his leather duffle on her lap, which was too large to cram into the minuscule storage space behind their seats.

Resting her arms across the duffle, she entered their address into the GPS on her phone. "We're lucky Greg wasn't using his house this week. A whole house to ourselves is so much nicer than even the best hotel."

Her former bank client, Greg Edwards, had often urged her to stay at the house whenever she wanted. Greg, the dedicated owner of Riverboat Rum based in St. Louis, only made it to Bermuda occasionally. Usually when corporate finances and Bermudian law dictated. The bungalow stood on a cliff on the outskirts of the historic Town of St. George. Painted peach, the two-bedroom cottage had an intimate covered patio at the rear that faced the glassy Atlantic—a perfect place to write her travel blog and enjoy the sun.

Thomas's claim about driving on the left was justified. He had no problem acclimating, and in short order, they'd gone the less than a mile to Greg's house.

After changing into swimsuits to lounge in the warm Bermuda sunshine, Thomas poured them each a glass of pinot grigio, and they settled onto the chaise lounges in the backyard.

The smoky scent of a neighbor's wood fire mixed pleasantly with the tang of sea air. Stefanie glanced around the yard and patio for a fire pit they could use but didn't see one.

"Bermuda is more colorful than I expected." Thomas's gaze went from the low wall painted to match the peach house color to the neighboring bright blue cottage beyond, with its white stepped stone roof. He shifted his gaze from the neighbor's house to her. "The view is stunning."

She smiled and set her wine on the small metal table between them.

"Just you and me," Thomas said. "Alone."

"Alone," she agreed. "With our peace and quiet. But you never know," she teased, "maybe it was the adventure that drew us together."

Swinging his legs off the chaise lounge, he sat up with his feet planted firmly in the grass and took her hand. "Is that all?"

No, but Thomas found the excitement of the chase irresistible. She smiled as he massaged her palm with his thumb, but didn't move closer to make it easier for him. Keeping him on his toes was delightfully entertaining, something that he enjoyed as much as she did.

"Where should we go tomorrow? A boat tour to spot sea turtles?" she asked.

Still holding her hand, he said, "Let's go snorkeling. Tobacco Bay. The fish and coral there are supposed to be worth seeing."

"I've never been snorkeling," she admitted. "I planned to try it in Crete, but there wasn't time. Have you?"

"At the Great Barrier Reef."

Australia. That didn't surprise her. As the son of the owner of Germany's largest publishing firm, he'd probably gone all over the world and done all kinds of activities that she'd never tried. Never tried because she'd dedicated all her time to working at Markham-Briggs Bank. That wasn't happening anymore.

"There's nothing to it," Thomas said. "You'll love it. And after we've done Tobacco Bay, we'll snorkel above shipwrecks. Bermuda is surrounded by them. Until then," he said, "I want you all to myself."

She gave in and swung around to a sitting position facing him. Bending forward, she lifted her lips toward his, stopping a breath away. "You have

4

me."

A discreet throat-clearing intruded on their moment. It came from the direction of the blue house next door. Reluctantly, Stefanie pulled back.

On the other side of the peach-colored wall, a thin man of about five foot eight or nine, tanned and with receding blond hair, peered at them from between two large palm trees. He'd changed from the sweat-stained blue polo and dusty dark grey knee-length shorts he'd worn when she'd met him two hours before and was dressed as colorfully as the houses in a pastel plaid shirt above coral Bermuda shorts.

Stefanie hid her disappointment. "It's Jeffrey Fitzsimmons," she said in a low voice. "I picked up the keys from him when I got here this afternoon."

She scooted further back on the chaise lounge and slipped her arms through her linen cover-up. Chatting with neighbors while dressed only in a skimpy bikini put her at a disadvantage.

"Good afternoon," Jeffrey called to them. "Sorry, don't mean to interrupt."

Thomas observed him without replying.

"Good afternoon," Stefanie called back as she stood up. Greg had cautioned her about always including a polite greeting when she visited Bermuda. "The locals are sticklers about common courtesy," she told Thomas. "We'll be outcasts if we forget that."

"Always the customer service vice president," he remarked.

"If I'd gotten that promotion," she said, "we never would have met."

He leaned in and kissed her. "A tragedy averted."

She smiled, then glanced at the neighbor. "Jeffrey's the kind who likes to talk. I had to make excuses so I could meet you at the airport in time. Luckily, the taxi was waiting." She gave Thomas's bicep a gentle squeeze. "We don't want to get on his bad side. We might want to use this house as a getaway again."

"Neutral territory?" he asked. "Conveniently located between the U.S. and Europe?"

"Something like that," she said, then turned back to Jeffrey.

The neighbor indicated the wall that separated the properties. "May I?"

"Yes, of course," Stefanie answered.

Jeffrey stepped over the wall. He'd come prepared, bringing his own bottle of beer.

There were only two chaise lounges, but two metal chairs at a small table against the house were available. Stefanie gestured toward them.

She and Thomas dragged their lounges around to face the patio rather than the ocean.

"Welcome to Bermuda," Jeffrey said to Thomas.

Thomas must have worried that the neighbor was settling in for an evening of conversation.

"Thank you," he replied. "We'll be trying your local cuisine at dinner soon."

"Here on St. George's Island? I can recommend places," Jeffrey offered as he pulled out a pink metal chair. "The Wahoo Bistro has fantastic fish."

"Hamilton," Thomas said, mentioning Bermuda's capital city on the main island.

Jeffrey nodded. "More nightlife there."

Thomas pointed a finger at Stefanie's empty wine glass. "Another?"

"Yes, please." She turned back to the neighbor. "Do you live here year-round, or part-time, like Greg?"

"Year round," Jeffrey said. "I'm with the National Museum of Bermuda. The lead archaeologist."

"Are you?" She perked up. "Thomas has a degree in archaeology, and I once interned at a dig on Crete. I didn't go into archaeology as a career, though."

"Oh, I know you're in banking," Jeffrey said. "Greg's told me all about you."

Thomas caught that last piece of info as he returned with the half-empty bottle of pinot grigio.

"Has he?" Thomas asked, filling Stefanie's glass.

She was surprised at that news, too, but didn't clarify that she wasn't in banking anymore. Her work with ART was confidential.

"Yes." Jeffrey turned back to Stefanie. "Greg told me about your involvement with the Akrotiri Snake Goddess in Greece."

Stefanie and Thomas exchanged glances. She hadn't mentioned her part in it to any of her former colleagues at Markham-Briggs. In fact, other than those directly involved, she hadn't even talked to anyone about the theft of the Akrotiri Snake Goddess. That had been left to the news media and whatever details the Greek police gave out. Thomas never boasted about his accomplishments. It was counterproductive to future cases.

"Jeffrey's an archaeologist here in Bermuda," she told Thomas.

The neighbor leaned forward, beer bottle in hand, elbows on knobby knees. "I'm hoping you can help me."

So he'd had something specific in mind when she brushed him off to get to the airport.

With that news, Thomas seemed even less receptive to the intrusion. He concentrated on pouring wine into his own glass. "Yes?"

Jeffrey gave him a brief smile but focused on Stefanie. "It's your help I want."

Stefanie and Thomas exchanged another look, one of surprise that time and amusement. Thomas had put in the major investigative work in their endeavors. She'd simply used the customer service skills she'd learned at Markham-Briggs Bank to her advantage. Yet Jeffrey approached them because of her reputation, rather than Thomas's stellar career. One point to her.

His eyes bright with humor, Thomas lowered himself onto the chaise lounge. Sipping his wine, he let her have the spotlight.

"My help?" Stefanie asked. "I'm not in banking anymore."

"Greg says you're known for your discretion." Jeffrey leaned even further towards them, sitting on the edge of his seat. "And from your time at the bank, that you have an eye for potential trouble."

You never knew what people would remember. She'd entertained Greg once with a description of what she noted about each person when they entered the bank, watching for signs of potential robbery.

Thomas's grey-blue eyes sharpened.

"Something has disappeared from the site I'm working on." Jeffrey spoke in hushed tones despite the fact that they were in the backyard, with the Atlantic on one side and empty yards on the others. "The theft hasn't been reported yet, and we—*I*," he emphasized, "hope it can be recovered before anyone has to know that it's missing."

She peered at Jeffrey. He'd gotten awfully close to their actual jobs. Disconcertingly close. "I'm not sure how discretion and an eye for potential trouble will help after the fact," she said.

Thomas was leery, too. "Why didn't you report the theft?"

"The homeowners didn't want the publicity if it could be avoided. I went along with that to protect our reputations." Jeffrey's gaze darted between Stefanie and Thomas. "If we don't get it back, our professional reputations are shot. Each one of us working the site."

"What kind of site?" Thomas asked.

"It's on privately owned land. There's a garden renovation going on at Carmichael House here on St. George's," Jefferey said. "The owner, Marlene Carmichael, our Minister of Economy and Labor, wants to make it a showplace. When a dead tree in the existing garden was removed, a small chest was exposed under the roots. That prompted a call for an archaeological assessment of the area to see if anything else was buried in the vicinity."

"A chest?" Stefanie asked, giddy as a child with an unwrapped present as she pictured a metal-strapped wooden treasure chest filled with gold and jewels.

Jeffrey held his hands about ten inches apart. "A small one. Brass and steel."

She cocked her head. "What was in it?"

A short laugh escaped Jeffrey's lips. "Nothing."

Thomas raised his eyebrows at that. "Any idea how it ended up here?"

Jeffrey sat back. "Most likely a Spanish shipwreck in the mid to late 1500s. Spanish and Portuguese sailors occasionally washed up on Bermuda before the *Sea Venture* wrecked in 1609 and we British settled here. We believe the ship this chest came from was on its way from Cartagena to Spain."

An exciting find. But the chest was empty. That was disappointing. And now it was missing. Having a reputation for discretion was nice, but the investigation should be carried out by the authorities, not two vacationers with few resources.

"I'm a travel blogger now, and Thomas is an assistant professor of archaeology," she said, using their completely legitimate cover occupations. "What you're describing sounds like a job for the police."

Thomas agreed.

Jeffrey's brows drew together, disappointment written in every line of his features. "We can't have another Tucker's Cross. We can't."

A spark of excitement flickered deep within Stefanie's chest. She'd read the story of Tucker's Cross in the guidebook she'd brought on the flight from the States.

"The emerald and gold cross that was recovered from the *San Pedro*," she said. "Replaced with a forgery, which was discovered just in time for Queen Elizabeth's visit in 1975."

Thomas set his wine glass on the table. "Stolen."

"When the archaeological record gets lost, the whole island loses. It can't happen again," Jeffrey said, his voice rising in desperation. "It can't."

Surely that emotion on his face wasn't for a small brass chest, even one that was 450 years old.

Thomas's eyes narrowed. "It isn't the chest that's missing, is it?"

Chapter Two

"You're right," Jeffrey said. "It isn't the chest that is missing." Taking out his cell phone, he brought up a photo and held out the screen for Stefanie and Thomas to see.

Pictured was a delicate gold bracelet. Each filigreed link held a finely cut deep green emerald.

Stefanie drew in a breath. "It's beautiful."

A little smile played on Thomas's lips. "There is the buried treasure."

"From the Spanish treasure fleets." Jeffrey turned his phone to better gaze at the photo himself. "Old mine emeralds. Harder and less brittle than those that have been mined since. Look at that color." He expanded the photo and again held it out for them to admire.

The photo was taken when the bracelet had been found. Even newly exposed in the soil, the gold gleamed brightly and she could see the saturated green of the emeralds.

"The gold work also looks exceptional," Thomas said, studying the photo. "Where was the bracelet found in relation to the chest?"

"Buried about a foot beneath it." Jeffrey took a swig of beer, letting that sink in.

"The box marked the spot," Thomas said, his eyes bright.

"A decoy," Jeffrey said.

"So maybe more than one sailor was shipwrecked," Stefanie speculated.

Jeffrey shrugged. "There's a story there, for certain. At least one person made it ashore. That's all we know for certain at this point."

"And now the bracelet is missing," Thomas said.

10

"Let me start at the beginning," Jeffrey said. "The back of the property at Carmichael House had gotten fairly wild, overgrown with plants and trees, and one of the oldest trees had died. Mrs. Carmichael—Marlene—wanted to renovate the garden, so she brought in a garden designer. Yesterday, Nathaniel Dimon, the landscape designer, was having the cedar tree removed when his men came across the chest, exposed in the ground when the dead tree was pulled out."

Stefanie pictured the scenario in her head. "If the Spaniard buried the chest at the base of a tree and never came back for it, the tree roots would have grown around it over the centuries."

"Explaining why it wasn't found until now," Thomas said.

"Maybe not the original tree," Jeffrey said, "but yes, that's our working theory. When the chest was found, work in the garden stopped immediately, and I was called in to conduct an archaeological assessment to see if it was likely that anything else would be found nearby. Of course I deemed further excavation necessary." He finished his beer. "After I recorded the location of the chest and removed it, I called on Dr. Ingram from the University of Virginia to help with the assessment. He was finishing up a field school project near the Dockyard and could spare the time, so he brought in his two remaining students, and we started the excavation this morning."

"Anything else found with the bracelet?" Thomas asked.

"Twelve gold coins," Jeffrey said. "Spanish, from the time of Philip II. Stamped with his name, but no date, so anywhere from 1556 to 1598. And five copper studs of a kind that possibly decorated a leather pouch, one that would have held the bracelet and coins. The leather itself hasn't survived."

"So not earlier than 1556, but the castaway could have landed later," Stefanie mused.

Thomas frowned. "You found the bracelet, then it disappeared."

"When did the bracelet go missing?" Stefanie asked, bringing her mind back to the present problem.

Jeffrey filled his lungs with air, then as he slowly let the breath out, his shoulders slumped.

"We found the bracelet and the coins mid-morning in our initial excavation square. Beryl, my assistant, and I were there along with Dr. Ingram and his two students. We called the Carmichaels out to see what we'd found. They were as excited as we were, though to be honest, I think Marlene didn't like the idea of a longer dig delaying her garden project. She's a trustee of the museum, so she knows that an archaeological assessment can either go quickly or expand."

"I photographed everything in situ with my camera," Jeffrey continued. "We all took photos with our cell phones. Hunter, one of the students, did a quick sketch. Then Beryl and I took everything up to the worktable in the buttery to examine them more closely."

"The buttery?" Stefanie asked.

"A small stone building, like a shed," Jeffrey explained. "Originally used for cold storage before electricity. There are quite a few left in Bermuda. The Carmichaels use theirs as a potting shed. It has a small table and some shelves inside."

"Go on," Thomas said.

"After initially cleaning them in the kitchen, we laid all the artifacts out on the buttery table for processing," Jeffrey said. "The bracelet, the gold coins, and the copper studs." His voice trailed off.

"And?" Thomas prompted.

"The buttery is small, not room enough for everyone in there at once. I left the artifacts there so we could all examine them as we wished. So everyone had a chance to photograph and sketch them if they wanted to. We were all excited. And of course we wanted to know if there was anything else to be found." His commiserating smile embraced them both. "Having experience with archaeology, you both know what that feels like."

She did know what it felt like. The rush of excitement, the anticipation. Not that she'd ever found anything except ancient Greek pot sherds. But they were valuable, too. Her sherds helped date the site that she'd found them on.

Thomas nodded as well, looking more wary than excited.

"The Carmichaels went back inside the house," Jeffrey went on. "We returned to work, eager to find anything else that remained, and started a second square to expand our investigation. At different times throughout the morning, each of us went into the shed for another look. That bracelet was like a magnet, drawing us in." He clamped his jaws tightly, then said, "By lunchtime, it was missing. After Hunter ate lunch, he went into the buttery to sketch and discovered that the bracelet was gone."

"The Carmichaels," Stefanie said. It would be logical they'd want to ooh and ah over the treasure buried in their own backyard.

"That was my immediate assumption," Jeffrey said. "That they'd taken it and put it in their safe. They own it, after all."

"The Town of St. George is a UNESCO Heritage site," Thomas said. "Wouldn't the artifacts belong to the museum?"

"Carmichael House is outside that boundary," Jeffrey explained. "The bracelet legally belongs to them. But both Marlene and Lawrence denied taking the bracelet inside for safekeeping. In fact, Lawrence had taken two of the coins into the house. The other ten were still on the table in the buttery, along with the copper studs. Only the emerald bracelet was taken."

"Anyone else enter the property?" Thomas asked. "While you were searching diligently for more artifacts?"

Jeffrey's countenance took on a sickly grey hue at the implied criticism. "The driveway is gated and kept locked, and the yard fenced. Not like these walls." He indicated the three-foot-high wall which surrounded the yard. "The Carmichaels' property has five-foot iron railings embedded in their stone wall. With the gate locked, there wasn't any reason to think anyone could come onto the property without being let in."

"What about security or cameras?" Stefanie asked.

Shaking his head, Jeffrey said, "No security cameras. With the gated property, they didn't feel any need. I searched the men, my assistant Beryl searched the women, Lawrence searched me, and Marlene searched Beryl. Lawrence searched our vehicles and bags. I privately asked to see in the Carmichael's safe, desk, and Marlene's purse. They were not only willing, but insistent that I do. Beryl helped me. The bracelet wasn't in their vehicle, either."

"The bracelet has been stolen, and you haven't called the police," Thomas said. "I see your dilemma. I don't see what you expect of us."

"It has to be a case of momentary madness. It has to," Jeffrey said. "I believe the bracelet will be returned. I've given everyone until tomorrow morning to return it, no questions asked. The Carmichaels agreed to that."

"Then why do you need us?" Stefanie asked.

Thomas tilted his head, studying the archaeologist.

Jeffrey appealed to them both. "Whoever stole the bracelet may get cold feet if they think they might be caught. I need another set of eyes. Someone I know isn't involved. If the bracelet isn't returned in the morning, what I want is your ability to suss out who is acting suspiciously, who looks guilty. Like you did at the bank. Looking for the troublemaker. And," he added, "I'm asking for your discretion."

A police inquiry would be followed by the media. With Marlene Carmichael being a government minister, Stefanie could understand the Carmichaels wanting to keep the theft as quiet as possible. That taint of suspicion wouldn't only fall on the archaeologists.

Thomas lifted his chin. "What makes you think the thief will give the bracelet back? It's gold, with high quality emeralds, historic. Valuable for many reasons."

"Our professional reputations are on the line," Jeffrey said. "Mine, Beryl's, Ingram's. We'll all end our careers under a cloud of suspicion. A stain on our reputations that will follow us for the rest of our lives. For Daphne and Hunter, the students, their careers will end before they begin. And if the thief doesn't see that, the rest of us need to be cleared."

Stefanie stared into her wine glass. She knew firsthand that what Jeffrey said was true. Artifact theft was all too common. Her own father had changed careers because of it. Thomas knew how that had affected her from their time in Crete.

And even though Jeffrey didn't realize it, he was asking them to help in an area that they were particularly qualified for. She glanced at Thomas. She didn't have to ask how he felt about a busman's holiday.

14

Chapter Three

Thomas raked his fingers through his hair. "Surely you reported the theft to your museum," he said to Jeffrey. "What did your director say?"

"I'm the museum rep at the site," Jeffrey told him. "Beryl is my assistant. The Carmichaels didn't want it reported, so we haven't said anything about the theft to our director. For now. Only the Carmichaels and the five of us working the dig site know it was stolen." He picked up his empty beer bottle. "If the bracelet isn't returned, and we don't find out who has it, none of us will be trusted with any job of magnitude again." Studying Thomas, he said, "As an archaeologist, I know you understand that."

Stefanie could see Thomas's mind working beyond his impassive gaze. He was running through all the possibilities, given the little they knew. She was doing the same thing herself.

"I know this would take away from your vacation," Jeffrey said. "I don't expect you to take it on for free. I'll hire you."

Thomas immediately shook his head. "No."

"Wait," she said. A little more experience investigating could only help her future with ART.

"Stefanie." Thomas's eyes darkened when he looked at her.

"I know it's a lot to ask, since you're on holiday," Jeffrey said. "Maybe I should have reported the theft to the Director earlier today. But reputations, once you've been suspected of theft in archaeology—" he shook his head. "Taking an extra day to report it is worth it to clear the innocent. Marlene and Lawrence will be able to weather any comments and suspicion. The members of my team won't."

Both Thomas and Stefanie nodded. Maybe they'd have made the same decision in his place, if there was reason to believe the bracelet would be returned.

Jeffrey stood up. "Please, talk it over before you make a decision. I can really use your help."

He wandered across the grass to the wall and stared out at the Atlantic, where the sunset slowly changed the sky from brilliant orange and gold to deep sapphire.

Thomas waited until Jeffrey was out of earshot. "We can't take money from him. For one thing, neither one of us is licensed to investigate in Bermuda."

Solving a theft when they weren't familiar with the situation or the people involved wasn't going to be easy, and there was no telling what René's reaction would be. It might even involve miles of red tape.

"No, I agree, he shouldn't pay us. But," she said, "I know what he's going through, and I could use the additional investigative experience." She never would lose that urge to plan seven steps ahead. As a member of Thomas's Artifact Retrieval Team, she had René's requirements to think of. The head of Interpol's Cultural Heritage Division hadn't totally accepted her, despite the success she'd had with Thomas on ART's last two cases.

"Just think," she said, "this is a way for us to develop a reputation for this kind of work, which will help with our covers in the future. We'll have investigative experience that we can actually admit to, to any of ART's targets, without worrying that they'll look more deeply past your college professorship and my travel blogging."

Thomas's stubborn expression didn't change. "We don't know the people. Including him." Thomas sent Jeffrey a disparaging look. "Leaving the artifacts in the shed was lax."

He was upset that his plans for a romantic week were being hijacked, but Thomas was just as intrigued as she was.

"Wouldn't you love the chance to see that bracelet?" she asked. "And anything else they might find?"

"We can fly back to Bermuda next year and see them," he countered.

Jeffrey turned away from the ocean view and walked back toward them. She only had a few moments to convince Thomas they could help and enjoy themselves, too.

She ran her palm up his arm. "I saw your eyes light up. You'll be thinking of those green emeralds while we're snorkeling."

The corner of his mouth lifted in a little smile. "Your eyes are emerald enough for me."

Flatterer. Her eyes were nowhere near that dark and dramatic. "It would be a shame if good archaeologists lost their careers when we could have helped."

She knew she'd scored a victory when he took in a deep breath.

"One day," he agreed. "We give it one day, and then we are back on vacation, whether the bracelet turns up or not."

She smiled. "Just one day," she promised. "Maybe we'll get lucky, and the bracelet will miraculously show up in the morning," she said. "We could be snorkeling by lunchtime."

"That is too much to ask."

Having made his way back to the patio, Jeffrey stopped at the edge of the concrete. "What do you say? Will you help?"

"We can give you tomorrow," Stefanie said. "As volunteers."

"Excellent." Jeffrey beamed at them, the first sign of hope on his face she'd seen.

Thomas subjected Jeffrey to his steady stare. "Twenty-four hours. That's all. You'll have to explain to the rest why we don't show up the day after."

"What happens tomorrow will dictate that," the archaeologist said.

"How do you suggest that we observe everyone?" Stefanie asked.

"I want to spend at least one more day on excavation," Jeffrey said. "I've never seen a dig that turned down an extra pair of hands. You both have experience. There's a tropical storm in the Caribbean, and I'll use that as my excuse for bringing you in. I'll say we have to get the dig finished before the storm comes in."

"The others won't like us being there, and neither will the homeowners after the theft," Thomas warned. "In fact, they'll be suspicious."

"And resentful," Jeffrey agreed. "The seven of us—the Carmichaels, Beryl and myself, and Ingram's team, have agreed to keep the theft quiet. I can't let them know that I've told you about the theft. Or the bracelet, for that matter." He watched them for their reactions.

Great. They were supposed to figure out who'd taken the bracelet without talking about it.

"Perhaps you should have mentioned that before we agreed to help," Thomas said.

"No problem," Stefanie said. "We'll help with the dig, keep an eye out for guilty behavior, and for the bracelet itself. I'll see if I can get one of them to bring up the bracelet."

Thomas searched Jeffrey's face. "You are aware that you might not like the outcome."

The archaeologist blew out a tired breath. "I'm aware."

"Who do you suspect?" Thomas asked.

Focusing on an azalea shrub next to the patio, Jeffrey said, "It had to be one of us. I hate to think it, but it had to be."

"Anyone you suspect more than the others?" Stefanie asked.

He shook his head. "That's why I need an objective view. I know these people. I've known Marlene and Lawrence for years. Both upstanding citizens. Marlene has always been in public service. Lawrence was a popular boat builder before he sold the business and retired. I work with Beryl. She's eager to get ahead, always puts the Museum first. I've known Ingram for the three years he's worked on his Dockyard project. The only unknowns are the two students, and I just don't think..." his voice trailed off.

Stefanie hoped the bracelet was returned. Being under a cloud of suspicion was no way to live.

"We'll keep a sharp eye out," she said. "Between the three of us, if the guilty person gives anything away, one of us should catch it."

And if they didn't, at least they would have tried.

"We start early," Jeffrey said. "The rest of the crew will be there at seven a.m. Let's leave at seven-thirty. Give them the opportunity to return the

18

bracelet before I get there."

With a pinched look on his face, he returned to his own yard.

Stefanie and Thomas picked up their wine glasses and went inside the house.

As she changed into a flowing calf-length dress more suitable for dinner out, Stefanie said, "We need to go shopping tonight. Nothing I brought to impress you is suitable for working a dig. And I need to find a new fedora after mine was crushed in Venice."

Thomas looked over her dress choice with approval. "Hunting down a Spanish bracelet isn't the way I pictured spending our time in Bermuda together."

She finished dressing and wrapped her arms around his waist. "Thank you."

He rubbed the tip of his nose against hers. "I told you a week of peace and quiet wasn't for you."

She laughed. "You do know me well."

"Even if you haven't accepted my proposal of marriage."

She smiled. His proposal had been thrown out so casually it deserved to be ignored.

Instead of responding to his comment, she said, "Jeffrey expects us to tell him who looks like the most likely culprit. I don't know how easy that will be. I'm better at spotting a criminal who is contemplating a crime than one who has successfully pulled one off."

"We'll have to do a little digging," Thomas acknowledged. He lifted her chin so she had to meet his gaze. "About that marriage proposal."

"What about it?"

His eyes sparkled at her sidestep. "I like a challenge. I'm up to it. Tomorrow we will go on a romantic moonlight cruise."

"Just the two of us?" she asked.

"You, me, and amorous glow worms in the dark," he said. "They put on a show after the full moon, and we are here at the perfect time."

She kissed him lightly, then grabbed her purse.

Who said an investigation had to interfere with romance?

Chapter Four

At seven-fifteen the next morning, wearing her sturdy new shorts and long-sleeved T-shirt to protect her arms from a long day in the sun, Stefanie tied on the running shoes that she'd brought with her.

"Jeffrey had a good point yesterday." She pulled the laces of the last shoe snug. "Maybe taking the bracelet *was* done in a moment of madness, one that the thief would give anything to take back. To have a chance to do over."

Maybe a night of feeling guilty was all the person needed, and the bracelet would be returned, as Jeffrey hoped.

"I don't have that faith in human nature." Thomas frowned after tapping into his cell phone.

"What's the matter?" she asked.

"The Glow Worm Cruises are fully booked."

"All of them?"

"Yes." He slipped the phone into the side pocket of his cargo shorts, then pressed the Velcroed flap closed. "They limit the cruises. To keep from disturbing Mother Nature too much."

"Tomorrow night, then," she said.

Thomas picked up their shiny new trowels and pristine leather gardening gloves. "The tours only run two nights a month. The glow worms stick to a strict schedule, only putting on their show for the two days after a full moon. Tonight is their last showing."

He looked so dismayed, Stefanie couldn't help but smile as she put on her sunglasses.

"It was a romantic thought," she said in consolation as they left the seclusion of the cottage.

They shared a wry smile at the sight of the square electric microcar in the driveway. Yet another blow to his plans for their romantic getaway.

"At least we didn't have to rent a Twizy," she said.

Folding themselves into the Tazzari seats, they buckled in and when Jeffrey left his driveway, they followed, headed for Carmichael House.

Stefanie tried to take in everything on the drive. Plastered square gateposts marked every driveway, whether attached to a surrounding wall or not. Though the posts were uniformly square and roughly about four feet high, finials allowed for individuality. Some were pyramidal, others conical, some flat or topped with a ball. A few were stepped like the unusual stone roofs on all of the houses she'd seen.

They left the built-up streets of low walls and pastel houses for the isolation of open grassy areas and random palm trees.

"We go straight through the Town of St. George," she said, looking out the window. "Carmichael House is on the other side of it."

The road narrowed as grassy verges gave way to walls enclosing the road on either side. On the left, angled striations in the living limestone showed upheavals from eons past, while on the right, the walls consisted of cut limestone block. Both were topped with luxuriant vegetation spilling over and softening the cold grey stone.

A horn blared as Thomas started to pull out at the next intersection. A Mini Cooper whizzed by inches from the Tazzari's front end, nearly grazing the wall. When traffic from both directions cleared, Thomas headed into the historic Town of St. George.

He darted a glance at her. "There's a good chance that if the bracelet is returned, it won't be to the table where it was taken from. It may be left somewhere else."

"Less chance for the thief to get caught," Stefanie agreed. "We'll need to keep an eye out for it in other areas if Jeffrey doesn't find it in the buttery. It's too bad the Carmichaels don't have security cameras."

"The crime rate isn't high here," Thomas said.

"Oh, you've done your research, have you?" she asked.

He chuckled. "Had to know what we're getting into."

As the GPS on her phone showed them getting close, she watched out the window for Carmichael House. Jeffrey, ahead of them in his small Ford, slowed down and pulled into the driveway of a pale yellow, two-storied house. Palm trees, oleanders and bougainvillea bursting through the iron fence railings gave a lush feel to the grounds.

On a corner lot, the Carmichael property was large by St. George's standards, at least judging by those they'd passed. The yellow property wall bordered a side street, then extended along the front of the property, which faced St. George's Harbour.

"That took us five minutes," she said.

"A kilometer and a half," Thomas noted, checking the odometer. "We could have walked."

In front of them, at the entrance to the driveway, Jeffrey leaned out his car window and entered a code into a keypad on the yellow gatepost. The six-foot-tall iron gate slid smoothly to the right.

The driveway ran parallel to the front of the house. Several vehicles were already parked there. Jeffrey parked behind two other cars, and Thomas pulled in beside him behind a small passenger van.

Stefanie unbuckled and got out of the car. Stretching her legs, she looked up at Carmichael House. Larger than the Colonial cottages in the historic area, it was by no means a manor house. It followed the regular lines of early Georgian architecture, with two windows above and below on each side of a central front door on the first floor and a door to a small cocktail deck on the second. Shutters at each window and door were painted pristine white. A stone paved terrace connected the driveway to the house, where low plastered walls flared out on either side of three wide steps leading to the front door.

"Hopefully, I will have wasted your time," Jeffrey said as he came up. He was once again in a blue polo and grey shorts, which Stefanie took to be the museum uniform.

Climbing out of the Tazzari, Thomas studied the gates and the fencing.

"You're right. With this gate locked, no one could walk in off the street. At least, not without risking being seen in broad daylight."

The house itself was located at the right front corner of the lot. A narrow walk led to the back of the house, with the iron fencing above the wall mostly hidden by rampant hedges of hibiscus and bougainvillea. A magnificent rubber tree at the front corner stretched its branches nearly to the driveway gate.

Jeffrey nodded toward the wider expanse of yard on the left. "I'll introduce you to the team before I check the buttery for the bracelet. If it hasn't been returned, you have my blessing to interact with them as you wish."

"We will impress them with our work ethic," Thomas said. "Who knows, we may find something worth reporting."

"I knew you wanted to help at the dig," Stefanie said.

He grinned. "Buried treasure. It's every boy's dream."

"If only it were pirate treasure, too," she teased.

"Perhaps it is," he said.

Jeffrey produced a weak smile for their efforts, then took a bright red and white insulated cooler from his car and lifted the lid. "I've brought lunch and plenty of water for us. It will be hot today."

Nestled beside six bottles of water were a stack of sandwiches in plastic bags and a pile of bright orange tangerines. Scattered across the top of everything were a half-dozen protein bars.

Helping herself to one of the bottles of water, Stefanie opened it and took a drink. She noted two large burgundy containers on either side of the front steps that spilled over with bright pink and purple petunias. Recapping her water, she set the bottle on the seat of the Tazzari. If the bracelet wasn't in the buttery, she'd make a point to look inside those planters later.

"Time to meet the crew." Jeffrey headed for the back of the well-manicured lawn.

She and Thomas followed. Along the left and rear of the property ran a deep border of palm and poinciana trees, viburnum, a hibiscus larger than any she'd ever seen at home, and other shrubs and vines Stefanie couldn't identify. The area was overgrown, but its tropical paradise style

23

was appealing.

At the back of the house was a stone patio lined with more burgundy flower pots. As she passed those closest to her, Stefanie peeked in the top of each tightly planted container, but didn't catch a glimpse of gold or emerald green among the plants. She'd check out the others around the patio later, during a break.

As Jeffrey led them to the excavated area in the back towards the left, Stefanie glanced at the buttery. The scene of the crime.

The building was on the opposite side of the property, about sixty feet behind the house. Tall and square, not very wide or deep, with a high stepped stone Bermuda roof. Like the house, it had been built about ten feet in from the wall. None of the bougainvillea or vines that grew exuberantly on the iron railings along that stretch were crushed or pressed down in a manner that would suggest someone had climbed over the day before.

She turned back to the excavation site, which consisted of two meter-square shallow pits, neatly marked off with string at the edge of the canopy of large trees. An older man dressed in a cargo vest and two young adults in shorts and T-shirts waited there, eyeing Stefanie, Thomas, and Jeffrey as they crossed the lawn.

"Morning," the man in the cargo vest said, stroking his salt-and-pepper beard. He looked to Jeffrey for an explanation.

"I've brought in reinforcements," Jeffrey said. "Stefanie Adams and Thomas Burkhardt."

Stefanie waved her trowel. "Good morning. Nice to meet you all," she said, hoping the Bermuda niceties would smooth the way.

Jeffrey gestured at the bearded man in the cargo vest. "Dr. Allan Ingram, from the University of Virginia. Goes by Ingram. And his students, Daphne Pasinski and Hunter Renko."

Both students looked to be about nineteen or twenty. Daphne's shoulder-length dark curls were pulled back into a ponytail. Hunter's lightish brown hair was cropped close on the sides, and the longer locks on top were the bleached blond of someone who spent a lot of time outdoors.

Ingram exuded wariness from his stance and expression. Daphne's wide open eyes looked fearful, and Hunter's compressed mouth and tight grip on the trowel in his hand showed his anger.

Thomas's glance at Hunter lasted longer than at the others. Because he saw something suspicious already?

"We're ready to help in any way we can," Thomas said.

"I didn't think we needed extra help," Ingram said pointedly.

A woman in her thirties stepped out of the buttery, halting when she saw Stefanie and Thomas. Her black hair was cut short, with longer points in front of her ears, giving a pixie-like look to her fine-boned features. She wore the same type of blue polo and dark knee-length shorts that Jeffrey did. She joined them in front of the excavation.

After a searching look at the woman, Jeffrey continued his introductions. "Beryl Swan, my assistant at the Museum. Stefanie and Thomas are staying at my neighbor's place, and I learned last night that they've both worked digs before."

"You want to hire more help now?" she asked, wiping away a trickle of sweat that slid from her temple.

Stefanie was feeling the heat already herself. She removed her new straw fedora long enough to brush her hair away from her forehead.

"With the tropical storm down in the Caribbean, I thought it best to wrap up the dig as quickly as possible," Jeffrey said.

Beryl pursed her lips. "That wasn't necessary. The storm is heading west. Not north."

Jeffrey gave her a steady look. "Don't worry, they're both experienced. Friends of my neighbor."

His crew were definitely unhappy that she and Thomas had joined them. Beryl, Jeffrey's assistant, was the angriest. With good reason, since he'd brought them in without letting her know and compounded an already touchy situation.

"Between Marlene on my case to finish so that the landscaping can get back on schedule and the tropical storm in the Caribbean, we need to get this done," Jeffrey insisted. "Thomas's degree is in archaeology, and Stefanie has worked at a site on Crete. Stefanie, Thomas, we've got notebooks for you in case you want to note any finds or make sketches. I'll get them, then we can get started."

When Jeffrey proceeded toward the buttery, all eyes followed him.

Would the bracelet be waiting, and their day of digging be done as soon as it started? If it had been returned, they'd finish the day out so Jeffrey could maintain the charade that they were only there to help with the dig, whether Thomas wanted to or not.

Stefanie hid her intense interest in the bracelet by studying the excavated squares. The one on the left was excavated to a depth of twenty-four inches, she estimated, the one on the right not quite as deep. A hillock of soil filled a tarp on the lawn nearby.

When Jeffrey entered the outbuilding, an attractive woman in her fifties with a grey-streaked bob and large almond-shaped eyes came out of the French doors at the back of the house. Dressed in a printed blouse and solid maroon skirt and wearing low-heeled black pumps, she stood on the stone patio, facing the buttery.

She had to be Marlene Carmichael, the Bermuda Minister of Economy and Labor. Far enough away that Stefanie couldn't read her expression, there was no doubt from the Minister's stiffly held posture that she, too, waited intently on Jeffrey.

Wanting to engage the archaeological team, Stefanie gestured at the pits. "You've made good progress."

Beryl gave her a quick glance, but that was all. The others watched the doorway of the shed. Ingram stood with one hand on his hip, while Daphne slowly pulled on a pair of work gloves. Hunter's eyes burned hotly, and he gripped his trowel as fiercely as if he intended to stab someone with it.

She'd be better able to gauge what they were actually feeling if she could bring up the bracelet, but Jeffrey made it clear the team and the Carmichaels didn't want anyone else to know about the bracelet unless it was found.

Jeffrey walked out of the buttery, two small yellow notebooks in hand, along with a couple of pencils and pens. He looked first at Marlene and gave the slightest shake of his head. Turning to Beryl, he did the same.

So the bracelet hadn't been returned. At least not to the buttery. They were still on.

Marlene turned and glared at the group by the excavation, her lips tightly pressed together.

Her scrutiny landed on Stefanie and Thomas, and she marched the fifty feet or so across the lawn to face them. "Who are you?" she demanded.

So much for Bermuda politeness.

"I've hired additional help for the excavation, Marlene," Jeffrey said, stepping in. "Thomas Burkhardt, Stefanie Adams, this is the Honorable Mrs. Marlene Carmichael, the homeowner and our Bermuda Minister of Economy and Labor."

"Do we need more people?" the Minister asked him. "This project isn't that big."

Jeffrey gave her the same explanation as he'd given to the dig crew.

Marlene gave him a piercing look in return. "Nathaniel wants the excavation cleared up as soon as possible as well. I'll be in my office if—" With a glance at Thomas, she caught herself. "If you need me for anything."

Emotions were amplified because no one would mention the bracelet. With any luck, she could leverage that. Marlene was angry. Because her emerald bracelet hadn't been returned? Or could it be guilty anger, because Stefanie and Thomas had added to the likelihood of discovery, Stefanie wondered.

Wishing she'd brought her lockpick with her, she watched Marlene Carmichael return to the house. It was a large house. Jeffrey couldn't have searched very thoroughly yesterday afternoon. But what purpose would it serve for the Carmichaels to pretend to steal their own bracelet?

"Should we get to work?" Thomas asked.

"Yes," Jeffrey said.

Everyone they'd met resented the fact that she and Thomas were there. Whether that was due to fear, anger, or disappointment, she couldn't tell. Yet.

Chapter Five

"Here," Jeffrey said, passing Stefanie and Thomas each a notebook and pencil. "Most of us take notes on our digs. More supplies are in the shed—paper bags, markers, string for guidelines. Help yourself if you need anything."

Stefanie eagerly took the yellow Rite in the Rain All-Weather Memo Book and rubbed her thumbs across the smooth cover. "I used these in Crete," she said. "This brings back memories of the summer I interned."

That first yellow notebook filled with measurements and notes and smudges of Cretan soil was the reason she'd carried a notebook in her purse ever since. Usually Moleskine, rather than Rite in the Rain, which were thicker and bulkier.

"This is my first internship," Daphne said.

Stefanie smiled at the girl and got a faint smile in return.

"Thomas," Jeffrey said, "join Ingram at Unit One, where we found the gold coins."

Flashing a glance at Jeffrey, Beryl's hunched shoulders seemed to relax. Jeffrey's abbreviated list of their discoveries seemed to put Ingram and Daphne more at ease as well.

Unit One was the deepest, and level and smooth across the entire surface. Where the cedar tree had been removed, Stefanie guessed.

"You take the far side," Ingram said to Thomas, pointing to the edge just two feet from a thicket of oleanders. "I'll work this one."

Thomas shouldered past stiff oleander branches and sat on the ground without complaint.

How long would Thomas put up with Ingram taking charge, Stefanie wondered, seeing Ingram settle easily onto a comfortable patch of grass on the opposite side of the square.

She tried to assess the power structure among the archaeological team. Jeffrey was in charge, but it was hard to tell if Beryl, as his assistant, or Ingram, as a visiting professor, came next in the pecking order. That would play a part in their reactions to the theft.

"Hunter and Daphne, continue on Unit Two with me," Jeffrey said. "Beryl and Stefanie, start a third unit, directly north of Two."

"I'll get the string and stakes," Stefanie offered, heading for the buttery and the chance to search more thoroughly for the bracelet. Jeffrey hadn't had time to do much more than take a quick survey earlier.

"No," Beryl said. "I know where they are." She gestured toward a large commercial tape measure on the ground. "There's the tape measure. Mark out a meter square."

Great.

At least it was fairly certain that Beryl wasn't taking the opportunity to return the emerald bracelet. She'd been in the buttery when they'd arrived, and returning it now was too blatant and wouldn't save her reputation. One thing was certain. Beryl liked to be in control.

Stefanie couldn't get into the buttery, but at least she knew what was expected of her. Picking up the tape measure, she rolled the tape out to just over a meter. She was in the palmettos, with an enormous oleander at her back and a thick patch of English ivy in the area that they would be clearing.

"Burkhardt," Ingram said, "you'll have to move faster than that if we're going to deepen this another ten or twelve inches, friend."

Thomas chuckled. "I don't want to damage anything. You go as fast as you like."

Pressing her lips together to hide her smile at the ease with which Thomas handled Ingram's heckling, Stefanie waited while Beryl returned with shovels, a folded tarp, and long metal pins.

"We don't want to rush this," Beryl said as she crossed the lawn.

Jeffrey replied without looking up from his trowel. "We're not rushing anything."

"It's happened before," Beryl answered. "We might lose valuable historic information."

He flushed red.

When Beryl handed her a shovel and one of the thin stakes, Stefanie leaned the shovel against a large palm tree, then pushed the stake into the soft ground at the one-meter mark. When all four corners were marked, Beryl took a ball of white cotton string from her shorts pocket and tossed it to Stefanie. Stefanie tied the end to the closest stake, then took it to the next corner, wrapped it tightly, then she did the same with the last two pins, marking off a neat square.

Since Thomas hadn't brought up the treasure, Stefanie did. The longer they waited, the cagier the guilty one would be about what they said. At least they could discuss the Spanish coins and the chest.

"You found gold coins," Stefanie said, trying to start a conversation. "That's incredible."

"And that's why you're here, isn't it?" Ingram eyed Thomas with malignant glee. "Why you're so eager to help out on a hot day when you could be sipping rum swizzles in the shade."

Thomas smiled. "Why not? Who knows what's still buried."

"Start there," Beryl said, directing Stefanie to a corner. "Take off as little as you can with the shovel. We'll load the turf and plants onto a new tarp." She picked up the folded plastic and whipped the tarp open with a sharp snap of her wrists, then finally addressed Stefanie's comment. "Twelve gold coins. Spanish," she said.

Pleased that Beryl responded, Stefanie picked up the shovel and got to work. "They were in the chest?" she asked. First cutting straight down for a vertical edge, she angled the blade toward the center and removed a shovelful of ivy and turf.

"Not in the chest, below it." Beryl took up another shovel and began on the opposite side of the square.

"You never know what you'll find with archaeology," Stefanie said.

In no time, the surface vegetation was cleared. Jeffrey moved to the freshly filled tarp. "I'll check these root balls and turf." He probed the clumped earth with a screwdriver and his trowel.

Wishing she'd bought a pair of pants to work in rather than shorts, Stefanie settled as comfortably as she could on the ivy. The lessons from her summer on Crete working with her father's friend Monty came back. Starting about two feet out from the corner, she held her trowel horizontally and scraped lightly with the flat of the blade, pulling it toward her as she watched and felt for anything hard, anything a different color or texture from the sandy Bermuda soil. She fell into a steady rhythm that produced a respectable pile of soil.

Daphne must have been listening to their conversation.

"The coins are stamped Philip II," Daphne said, sitting on one hip and scraping along the edge of the neighboring square.

"Any chance I can see them, or have they been taken away already?" Stefanie asked.

When Beryl and Daphne exchanged a look, Stefanie smiled expectantly. Trying to trap them into talking about the bracelet was almost as fun as the excavating. Once the topic was out in the open, conversation would reveal more about how people felt and where they'd been when the bracelet disappeared.

"That's up to Lawrence," Beryl said. "Marlene's husband. He put away the gold coins. They're inside the house with the brass chest."

She noticed the pile of dirt collecting in front of Stefanie. "We screen over the tarp. Grab a bucket for your soil."

Disappointed that her efforts hadn't turned up any artifacts, Stefanie grabbed a dirty white bucket from the stack against the enormous palm trunk and pushed the pile she'd made into it.

Daphne hopped up. "I'll get the screen." She removed the band which held her hair into a ponytail, pulled her hair back again, then rewrapped the elastic band. Going into the canopy of trees, she brought out the screening frame and placed it in the center of the fresh tarp.

"Thanks," Stefanie said, going to the screen, a three-feet-square wooden frame on legs that had quarter-inch metal screening stretched across it.

After dumping the contents of her bucket onto it, she spread out the loose soil with her gloved hands. Finer particles dropped through the mesh onto the tarp below.

"Who found the gold?" she asked as she continued to screen, breaking down larger bits of soil and sending them through the mesh. "I found a few potsherds on Crete."

Daphne glanced at Hunter, who ducked his head to his excavating after darting an angry look up.

"Hunter found it," Beryl said. "Them," she corrected. "The Spanish coins."

Stefanie rubbed across the remaining dirt until it all fell through, then peered closely at the remaining pebbles. Most were bits of limestone, but an angled fragment with blue on one side and white on the other stood out among the small rocks.

"Looks like I've got a bit of ceramic here," she said, taking her gloves off to pick it up. "Anyone else found pottery?"

Beryl pointed to a canvas duffle bag off to the side. "Bags and markers in there. Date, location, and our names, because we're the ones working the location."

Fantastic.

Squatting near the supplies, Stefanie took a paper bag from the stack and wrote the information on it. How disappointing that everything was handy, and she had no excuse to go to the potting shed without making it a big deal. She studied the buttery, wondering what excuse would work. Just getting up and going in would seem too blatantly curious after Beryl's comments. She needed to stay on Beryl's good side to get her to talk.

"Are you looking at the roof?" Ingram asked her. "That stair-stepped design is to catch rainwater. All the houses in Bermuda have cisterns. There's no fresh water source here."

"That's interesting," Stefanie said. "I wonder what the sailor who buried the gold did for drinking water."

"Probably drank from catch pools in the rock," Beryl said.

Thomas tried to engage the others in conversation as well, but the team fell silent, no one willing to give anything away about the bracelet that was found yesterday. The Carmichaels might be easier to pry the secret out of.

Plus, she really wanted to check out those flower containers and surreptitiously search the perimeter landscaping of the house. The other members of the dig team had arrived earlier than they had. As Thomas suggested, the culprit could easily have dropped the emerald bracelet as they walked, and no one would be the wiser. Leaving the thief's reputation untarnished.

Stefanie put the annotated paper bag to the side. "I'm going to grab my water."

Jeffrey looked up from his labors. "If you need to wash your hands, we use the kitchen door on the far side so we don't track dirt in." He pointed past the patio.

"Thanks." She smiled as she headed for the house.

She wasn't actually dirty, other than sweating in the heat, but using the kitchen door gave her more opportunity to search the grounds.

Making a point to stop and admire each of the glazed ceramic flower pots on the patio, as well as the sedum that served as ground cover edging the house foundation, Stefanie went to the Tazzari first. She picked up her water bottle.

The bracelet could have just as easily been taken by the Carmichaels as anyone on the dig team. If they were occupied, she could do a little searching.

Taking a sip of water, she sauntered across the front and checked out the two pots that flanked the front steps. Nothing but lush petunias in them. She went around the corner of the house. Only an occasional chunk of striated limestone for decoration in the landscape bed. No filigree bracelet revealed itself in the tiny yellow flowers of the sedum. She didn't sift through the fleshy stems for the bracelet. If the thief wanted to return it, he or she wouldn't make it that hard to find. The bracelet would be lying on top.

She stopped and drank deeply from the plastic bottle. The iron fence and thick, overgrown plantings would have made it difficult for anyone to climb over, and the branches of the rubber tree were too high. As with the area near the buttery, there wasn't any evidence that anyone had tried, no crushed or broken limbs in the bougainvillea. And how would a stranger or random thief know to try? The bracelet and gold pieces had just been found; it wasn't as if they were common knowledge.

Capping her bottle, Stefanie returned it to the car, then made her way to the kitchen door, studying the groundcover next to the house as she went. Hoping one or both of the Carmichaels would be the weak link in the chain of silence, she knocked, then stepped inside when no one answered. Marlene had been reserved and angry, but that anger might cause her to reveal more than she planned.

The modern kitchen with richly polished wooden floors, dark wood cabinets, and granite countertops was empty. She found the powder room beside the kitchen and washed her hands.

Creeping into the short hall, being careful to step lightly on the wooden floor, she considered the room to her left. The door was open, a clear invitation. It was a den or office, paneled with dark oak. A sturdy wooden desk stood by the window, and on it was a small brass chest, about ten inches long, six high, and six deep.

Her pulse quickened. From where she stood, it looked like it had weathered its burial quite well. It had been cleaned, if not polished. The lid was open. Could the bracelet be inside? She hesitated in the hallway, not wanting to get caught snooping by Marlene or her husband.

She was glad she waited. A short man with a shock of white hair and a neatly trimmed white beard walked into view near the window, a cell phone to his ear. Like every man she'd met in Bermuda, he wore shorts.

"I'm good for it," he said. "I'll be in touch."

When he clicked off, his pensive expression didn't reflect the confidence of his voice.

A sharp voice spoke out from over Stefanie's shoulder. "What is it that you are good for, Lawrence?"

Stefanie spun around, her hand to her chest.

Chapter Six

With a critical eye on Stefanie, the Honorable Marlene Carmichael moved past her into the room and stood near her husband. Lawrence Carmichael set his cell phone on the desk, and the two of them waited expectantly for Stefanie to explain herself.

She took in a deep breath. Of course they'd be wary of a stranger in their house. Yesterday they'd had a valuable bracelet stolen.

"I'm sorry," Stefanie said, holding her hands out. "I came in the house to wash my hands, and I was struck by the chest and hoped for a closer look. Stefanie Adams," she added for Lawrence's benefit. She crossed to the desk and stuck out her hand, hoping the habit of courteous greeting would smooth over her intrusion. "Nice to meet you. My partner and I joined the dig team this morning. Jeffrey hired us."

"You're with Jeffrey." After a moment, the bearded man shook her hand. "Lawrence Carmichael."

"We met earlier," Marlene said, her fingertips resting on the desk.

Was that curtness Marlene's normal manner, the impatience of a busy woman, Stefanie wondered, or could the Minister's brusqueness possibly be because the emerald bracelet was close at hand, possibly in the chest?

Wanting to diffuse the awkwardness and make a connection, Stefanie deflected. As she'd entered, she'd noted framed photographs on shelves along one wall. Sailboats and sailors in shorts and T-shirts. She was in the office of a seafaring man.

Speaking to Lawrence, she said, "I see you're a sailor." She gestured toward the brass chest on the desk. "And is this a sailor's chest? Jeffrey said one was found Monday."

"Yes. Take a closer look." He turned the chest toward her.

"Thank you." She leaned forward. The brass chest was empty. She'd been naïve to expect anything else.

Lawrence pointed to the brass rings that formed handles on either side. "The rings were so the chest could be suspended on the ship, keeping anything inside safe from loss or breakage."

Up close, she could see that the metal was slightly corroded, with a dull verdigris patina. The chest was more detailed than she'd noticed from the doorway. The flat panels on the sides and top were etched with a floral and leaf design, one that was repeated on the heavier metal that reinforced all edges of the chest. A larger handle was welded to the lid.

"Brass and steel," Lawrence said. "It should clean up well, Jeffrey tells me."

She was dying to ask why he thought the bracelet hadn't been buried inside the chest, but couldn't bring it up until they did. However, she could talk about the coins.

"Any chance of a peek at the coins that were found?" she asked. "I heard there were twelve."

Lawrence glanced at his wife.

"We've asked Jeffrey and his people to not speak to anyone about what was found here," Marlene said. "I would ask the same of you. We don't want the news media getting hold of the story. We'd be hounded day and night."

"Of course," Stefanie said. "I totally understand. If the public knew, that would also bring the risk of theft, and you don't want that."

Marlene's lips closed in a firm line.

Darn.

Taking a key from his chest pocket, Lawrence unlocked the center drawer of his desk and took out a folded blue flannel cloth. Laying it on the desk, he unfolded the flannel to reveal a dozen gold coins, each about the size of a quarter.

"Spanish gold." Stefanie grinned up at them both. "Incredible."

"From the time of Philip II," Lawrence said. He picked one up and gave it to her.

The front featured the profile of the king. She turned it over. The other side was stamped with a crowned shield. It was beautiful, shining with the enticing brilliance of high karat gold.

She handed it back. "What a fantastic find. You must be so excited."

Neither of the Carmichaels felt compelled to mention the even more fantastic find that had been discovered.

"Jeffrey tells us this was probably the sailor's personal hoard," Lawrence said. "They were minted in Europe, you see, not in the Spanish colonies. That's the Hapsburg coat of arms on the back."

He folded his coins back in the blue flannel and relocked them in the desk drawer.

"We're quite pleased with the find," Marlene said. "Let me walk you out."

Stefanie gave them both a quick smile. "Yes, I'd better get back to work."

Leaving, she paused to examine the collection of photos displayed on the wall of shelves behind her. The matching shirts in the largest photo told her those pictured were on a team.

"America's Cup. Back in the day," Lawrence said with pride. Coming to stand in front of the bookcase, his gaze caressed the photo. "I was helm."

She didn't know much about the race, or sailing in general, but that didn't matter.

"Quite an accomplishment," she said. "The America's Cup. You won?"

His pride turned to regret. "We only made it to the semi-finals." He straightened the photo.

"Making the semi-finals is an accomplishment in itself," Stefanie said. "And now you've found a dozen gold Spanish coins on your property."

He smiled at the photo. "It takes a lot more money than that to finance one of these. Had to be tight-lipped about that boat. Didn't want the competition to know our design modifications. Unfortunately, the hull was too bulky."

Too bad he was also tight-lipped about the emerald bracelet. Seeing that he was the kind to chat, she'd thought he'd let it slip that they'd found more than coins.

"Have you found anything new out there?" Marlene asked Stefanie.

That took Lawrence's attention away from his boats. He looked at Stefanie hopefully.

"No, I'm sorry," she said.

Marlene's nostrils flared. "Perhaps they've found all there is. The sooner the archaeological work is done, the sooner Nathaniel Dimon can get back to work on the garden."

So much for getting them to talk.

Marlene led the way to the living room, a beautifully constructed room with a carved mantelpiece over the fireplace. Though not large, the house was charming. The dark woodwork throughout on the door frames and deep window casings stood out against the cream color of the wall paint. Through the French doors, Stefanie could see the crew at work in the back garden. If the Carmichaels were the ones who'd taken the emerald bracelet, there was no way she or Thomas would find it in one day. If they were innocent, the Carmichaels would have to be more forthcoming with the police, whether the news media found out or not.

Still, she had one more chance before Marlene showed her to the door.

"I'm Jeffrey's neighbor," she said, hoping to thaw Marlene's icy reception. "Temporarily, at least. I'm staying at a friend's place."

Marlene really looked at her for the first time. "His neighbor?"

"Greg Edwards," she said. "You might know him. CEO of Riverboat Rum?"

"If it makes money in Bermuda, I know about it." Marlene gave a little laugh.

"That's right, Jeffrey said you're the Minister of Economy."

"And Labor." Marlene smiled briefly.

"Economy and Labor, apologies," Stefanie said with a warm smile.

"So you're a friend of Greg's," Marlene said.

"Yes." Admitting he was a bank client wouldn't establish the relationship she wanted with Marlene. "He's often encouraged me to stay at his place here, and my friend and I have finally taken him up on it."

"Greg's headquarters is an interesting place. Have you been?"

"Not yet," Stefanie said.

"I make a point to visit my constituents. The building has a lovely moon gate in front," Marlene said, opening one of the French doors to the patio.

Stefanie stepped outside. "Will you have a moon gate installed in your garden?"

"It's in Nathaniel Dimon's plan, along with paths." The Minister indicated the buttery. "We save historical elements when we can. Have you gone inside? It makes a lovely potting shed."

Stefanie studied the square stone building across the yard.

"I haven't been inside yet," she answered. Not for lack of trying. Chagrined, she saw Thomas exit the buttery. How did he manage that? Beryl must not have felt the need to block *him*. Not that anyone could stop Thomas when he was determined.

"I'll make sure I do." With what she hoped was a natural segue, Stefanie asked, "Have you been watching the archaeologists' progress?"

Marlene didn't question her curiosity. "Jeffrey tells me when they've found something of interest." A shadow of anger crossed her face, but she didn't mention the missing bracelet.

Fine.

Stefanie smiled. "I'll get back to my labors," she said. "Maybe we'll find more treasure."

"One can hope." Marlene's gaze rested on the crew at the back of the garden. "And if not, I trust the work will be wrapped up soon." She flashed a smile at Stefanie. "I am looking forward to my new landscape."

Stefanie crossed the expanse of lawn at the same time as Thomas and met him at the excavation.

Daphne had taken over screening while Beryl and the men scraped the soil, deepening all three units.

"Find anything exciting?" Stefanie asked the group.

Daphne frowned. "No."

"Did Marlene tell you to hurry us up?" Beryl asked. "She can't wait to impress her friends in Tucker's Town with the garden once it's finished."

"She did," Stefanie said with a commiserating smile.

Thomas wiped the sweat from his forehead with the back of his arm. "I'm ready for a break."

"That's because you spend your summers teaching instead of doing the real work out in the field," Ingram said with a derisive smile.

"Something like that." Thomas bent down and set his trowel and gloves off to the side.

"Come on," Stefanie said. "I've got water in the car."

"If you can call that toy a car," he said.

That brought smiles from the dig team, a welcome show of friendliness.

"What excuse did you use to get in the buttery?" she asked when she and Thomas were halfway across the lawn. "Beryl blocked me every time I tried."

"I didn't. I just walked over."

That figured. One point to Thomas. "Find anything?"

He shook his head. "I searched the entire place, hoping Jeffrey missed the bracelet. Not that I think he would."

At the car, Stefanie reached into the open window for the water and handed the bottle to him. "It's hot," she warned.

"But a good excuse." He gestured with the bottle toward the burgundy flower pots on either side of the front steps. "You? Any luck?"

"No, and I couldn't get the Carmichaels to mention the bracelet. They are both uptight. Lawrence is friendlier than Marlene, although I am getting her to thaw a little," Stefanie said. "She requested that we not mention the gold coins to anyone. More of a demand, actually. The Carmichaels really want it kept out of the news. They don't want the public to know."

"A wise decision," Thomas said. "Especially since they don't have security cameras. Even if crime in general is low in Bermuda, greed is everywhere."

"I'll work on Beryl—she made that comment about losing artifacts earlier." Stefanie took the bottle from him and finished it off, not caring that the water was warm. "I can't say any of them strike me as acting guiltier than the others."

He walked over to the driveway gate. "Someone off the street would have to scale the gates to get in. It could be done."

"But they'd risk being noticed by anyone in the house and five people out in the yard," she said.

"Not a likely possibility," he admitted. "It was one of the people here."

"If it was the Carmichaels, we'll never find the bracelet in the house. And

I just can't come up with a reason they'd pretend to steal something they legally own," Stefanie said.

Thomas frowned. "It wouldn't be for the insurance. The bracelet was found yesterday and hadn't been appraised." He shook his head. "That's the usual reason people claim their property was stolen, but it doesn't fit in this situation."

She took off her fedora and wiped the sweat from her forehead with the back of her hand. "We only have today to help Jeffrey pin down the thief. What about using your phone app that clones calls and texts?"

"I did one better," he said, smiling at her. "My phone is recording whatever they say without us there."

"Is it now?" Stefanie smiled back. Thomas was always so resourceful. That taped conversation would be far more revealing than anything the crew might say in their presence.

Returning to their microcar, he took her hand. "I want this job finished. This is our vacation. Tonight I'm taking you out for a romantic dinner."

"This isn't romantic enough?" she asked. "I'm having fun. Are you?"

"*Ja*, I enjoy being bullied by Ingram."

"Think it was him?" she asked.

Thomas shrugged. "They are all skittish. Ingram thinks I want to publish this find before he can. There is one I suspect more than the others, though." He paused. "Hunter Renko."

Hunter had been quiet all morning. And angry. It could be because he didn't like being in a situation where he was suspected, as they all were, or it could be that his anger was a cover for his guilt.

"Because Hunter has less to lose than the professionals?" she asked.

Thomas looked toward the back, even though the archaeologists weren't visible from where they stood. "I recognized his name."

"Hunter Renko?" It didn't ring any bells for her, but she wasn't knowledgeable about wider archaeological circles like Thomas was.

"He's the son of a well-known shipwreck salvager," Thomas said. "His father locates shipwrecks and sells what he can salvage. Perhaps Hunter thinks that's an acceptable business model for archaeology."

Chapter Seven

"Hunter's father salvages shipwrecks," Stefanie said, striding to the end of the drive, where she could see past the house to the excavation. That was a red flag.

The student was on his hands and knees, scraping away in the middle of his square.

Thomas followed her. "Salvage divers are used to taking what they find."

Hunter would have the resources to sell the bracelet, if that was his aim.

She turned around. "His backpack was searched yesterday. How would he have managed to leave with the bracelet?"

"Perhaps it was deposited somewhere inconspicuous, then picked up on the way out," Thomas suggested.

"That would be difficult to pull off," she said. "The other members of the dig team would have been watchful, not to mention Marlene and Lawrence."

"True. They were all under suspicion."

"Hunter hasn't said a word all morning," she said.

"Jeffrey needs to report the incident to the police," Thomas said. "We have better things to do."

"Snorkeling." With the sun blazing down on her, causing her sunglasses to slide from her sweat, a dip in the ocean sounded heavenly.

"Tomorrow," he agreed.

Too hot and sticky to hold hands, they walked side by side back to the excavation.

At her square, Stefanie dropped to the ground and picked up her trowel, watching Thomas palm his cell phone from its hiding place under his gloves.

He tucked it into his cargo pocket and got to work.

She rubbed her shin where the ivy stems scratched her, wondering how best to provoke Hunter. "So," she asked the group at large, "What's the plan? For the garden?"

"Marlene hired a big-shot garden designer, Nathaniel Dimon," Jeffrey said from his position on the screening tarp. He accepted a bucket of soil from Hunter, then dumped it onto the screen. "They want to make it into a showplace."

A derisive snort came from the direction of Dr. Ingram.

Stefanie looked up from her careful scraping. Ingram worked his trowel with vigor.

Had his reaction been for the landscaper, or the garden? The border of trees and shrubs was about fifteen feet deep, giving it plenty of scope for a moon gate and structured paths.

"It'll cost them," Ingram said.

Daphne sat back on her heels and took stock of the house. "They can afford it."

Hunter took the empty bucket back to his square and resumed his task of removing layer by layer of soil.

"I imagine the Carmichaels will be having lots of visitors stop by to see the artifacts once the finds are made public," Stefanie said.

"Marlene mentioned donating part of the find to the museum," Beryl said.

"Oh?" Stefanie asked. "Which part?"

Ingram paused in his scraping.

Buzzing bees and calling seagulls filled the silence, along with the occasional passing traffic on the road. Beryl shrugged.

Stefanie caught Thomas's eye. This group wasn't going to crack.

"Donating artifacts to museums benefits everyone," Thomas said. "The public and researchers from all over the world can study and learn from artifacts they wouldn't have access to otherwise."

"That's our goal at NMB," Beryl said.

"Private owners loan their artifacts to museums, too," Hunter said.

If Hunter had the emerald bracelet in his backpack and was on the fence about whether to return it or not, she needed to give him as much encouragement as she could.

"They must take great pride in knowing that what they've contributed adds to public knowledge," Stefanie said. "Like the Spanish coins found here. Lawrence told me they weren't gold from the Americas at all, but the sailor's personal savings. I wouldn't have known that without being told."

"For all the good it did him," Ingram commented.

Hm. Was Ingram frustrated with hard work that hadn't paid off? Enough to tempt him into taking the bracelet for a long-awaited personal reward?

"Let's break for lunch," Jeffrey said. "We're down several more centimeters, thanks to everyone's diligent efforts."

While Hunter took a sack lunch out of his nearby backpack, Beryl went to her car and returned with a plastic lunch case. Ingram and Daphne headed to the passenger van. Daphne returned with her backpack, and Ingram with a paper sack lunch.

Stefanie and Thomas picked up sandwiches and tangerines from Jeffrey's cooler. "Thomas and I are going to stretch our legs and explore," Stefanie said. "I'd like to check out the buttery. Marlene told me a little about it. I've never seen one before."

"Sure," Jeffrey said.

When they were out of hearing range, she asked, "Think the bracelet is in Hunter's backpack?"

She looked back. The five members of the dig team seemed to have retreated into separate worlds, browsing their cell phones or eating silently.

"It's Jeffrey's call whether or not to search it." Thomas handed her his sandwich, then played back the audio his phone had recorded.

The first voice was Beryl's. "What were you thinking, bringing them here today?"

"We need to get the excavation done quickly," Jeffrey replied. He cleared his throat. "Whether anyone else is here doesn't matter."

"We each went into the buttery before you got here, so no one would be singled out," Ingram said.

"Smart. But the bracelet wasn't there. I searched every shelf," Jeffrey replied. "That doesn't mean whoever took the bracelet hasn't returned it. I expect it to show up. Soon," he said ominously.

The abrupt sound of metal slicing into gritty soil told them a trowel had been shoved into the ground. "I don't need this trouble," Hunter said.

No one spoke after that. Only sharp scraping and the occasional ping of one rock tossed against another broke the silence.

Thomas ended the recording. "No revelations. Except that they each went into the buttery."

"So Beryl coming out of it earlier didn't mean anything," Stefanie said. "She must have been afraid I'd find the bracelet if Jeffrey had missed it."

They were no further, really, than they had been before.

"At least Jeffrey is pushing the thief to return it," Thomas said.

When they reached the buttery, Stefanie stepped through the open doorway into cool shade. Directly opposite the doorway, a small table butted up against the wall beneath a single small, high window. Wooden shelves lined the walls on either side of the door.

"Maybe the bracelet had been returned, but the guilty party wasn't about to point that out. Maybe Jeffrey missed it because he was stressed," she said.

"I searched," Thomas said. "Perhaps you'll have better luck than I had. Fresh eyes."

"I'll bet Beryl searched again as well," she said, "when she came in for the string and tarp."

Still, she sifted through the fertilizers, garden tools, and stacks of unused pots on the floor and on the shelves, then, without much hope, through the notebooks, black and white rulers, toothbrushes and other archaeological supplies on the table. Despite the shade and stone walls, she was hot and sweaty, and her efforts were completely unrewarded.

"No luck," Stefanie said. She'd had to try.

Leaving the stone building, she and Thomas returned to the units and once again took up their trowels. One by one, the others packed away their sandwich wrappers, plastic bags, and containers and joined them.

Stefanie eyed Hunter's backpack, wondering again if he'd brought the bracelet back, yet not taken the difficult step of returning it. She really wanted a chance to go through it. No excuse came to mind, though, and Thomas was right. That would be up to Jeffrey.

Hunter caught her watching him.

"Nathaniel Dimon was here yesterday," he said as he scraped the soil with quick strokes. "The landscape designer. I saw him."

"What?" Jeffrey exclaimed, wiping sweat from his forehead with the back of his hand. "Nathaniel Dimon was here? Yesterday?"

The thought seemed to give Jeffrey hope. Beryl sat up, too.

Stefanie hit an impediment with her trowel and leaned forward for a closer look.

Thomas scooped soil into his bucket and took it to the screening table. "Does the landscape designer come every day to check on your progress?" he asked.

Wanting to listen, but discerning a tiny triangular point of metal in the soil, Stefanie concentrated on the patch before her. Probably an iron nail. But still, the bracelet, coins and brass chest had been found in the same area. Her pulse quickened.

Getting up on her knees, she leaned on her left hand and dug carefully with the tip of her trowel around the object, excavating deeper into the soil. The item was at least an inch wide, yet thin. A thin bright edge glinted in the sunlight. Stefanie pressed her lips together. Whatever it was, it wasn't a nail.

"Thomas," she said quietly, "I've got something."

The triangle widened out as she cleared the sandy soil from around it.

He came over, squatting beside her while she cleared the earth away. Everyone else stopped working and waited. She picked quickly, brushing the dirt away bit by bit until the entire object was revealed.

She sat back on her heels. It was a diamond-shaped insignia of some kind, chipped enamel on gold.

Chapter Eight

Stefanie looked up at Thomas. Bursting with elation, she could hardly believe she'd discovered something.

Thomas knelt on one knee, his hand on her shoulder. The diamond shaped badge lay exposed in the earth. Outlined in gold, an enameled red cross was centered on a background of chipped white enamel. Each arm of the cross ended in a red fleur-de-lis. Glints promising more gold showed through the chipped spaces.

Jeffrey and Ingram crowded around, peering at the artifact, as did Hunter and Daphne. Beryl's face registered little emotion from the opposite side of the square.

"That's nice," Beryl said. "I've been out here two days and haven't found a single thing."

"What is it, exactly?" Stefanie asked.

She moved out of the way for Jeffrey, who'd taken a digital camera from his bag and started photographing the badge in situ.

Before Jeffrey could answer, Hunter spoke up. "It's a Spanish medal."

When Daphne scoffed, his face flushed red. "I've seen them before. I don't know which order, but I bet it's a Spanish medal." He put down his trowel.

"I'll get the photo scale and meter sticks," Daphne said, heading for the buttery.

Jeffrey lowered his camera. "Beryl, get Marlene and Lawrence."

Beryl didn't need to, because the homeowners hurried across the lawn. They must have seen the activity from the French doors.

"You found it," Marlene called.

So focused on the missing bracelet, Marlene wasn't thinking clearly.

"No, Marlene, this is something new," Jeffrey said.

"It wasn't buried with the coins," Thomas pointed out.

No one picked up on the fact that Thomas wasn't supposed to know that Marlene had mistaken the discovery of the new artifact with the recovery of the missing bracelet. A sign that they were letting their guards down.

"No," Ingram said. "Different location, and closer to the surface." He extended an expandable tape measure between a flag in Unit One to the new find. "One point eight meters apart."

"Huh. Another Spanish artifact," Lawrence said, squatting at the edge of the shallow pit.

Daphne returned with two black and white meter sticks, which Beryl took and arranged at right angles along the edge of square. Each ten-centimeter-long color block allowed for a quick visual reference of the medal's location.

Daphne stepped into the square and placed a small black and white ruler next to the enameled diamond.

"Point goes north," Thomas said.

"Right," Daphne said, smiling for only the second time that day.

Hunter took a compass from his backpack and tossed it to her. After finding north, Daphne repositioned the ruler next to the medal, then stepped back.

Stefanie took photos with her own phone, as did each of the archaeologists, as well as Marlene. Hunter also grabbed a notebook from his backpack, a larger notebook than the yellow ones provided, and quickly sketched the artifact.

He'd left the pack unzipped. With the others concentrating on the medal, the opportunity was too great to miss. Stefanie squatted close to the pack and balanced on her heels, ready to stand up if Hunter turned around and saw her. Picking up the backpack by the unzipped flap to move it out of her way, she peered inside. If Hunter was the thief and intended to return the bracelet, he'd make sure to have it easily accessible, waiting for an opportunity to drop it.

Inside the backpack were two more notebooks, several pens and pencils, and a pencil sharpener. That was all. Disappointed, Stefanie set the backpack off to the side. She should have expected as much. Leaving the bag open and unattended was proof enough that Hunter had nothing to hide.

Standing up, she went to Thomas's side. She peered over Hunter's shoulder, pleased that he did justice to her find. But, of course, the medal belonged to the Carmichaels. Laughing at how possessive she felt about it, she squeezed Thomas's hand.

He grinned. "We'll get a photo of you with the medal," he said. "We'll frame it and put it on our wall."

"Will we?" she said, just as pleased at the thought that they'd have a shared wall as she was with the medal.

"Everyone get their photos?" Jeffrey asked. "Hunter, have you got enough?"

"Almost." The young man flipped his pencil, swiped with the eraser, then added a few more strokes. "Done."

Jeffrey turned to Stefanie. "You found it. You do the honors. Let's see this medal up close."

Even knowing it was simply a matter of luck that she'd found the medal rather than any of the others, Stefanie's chest filled with pride. She knelt at the edge of the square and gently pried the medal up with the sharp point of her trowel. She turned the flat piece over. Smooth, satiny gold.

"I assume a ribbon was once attached. Silk would have decomposed long ago," Jeffrey said.

Stefanie stood up, holding the gold diamond in the palm of her hand, and both Jeffrey and Thomas took a photo.

As Jeffrey put his camera away, Beryl skewered him with a relentless stare. "We have to report it," Beryl said.

Daphne and Hunter looked up, and Ingram got to his feet. Marlene was not happy.

"Of course you have to report it," Thomas said, tucking his cell phone into his chest pocket. "This is more proof of a Spanish shipwrecked sailor, if Hunter here is correct. That's important information."

Stefanie pressed his hand again, confident he'd get them to speak openly about the emerald bracelet.

"I'll report it to Roberta if you don't," Beryl said.

Finally, Stefanie thought.

"Must you?" Marlene demanded of Jeffrey. "You're the senior museum representative. We do not want to deal with strangers at our gate, clamoring to see the treasure. In addition to that, Nathaniel is pressuring me to get back to work on the garden. He has deadlines he needs to meet. It's our property, isn't it?"

"It is," Jeffrey said.

"Why wouldn't you report it?" Stefanie asked, as if she didn't know they were talking about the emerald bracelet rather than the Spanish medal.

"We don't want to bring the police into it," Lawrence said.

"The police?" Thomas asked innocently.

"The news reporters will have a field day," Lawrence warned.

"We need to report the medal anyway," Jeffrey said. "So I'm reporting the theft of the bracelet as well. For the record. The sooner, the better." Walking off to the side, he punched a number on his cell phone and held it to his ear. Then he called out to the professor. "Ingram, will you take the medal inside and clean it? Then have Lawrence put it in his safe with the coins."

Ingram took the gold and enamel medal from Stefanie and trudged to the house with Lawrence. As the two men headed for the kitchen door, Ingram passed the medal to Lawrence.

Wistfully, Stefanie tore her attention away from them and her find.

"The bracelet?" she asked Marlene, hoping Marlene would indulge her curiosity.

Ignoring Stefanie's question, the Minister clenched her jaw. "I gave your team time to return it," she said to Jeffrey. "I want that bracelet back. I had planned to donate it to the National Museum."

Crossing her arms, Daphne hugged herself and studied the trampled grass underfoot. Hunter carefully closed his notebook and adjusted his grip on his pencil.

Beryl threw her chin up. "We want that too."

After returning Beryl's defiant stare, Marlene turned on her heel and returned to the house.

50

Stefanie considered the suspects, as she thought of them. Marlene was angry enough to reveal the theft of the bracelet with Stefanie and Thomas present. Beryl was angry too, defiant over Marlene's insinuations about the archaeologists. Daphne was worried, and Hunter controlled his movements, and his emotions, rigidly, while Ingram and Lawrence shared an excitement about the new artifact. Jeffrey himself finally did the right thing and made the call about the theft. Was it Hunter, like Thomas thought?

"What bracelet?" Thomas asked loudly, guilelessly, as if he didn't know all about it.

"We found a bracelet yesterday," Beryl admitted. "Gold, with rectangular cut emeralds. It was in the buttery, but then went missing."

Relieved to be unfettered, Stefanie said, "You were in the buttery when we arrived. Did you find it?"

"We all went in there this morning," Ingram said, having returned to the site. "To encourage the thief to return the bracelet, without backlash. So we could all put this debacle behind us." He glanced at Jeffrey, who stood away from the others, still on the phone. "Let's get to work. The wind is picking up. We know what that means."

Stefanie took off her fedora, thankful for the breeze. The suspects showed openly how they felt about the bracelet, but the problem was that she was seeing the same emotions as before. Worry, disappointment, fear, and anger.

Pulling out her ponytail holder, Daphne gathered her curls in one hand, then rewound the elastic band around her hair. She picked up a bucket and trowel and moved to Unit Three with Stefanie.

Ingram nodded at the girl. "We should be able to find other pieces of the medal. A suspension ring for the badge, and a bar which the ribbon would have been folded over. They'll be small."

Except for Hunter, who continued to work in his sketchbook, they all settled onto the ground and once again resumed the steady scraping away of the layers of soil. Stefanie was careful to go slowly, searching for the other vestiges of the medal.

"The bracelet was a fine example of Spanish Colonial goldwork," Ingram said. "Old mine emeralds. Real beauties."

51

With her head lowered, Stefanie studied them, one by one.

"I didn't take it," Daphne said when Stefanie's scrutiny landed on her.

"Nathaniel Dimon was here yesterday at lunchtime," Hunter insisted. "He needs to be questioned."

Tossing her head, Daphne said, "He didn't come back here."

With an impatient gesture, Hunter flung down his notebook and pencil and took up his trowel again. He worked the soil angrily.

"Jeffrey's reporting the theft," Thomas said. "The police will find out who took the bracelet."

Ingram stabbed his trowel deep into the grass. "This is going to kill my reputation."

Murmurings of assent rose from the others.

Beryl studiously worked the soil, her mouth pressed in a worried line.

By the end of the afternoon, nothing else had been found, not even the expected additional parts of the medal.

Jeffrey stood up. Putting his hands on his hips, he addressed the team. "Let's wrap things up. We'll finish tomorrow morning, be gone by noon. What do you say, Ingram? Beryl?"

Quick to voice her opinion before Ingram could, Beryl said, "I agree we've found all we're going to here. A Spaniard buried his valuables for safe keeping and for reasons unknown, never came back for them."

Ingram surveyed the three units, each down at least two feet, with Unit One deeper and exposing the bedrock. "We've made good progress. I agree. We're unlikely to find anything else."

Beryl came to her side as Stefanie wiped the soil from her trowel with her gloved finger.

"Our office scheduled a glow worm cruise tonight as a thank you to Dr. Ingram and his team. There'll be drinks and appetizers for dinner. Join us?"

"Thank you for the invitation." Stefanie grinned at Thomas, who took her trowel and gloves. "A glow worm cruise? Sounds romantic."

In a quieter voice, Beryl said, "You two weren't here yesterday. You aren't suspects in the theft of the bracelet. We all are. It would really relax the atmosphere to have you there."

Ingram joined them. "Come with us," he said, clapping Thomas on the back. "I want to hear your stories, now that you've listened to mine all day."

"Go ahead, you'll enjoy it," Jeffrey said. "I've seen glow worms many times, so I'm going to sit this one out." He picked up his backpack and cooler and headed for his car.

They needn't have bothered with the extra persuasion. Thomas grinned from ear to ear.

"*Ja, danke*," he said, preening over his plans working out after all. "We will go."

And alcohol would loosen reluctant tongues. They hadn't been any help at all to Jeffrey, but with the cruise, maybe they could end the evening on a high note with a likely culprit to point out.

Beryl took her yellow memo book from her pocket, wrote in it, then tore the sheet out and handed it to Stefanie. "This is the boat. It leaves from the St. George's dock at seven p.m."

Stefanie read the words written on the paper. *Sea Breeze*. Sounds delightful, she thought as she folded the note and tucked it into her shorts pocket.

Daphne and Hunter lugged one tarp to the other and dumped the soil, forming a single pile, then laid the loose tarp over the dirt. When Ingram got a third folded plastic sheet from beneath the canvas bag, Thomas took one end of the tarp and helped cover the open squares. Beryl placed the buckets at the corners to keep the tarps from drifting across the lawn.

"Why didn't you report the theft of the bracelet to the museum, even against the homeowner's wishes?" Thomas asked.

Beryl and Ingram grimaced at each other.

With a glance toward the house, Ingram answered. "Because of the Spanish question."

Chapter Nine

They didn't learn more about the Spanish question until they were on the cruise.

Dressed in a flowered halter-topped maxi dress, with Thomas at her side, Stefanie looked for the *Sea Breeze* at the Town Square dock in St. George's.

"There it is," Thomas said, placing his hand on the small of her back to guide her toward the forty-five-foot catamaran.

A man of about forty with close-cropped blond hair greeted them. "Here for the Glow Worm Cruise? Welcome aboard. Captain Craig."

Stefanie held onto the rope railing as they walked the gangplank.

"Take your shoes off when you come on board. Make yourself comfortable," Craig told them.

A woman of about the same age, just as blond and tanned, with lined, weathered skin, ran up from below. "Helen," she announced, waving to them.

"My wife Helen will take care of drinks and snacks. Just let her know what you want," Craig said.

From his seat at the front, Ingram lifted a glass of beer in greeting.

"Local brew," the captain told Thomas.

"You'll be set for the night," Stefanie commented over her shoulder to Thomas.

"I'm ready for one," he said.

"Also wine, champagne, and rum swizzles," Helen said.

"White wine for me," Stefanie said. No telling how heavy-handed they'd

54

be with the rum, and she needed to stay sharp if she were going to find out anything from the other passengers on the cruise.

Helen nodded. "Coming right up."

Once on the boat, Stefanie reached down and slipped her sandals off by the heel straps, then set them down near the five pairs already lined up. Thomas paused before he removed his and gave her a reluctant smile.

He wasn't comfortable in any situation where he couldn't be ready to get up and go at a moment's notice. Still, he took them off.

"We're just going to be talking to them," she whispered, taking his brown leather sandals and nesting them near her own gold-colored ones.

Squeezing between the cabin and the side, Stefanie held onto the rope railing as she made her way to the front of the boat. Once there, she considered seating options. White benches lined three sides of the square, open prow. A net hung in between them, revealing the water sloshing gently below. Daphne and Hunter, with several feet between them, sat against the rail opposite Ingram. Since she and Thomas needed to be thick in the middle of conversations, Stefanie chose the bench in the center, with its back to the cabin window.

Across the parking lot, Beryl sauntered to the dock, tanned and sassy in her shorts and T-shirt, quite a far cry from the grey Bermuda shorts and polo shirt she'd worn during the day.

As she boarded, Beryl checked that they were all there. "I'm the last one. Jeffrey isn't coming." She slipped off her tennis shoes without any prompting.

Stepping onto the springy net, Beryl bounced past Ingram and sat at the farthest point in front, then raised her face to the sunset.

"I'll have your drinks in a jiffy," Helen said. She cast off, then the captain turned the vessel and aimed out into the bay.

"Rum swizzle," Beryl said.

"The glow worms won't come out until dark," Captain Craig told them. "Until then, sit back and enjoy the ride."

Helen must have turned on the sound system before she started pouring drinks, because eighties pop music emerged from the speakers, the volume low enough for romance and conversation.

Stefanie leaned against Thomas. "We have our romantic cruise after all," she said in his ear.

He held her hand, then released it to take their glasses from Helen, who'd brought several drinks up on a tray. The blonde stepped onto the netting and swayed with the motion of the water as she held the tray out to Daphne and then Hunter, who each took a glass, and finally to Beryl.

"Cheers," Beryl said, accepting her rum swizzle. "It's been a day."

Ingram stared into the water beneath the net. "It has."

"What is the Spanish issue?" Thomas asked after sampling his beer.

Stefanie smiled to herself. No matter how much he protested, the pull of the investigation drew him in, as she knew it would.

"Fabiola was in the office last week," Beryl said.

Ingram nodded.

"Fabiola?" Thomas asked.

"Dr. Fabiola Ortiz, a tenacious researcher for the Spanish Cultural Ministry team," Ingram said.

"The Spanish have made a point to document as many of their shipwrecks from centuries past as they can and are campaigning to have them declared UNESCO sites, so looters will be prosecuted," Beryl said.

Stefanie considered that. "Marlene thinks they'll want the things found on her property?"

Ingram leaned back. "With the trend towards returning archaeological artifacts to original cultures, the fear is that the Spanish will step in and claim any items of Spanish origin."

"We know her well at the museum," Beryl said. "Once she hears rumors of the bracelet, Fabiola will do what she can to claim it for Spain."

Thomas addressed Hunter. "You know something about Spanish history. You knew the medal was from a Spanish order."

"Spanish Colonial archaeology is my field of study," Hunter said. "I work hard at it."

"I *wish* whoever stole the bracelet would return it," Daphne said, weaving her toes into the rope mesh in front of her. "If my school thinks I've been accused of stealing an emerald bracelet, I'll lose my scholarship."

CHAPTER NINE

That evening Daphne wore her hair down, and her curls billowed around her shoulders. The setting sun reflected off the copper of her cheeks and highlighted the worry in her eyes.

"Bad situation for all of us," Ingram said. "My God, why didn't they put the bracelet in the safe? I don't know how I'm going to explain the situation to the university board."

"I thought for certain the guilty party would return it," Beryl said, studiously avoiding eye contact with the others by maintaining an interest in the darkening water.

"Nathaniel Dimon was there," Hunter grumbled.

Again, Daphne took exception. "He didn't come out back. I would have noticed."

"You would, wouldn't you?" Hunter accused her.

"But you noticed, Hunter," Thomas said. "Where were you that you saw him and no one else did?"

Instead of answering, Hunter stared morosely out at the sea and the setting sun.

Thomas turned to the college professor. "Ingram," he said, "your reaction earlier, to Nathaniel being there yesterday afternoon. What was that about? Did you see him?"

Ingram rested his glass on his knee. "No. No, I didn't see him." He glanced sideways at Thomas. "But I know him. Or, at least, I used to. We were college roommates our freshman year at University of Virginia."

"And that look?" Thomas asked before taking a drink.

"He was a cheat. It's hard to see someone get ahead by cheating when you work hard for every grade." Ingram shrugged. "That was twenty years ago. He's done well for himself. Maybe through hard work. Maybe not."

Beryl drew one leg under her. "Nathaniel is ambitious. He doesn't let anything get in the way of his dream."

Anyone who'd been at Carmichael House over the lunch hour was suspect.

"What dream is that?" Stefanie asked.

Beryl gave a short laugh. "To be the biggest name in garden design since Gertrude Jekyll."

57

"And Marlene is going to help with that, to impress her friends in Tucker's Town," Stefanie said, repeating Beryl's comment from earlier.

"There's one who comes from humble beginnings." Beryl sipped her rum swizzle.

"Does she? I'm surprised," Stefanie said. "She's friendly with Greg Edwards, the CEO of Riverboat Rum. We're staying at his house."

Beryl looked her up and down. "She would be, wouldn't she? They're both trustees of the museum." Bitterness set her lips in a rigid line. "Some people try to put the past behind them. That's not always possible."

What would Beryl like to put behind her? The theft of the emerald bracelet?

"Even small acts in the right direction help," Stefanie said, hoping to encourage Beryl, if she were the thief.

In response, Beryl drank her rum and returned her gaze to the water.

Stefanie sipped her wine and took Thomas's hand. Beryl herself was ambitious. She'd been envious when Stefanie found the medal, and it seemed that she wanted to move up in the ranks at the museum. That ambition spoke against risking her career by taking the emerald bracelet. Envy, though, was a motive.

But was that motive any stronger than Hunter's, with his family history of salvage? They couldn't discount Nathaniel Dimon, either, it seemed.

The setting sun spread a glorious rainbow of color across the clouds, and Stefanie settled against Thomas, enjoying the light show and the gentle sloshing of the waves that splashed up through the net below her feet.

"What brought you to Bermuda from the University of Virginia?" Thomas asked Ingram.

"I started out in Jamestown, Virginia," the professor said, "at the archaeological site there. Moved on to studying military arms in Virginia in the 1800s, which led to comparing those in Virginia to those here in Bermuda during the same time period. Not as exciting as studying the Spanish Treasure Fleet. Hunter has that covered."

Darkness fell, and Helen kept up a steady supply of drinks and snacks.

"I wonder what his story is, the Spaniard who buried the gold," Stefanie said. "And who the bracelet was meant for."

"His woman," Thomas stated, entwining his fingers in hers.

Daphne pursed her lips while Hunter rolled his eyes. Beryl met Stefanie's gaze with a repressed smile and lifted her eyebrows at their response. Ingram took a drink of beer, refraining from comment.

"Maybe he had the chance to catch another ship and gave up his valuables to escape the island and return to Spain," Beryl suggested.

"Or someone tried to steal them from him," Ingram said. "Had to be some reason that chest was buried empty. It was a decoy, buried so whoever found it would stop looking."

"Or look somewhere else," Hunter said.

A massive sigh escaped Ingram's barrel chest. "We'll never know for certain."

Captain Craig leaned against the cabin. "Get ready. We're almost to the cove. I'll let you know when you can expect to see the glow worms."

Stefanie got up with her empty glass. Two generous glasses of wine had taken their toll. "Be back in a sec. I don't want to miss the main event."

She climbed down the narrow steps and squeezed into the tiny bathroom.

After pumping the flushing mechanism, she thought she heard a raised voice in the galley. Not one to miss an opportunity, she leaned her ear against the door.

"I saw you with him," a voice hissed. Then, bare feet padded quickly up the steps.

Beryl? Daphne? Helen? The voice sounded female, that's all she could tell. And who was the woman talking to? Giving her hands a quick wash, Stefanie dried them on her dress and opened the door.

No one waited on the stairs or in the tiny galley kitchen. She hurried up on deck. Thomas had moved to the back of the boat with Craig, and both peered into the dark water.

"Almost," Craig said when he saw her.

Thomas cocked his head.

"Was someone waiting on the restroom?" she asked.

"I didn't see anyone," Thomas said.

At the front of the boat, Beryl stood facing the water, her back to the boat. Daphne was seated where she had been before, and Helen held out a tray of appetizers to Ingram.

"I'm out of the bathroom," Stefanie said.

"We see," Hunter said with detached amusement.

The women didn't respond.

"I thought I heard someone knock on the door." Still no response from the women.

At that moment, Craig called out. "Get your phones and cameras ready."

Stefanie joined Thomas at the back of the catamaran as they all huddled to see the bright green luminescent spots in the water. Even Daphne let Hunter stand close to watch. One by one, glowing masses rose in the shallows near the dark shore.

Beryl stood apart. Preoccupied, or had seen glow worms perform many times before?

Thomas leaned his head against Stefanie's. "It's the way of nature. Women call, men respond."

"Is that what our relationship is?" she asked with a smile. "A phenomenon of nature? A particularly appealing phenomenon?"

"Destiny," he said, kissing her cheek in the moonlight.

She lifted her cheek against his lips, savoring that touch, then wrapped her arm around his waist and watched the glowing courtship dance in the dark water.

When the glow worm display was over, Craig steered the catamaran back to the dock, slowly gliding under the starry sky. Stefanie snuggled close to Thomas, content in the moment.

"Where are you staying?" Thomas asked Ingram.

"The university rented a house for us near the Dockyard."

"The house is mint green, but it's nice inside," Daphne said. "And it's across the street from the beach."

At the dock, Stefanie and Thomas said their goodbyes. With their part in the investigation over, she could relax. Except for the disappointment that they hadn't been able to suss out which one of those at Carmichael House had stolen the bracelet. No impressing René at Interpol with her additional investigative experience. At least they'd seen glow worms.

She and Thomas climbed into the Tazzari as a fine mist began to fall.

"These headlights are bright," he said, with grudging admiration for the car.

Thomas whipped through the dark streets, around corners where there was little room for error between the road and walls surrounding yards. Her muscles had been tense on the cruise as she stayed alert for clues and worked the others for information. Hunter or Beryl were the strongest contenders. She rested her head back, but Nathaniel Dimon's presence on the day of the theft nagged at her.

Stefanie repeated what she'd overheard. "I couldn't tell who was speaking, but the 'him' mentioned had to be Nathaniel Dimon, don't you think?"

Thomas narrowed his eyes. "Maybe."

"It wouldn't cause remark if the "him" were Hunter or Ingram. Or Lawrence Carmichael. Whoever hissed those words felt it important to hide that conversation from me," she said. "I wasn't subtle about someone being near the bathroom." She drummed her fingers on her thigh.

"It could be Hunter."

"I noticed you grilling him." It had been subtle, but sometimes that worked better than being obvious.

He smiled in the dark. "Not that he gave anything away."

"I suspect him, too. But wouldn't both Jeffrey and Ingram be well aware of Hunter's father and have kept a closer eye on him than on anyone else?" she asked.

"I suppose," he conceded.

"Jeffrey didn't know that Nathaniel Dimon was at Carmichael House yesterday. I wonder if Nathaniel saw anything."

"Our favor for Jeffrey is taken care of," Thomas reminded her.

"Very true. However unsatisfactorily. My best guess is Hunter, Beryl, or possibly Nathaniel Dimon, as unlikely as that sounds."

Thomas glanced at her, then back at the road. "You really want to follow this. All right. Let's check out Nathaniel Dimon tomorrow morning, verify that he was at Carmichael House yesterday, and see if he saw anything. Then we snorkel at Tobacco Bay."

One point to her.

The awkwardness between Daphne and Hunter on the boat reminded her of her own recent misunderstanding with Thomas. She never wanted that to happen again. Though she and Thomas were older than Daphne and Hunter, new relationships suffered growing pains, no matter how experienced you were.

"I was insecure in Venice," she said. "Not because Francesca was beautiful— she is. And not because you flirted with her—you did and you will flirt with women again," she said when he started to protest. "Because you and she come from the same kind of background. One of privilege and power. I don't."

He searched her eyes. "I'm a German policeman, working for Interpol."

She tilted her head at that.

"The rest doesn't matter," he said quietly. "We're right for each other. You know that, and I know that."

She did. She didn't need to worry about Thomas's commitment.

"In Venice," he said, "I should have seen that being honest about my past wasn't enough. I will show you that you are the only woman for me."

"I'm looking forward to that," she said tartly.

He shot her a look, his eyes dark and full of emotion, sending a thrill of anticipation up her spine.

As he slowed for the driveway, Stefanie saw a car in the driveway and a man standing in the shadows. No, two men. The one at the corner of the garage talking to Jeffrey was medium height, thin, with dark hair, expensively cut, and had an athletic grace to his movements.

With a start, she recognized Greg Edwards. A suitcase rested at his feet.

Chapter Ten

S tefanie's anticipation for the evening bottomed out. But maybe that suitcase at Greg's feet didn't mean what she thought it did.

"Who is that?" Thomas asked as he shut off the engine. The force with which he hit the emergency brake button expressed his feelings about yet another intrusion into their getaway.

His disapproval of unwanted company didn't extend to the sleek Jaguar they'd parked next to. The car sat low and lean, a metallic silver sedan.

"Jaguar XF," Thomas said, angling for a better look. Then his lips pressed in a tight line as his approval for the car morphed into envy. "Must not be a visitor to the island."

"It's Greg Edwards." She put her hand on Thomas's. "I didn't think he'd be coming to Bermuda this week."

A muscle in his jaw worked as he took stock of Greg. "I'll pull Jeffrey aside and tell him what little we learned, let him know that we'll do one last thing for him and check out Nathaniel Dimon in the morning. See if Dimon saw anything since he was at Carmichael House at the right time."

"Tell Jeffrey what I overheard. I just wish I knew who said it. And to whom." With a deep breath to fortify herself before talking to Greg, Stefanie tucked her purse under her arm and got out of the car.

Greg turned and beamed at her. Dressed in slim-fitting dress pants, a checked button-down shirt and tie, he looked every inch the suave, successful distillery owner she'd known at the bank.

"Greg," she said, "how nice to see you." And how unexpected. She met Thomas at the front of the Tazzari and slipped her arm through his. "This is

Thomas Burkhardt."

Greg leaned forward and shook hands with Thomas.

"Nice Jag," Thomas said, leveling his stern police officer gaze on the other man.

Greg grinned at the silver car. "Thanks."

"I'll be off," Jeffrey said, with a significant look at both Stefanie and Thomas.

"I'll walk with you." Thomas touched Stefanie's fingers. "Be inside in a minute."

He and Jeffrey walked to the end of the drive and stood talking by the driveway pillar. If Jeffrey hoped they'd overheard a confession about the bracelet, he was out of luck.

Stefanie turned back to Greg and glanced down at his roller bag, which sat silently, yet said so much. Hopefully, her dismay didn't show on her face.

"Come in," she said. "Make yourself at home." She laughed lightly.

Chuckling, Greg held the door, then followed her in.

The cottage had an open plan, with a living room/dining room combination, light wood flooring, and a modern kitchen complete with granite countertops and stainless-steel appliances. Perfect for two. A little crowded for three.

"Want a drink? The wine is yours, too," Stefanie joked over her shoulder.

Thomas had finished informing Jeffrey and was on his way in.

Greg held the front door for him as well, then closed it. He left his suitcase by the door, she noticed.

Thomas eyed it as he passed. "Very good wine it is, too," Thomas said.

He must have been straining his ears to have heard her comment to Greg. "Ah, but you should try the rum," Greg replied.

Thomas flashed a humorless grin. "Not tonight."

Either not catching Thomas's attitude or choosing to ignore it, Greg took a bottle of pinot grigio from the refrigerator and opened it.

Stefanie took glasses from the cabinet, then poured three conservative glasses of wine. Surely Greg would get that hint.

"How does it run?" Thomas asked, with a nod in the general direction of the driveway.

"Purrs like a kitten," Greg said, taking his glass and settling in the overstuffed leather chair in the living area. "I would have gone for the two-door model, but I needed the extra room for business associates."

Thomas took the corner of the matching leather sofa.

"Jeffrey says he put you to work," Greg remarked.

"Thanks to you," she said, bringing her glass to the couch. She pushed her sandals off with her toes and curled up beside Thomas. If Jeffrey had shared the reason he'd asked them to help, Greg would have to mention it before she shared any specifics with him.

"The excavation is at Carmichael House," Thomas said. "Stefanie and I both have experience in the field, and Jeffrey mentioned the threat of a coming storm."

"Carmichael House," Greg said. "Marlene and I go way back." He settled more comfortably in his chair, resting his elbows on the cushioned arms. "Anytime I have an issue with the business, she finds a way to make things work. For that matter, Lawrence and I go way back, too."

Thomas threw his arm across the couch back and stretched out his legs.

"What kind of issues do you have with your business?" he asked.

Greg smiled. "Small ones. We've got some of the most contented employees in Bermuda and are aiming toward a zero carbon footprint. We should reach it within five years. What is it you do, Thomas?"

"Is that polite curiosity, or do you really want to know?" After taking a sip of wine, Thomas glanced at Stefanie. "Worked an archaeological dig today. Tomorrow it will be snorkeling, and sea turtles after that."

"Right, you're on vacation," Greg said easily.

"And we appreciate the loan of your house. Great location," Thomas said. Stefanie stared as he drained his wine, almost in a single swallow.

"It has been a long day, between the excavation and the moonlight cruise," Thomas remarked. "If you'll excuse me." Setting his glass on the end table, he left them alone in the living room.

"It has been a long day," Stefanie agreed. And getting longer by the minute. She picked up Thomas's glass and took it into the kitchen.

Greg followed her. "Has a great view of the Atlantic, doesn't it?" he said.

"It does. We sat out back this afternoon," she said.

While she rinsed out the glasses, he jerked his head in the direction Thomas had taken. "I somehow thought the friend you were bringing was female."

Uh oh. She smiled to cover her discomfort. How awkward was he going to make it?

Leaning against the kitchen doorway, he looked her over. "You didn't have any special male friends when I knew you at the bank."

Very awkward. How her life had changed. Those long hours she'd happily spent working customers for Markham-Briggs Bank had been traded for travel with Thomas, and she wouldn't have it any other way.

"That's because I spent all my time working," she said. "I was married to the job, I'd almost say. Thomas and I met in Greece."

Greg looked pointedly at her bare fingers.

"We're a couple," she clarified.

He gave her a rueful smile. "I'd promised Jeffrey a double date. That won't be happening."

"Maybe with someone else," she suggested.

Thomas came up behind him. "You're welcome to stay. There are two bedrooms."

Greg turned smoothly. "No, I promised the house to Stefanie for the week, and it's hers. I may stop in occasionally to pick up something, if you don't mind."

"Of course," she said. "At least stay tonight. It's past eleven."

"Jeffrey has an extra room." Greg raised a hand in farewell as he sauntered to the door. "He'll put me up."

"Thank God for that," Thomas said as the front door closed.

He took her hand, and she turned out the lights.

Hopefully, Greg wasn't going to be a problem.

Chapter Eleven

The next morning, Stefanie chose her outfit with care.

"Nathaniel is something of a star," she told Thomas as she wavered between a tailored navy sundress accented with white buttons and a white peasant top over loose linen beach trousers. "I looked him up online while you were in the shower. He's won a ton of prestigious awards."

"The dress. He's used to high-end clients." Thomas pulled on a grey-blue shirt that matched his eyes.

"Peasant top and trousers," she decided, whisking the two hangers into the bathroom to change. "High-end women know how to relax in style when on vacation."

She caught Thomas's grin in the mirror as he buttoned the tailor-made shirt. She let her gaze linger, approving of the way the cotton stretched across his chest and tapered at the waist.

He went to her side and bent his head to hers. Nuzzling her behind the ear, he inhaled slowly. "Citrus," he said. "And...rosemary?"

Stefanie smiled at their reflections. "What a discerning nose you have. That's my Lili Bermuda perfume. Fresh Water."

"I know," he replied. "You were wearing it the night we met."

She remembered the way he'd smelled the night they'd met, as well. Like sea air and hops.

Neither of them brought up Greg Edwards.

Later, in the driveway, Thomas held up the key fob. "Want to drive?"

She pretended to consider, but declined, knowing the way the drivers took the narrow streets and curves.

"I'm not tackling this traffic. You can drive," she said. "You can be my chauffeur."

He clicked the remote. "I prefer to think of us as a power couple."

She tossed her leather carry-on, doubling as a beach bag filled with towels, sandals and their swimsuits, into the micro space behind the seats.

"We're questioning Nathaniel Dimon as ourselves, right?" she asked.

"Completely ourselves. On vacation here in Bermuda, away from the demands of life, but interested in his services after our friends Marlene and Lawrence highly recommended him."

On the drive from St. George's Island to the larger island where Hamilton was located, they ran into morning rush hour and tourist traffic, including frequent stops behind the buses that seemed to stop every half mile for an eclectic mix of commuters dressed for work and vacationers dressed for the beach.

"First we need to find out if Nathaniel actually was at the house Tuesday," Stefanie said. "No one saw him except Hunter."

Thomas nodded, keeping his eyes on the road. "Then we work the conversation around to what and who he might have seen."

He found a parking spot a few doors down from the landscape designer's office.

"I'll bet Nathaniel Dimon saw something, whether he realizes it or not," Stefanie said.

"Unless he went straight inside to talk to Marlene."

Thomas entwined his fingers in hers. Their arms swung together comfortably as they walked down the sidewalk.

He raised her hand to his lips and brushed a kiss on her knuckles. "Just this one last effort to help Jeffrey figure out who stole that bracelet."

Before he stepped off the curb, Thomas reflexively looked left for traffic, then stepped back as a car horn honked from the right.

"*That* will definitely go in my travel blog," Stefanie said. "Oh, that reminds me. A nice payment from the magazine was deposited in my account this morning. For the Italy piece." She couldn't help but smile.

"We'll have to celebrate."

"We will," she said, knowing exactly what he had in mind and looking forward to it.

They arrived at the address, an attractive two-story building with six-paned windows. Nathaniel Dimon Garden Design was written in a flourished script on the wooden sign out front. Thomas held the door for her.

They entered a small reception area. Beyond it, two doors led to offices, one of them slightly ajar. Maybe they were in luck, and the designer was present rather than out on a job.

Stefanie decided to take charge.

"Good morning," she said to the grey-haired, fashionably dressed recep-tionist. "It's a lovely morning out."

"Good morning," the woman greeted her. "How are you today?"

"We're fine, thank you. We're hoping Mr. Dimon is available for a garden consultation." Stefanie removed her fedora and held it with both hands. "We've heard the most divine things about him from our friends Marlene and Lawrence Carmichael."

The receptionist smiled primly. "Mr. Dimon isn't in at the moment. Let me see when he's available." She tapped a few strokes on her computer keyboard and scanned the screen. "I'm sorry, he's completely booked until October."

"That works for us," Thomas said. "We can just touch base today."

The secretary blinked at him over her glasses. "October next year."

An electronic chime dinged subtlety as the outer door opened.

Without checking to see who'd entered, Thomas put his hand on Stefanie's elbow. His voice full of consolation, he said, "I told you it was too much to expect a big name like Nathaniel Dimon to fly to Munich on such short notice."

Going with his bit of deception, Stefanie's mouth turned down. "And we have that reception for the ambassador in the spring. I had hoped—"

Out of the corner of her eye, she saw a handsome man enter and close the door. Very handsome, with high cheekbones and a chiseled jaw, short dark curls and eyes just as dark as they were sharp. No wonder Hunter thought Daphne would notice if Nathaniel Dimon entered the area. Any woman would.

Meeting them at the reception desk, the man said, "Nathaniel Dimon."

He shook their hands.

"Thomas Burkhardt. And Stefanie Adams."

Stefanie noticed the slight hesitation before Thomas announced her last name. So they weren't to be married for this little charade. Completely themselves. Was she disappointed or not? Time enough to think about that later.

"Munich, you said." Nathaniel's glance took them in, possibly assigning a cost to their clothes, certainly assessing their potential worth as clients. "I don't get much business on the continent."

"But you're not available until next year?" Stefanie asked, feeling herself drawn to that dark gaze. "Marlene and Lawrence raved about the plan you designed for them."

He acknowledged the praise with a smile. "The garden at Carmichael House will be an inviting and peaceful refuge when I'm done with it."

"Speaking of important projects," the secretary said, "The Governor's office called." With a pressing vigor, she tapped the paper calendar on her desk. "They've gotten the dates cleared that you asked for."

Thomas brought up a picture on his phone. "We'd need something much larger than the project at Carmichael House," he said, holding his screen out to the designer. "We're looking for a redo of our place in the country."

Stefanie managed a quick peek. The house was huge, maybe even a small castle. Germany was rolling with them. Which one had he shown?

The garden designer's eyebrows rose.

His secretary tapped the calendar again.

Had Thomas's property been enough of a lure? If the secretary continued to pressure the designer, they wouldn't get a chance to bring the conversation casually around to anything he'd seen at Carmichael House.

"At Carmichael House, I noticed only decorative rocks and containers for garden ornaments," she said.

"Our native limestone," Nathaniel said. "Their landscape blends with the natural environment. The paths I'll install at Carmichael House will tame Mother Nature while maintaining the rural abundance that Bermuda is known for."

"We'll have several pieces to install as focal points." Stefanie turned to Thomas. "There's the large Sykes' piece we commissioned when we were on Santorini."

"And the Roman statues." Thomas checked the date on his watch. "The auction house promised they will be delivered in two weeks."

Nathaniel's jaw clenched, for just a moment. To his secretary, he said, "I'll call the Governor's office back when I'm finished here." He gestured toward a white painted door on the left. "Come into my office. Let's talk landscapes."

Inside the room, he indicated two white painted chairs in front of a whitewashed desk, then sat down facing them.

"When you want to make a statement, that first impression is of utmost importance," Nathaniel said. "At times, the plants I initially choose don't have quite the impact that I planned for, and I substitute for the proper effect. That's why I insist on being present when my designs are being implemented."

The in she was hoping for. "So you go to Carmichael House every day?" Stefanie asked. "We must have missed you Tuesday. What time were you there?"

"It might have been around noon," he said.

"Beryl showed me what they were doing," Thomas said. "The things they'd found. The brass chest."

"Beryl Swan. Yes," Nathaniel said. "She works for the National Museum of Bermuda."

"So you know her. Did she tell you how the excavation was going?" Stefanie asked.

Nathaniel's expression closed. "No."

"She was probably hard at work," Stefanie said. "Or maybe in the buttery. I understand that's where they keep their discoveries during the day."

He gave a little smile. "I was there, but only for a moment. The archaeological work, you know."

"Hunter specializes in the Spanish Colonial era. I'll bet he had tales to tell," Thomas said.

The landscape designer tapped the end of his pen on his desk. "I only spoke with Marlene on Tuesday."

How frustrating. Nathaniel Dimon apparently had a one-track mind, and that was on landscaping.

She turned to Thomas. "We'll have to get Marlene to invite us over again after the garden is done."

Nathaniel's radiant smile showed perfect confidence. "Tell me what your plans are for your…" his voice trailed off.

He must be wondering if the place Thomas had shown was a castle, too, she thought, amused.

"The family home," Thomas said. "We want something formal, but not stuffy."

"Environmentally sustainable," Stefanie said. "We'll consider natives."

"No weeds," Thomas insisted. "We're not growing weeds and calling them natives."

Nathaniel grinned. "I'm certain that I can design a plan that will satisfy both your needs."

The secretary knocked on the door frame. "It's the Governor's office calling again." Her eyes widened, urging him to heed her.

"I'll get back to them shortly, Sandra." Nathaniel turned his attention back to Stefanie and Thomas. "Busy morning," he said with a tone of apology. "I'm doing some alterations for the grounds of Government House. I believe I heard you say you had an important reception this spring? We can set up an appointment to discuss preliminary details. Acreage, budget."

Thomas opened the calendar on his phone. "Next week, Thursday?"

"Yes, that will do."

Bring up the theft, or not? Not. Even if he had seen something, he'd shown he had no interest in talking about it with them.

"And can we call you if we think of something we must have?" Stefanie asked. "Bermuda is inspiring me."

Nathaniel stood up. "Of course. If you leave me your number, I'll have Sandra contact you with the time of the appointment."

After Thomas exchanged business cards with the landscaper, they left the office.

"Now we know. He was at Carmichael House Tuesday. Around lunchtime," Stefanie said when they got in the car. "And a little cagey about it. At least concerning Beryl."

"We can let Jeffrey know," Thomas said, "and leave the follow-up to him. And the police."

Still, it was disappointing that Nathaniel hadn't given them anything for Jeffrey to go on.

"What was that building you showed him?" she asked. "It certainly impressed him." Linderhof, she thought. Or maybe Mespellbrunn. Anticipating a trip to Germany, she'd researched castles to visit in Bavaria.

Turning his head, Thomas gave her a steady look.

Stefanie blinked. Oh. It *was* the family home. "We're here as ourselves."

Absorbing the unexpected possibility of moving into some grand mansion with Thomas and all that entailed, she was surprised when they made it back to St. George's, and he pulled up beside a white two-story building instead of Carmichael House.

She smiled when she read the sign.

"The Lili Bermuda Perfumery," she said, pleased. "I thought you'd want to finish with Jeffrey and zip off to Tobacco Bay."

"Not yet. This is on the way." Thomas opened the door to the perfumery. "You're running low."

Inside the salesroom, Stefanie inhaled deeply. Scents of rose and greenery reminded her of a bouquet of flowers. An array of fragrances, yet light and fresh. The very thing she loved about her Fresh Water cologne.

Wooden beams crossed the ceiling of the historic building. Glass shelves were full of Lili Bermuda's signature square bottles, artfully displayed, and racks of essential oils in blue bottles added to the sophisticated quaintness.

"Feel free to sample anything you like," the young saleswoman said. "Or all of them."

"No need," Thomas said. "She knows what she likes. Fresh Water eau de cologne."

When the sales clerk brought a box from beneath the counter, Thomas asked, "Do you ship?"

"Anywhere in the world," the woman said.

"We'll take a bottle to ship, also."

"Thomas, no," Stefanie protested. "This one will last plenty long enough."

He gave her a sideways smile, then gave the sales clerk an address in Munich.

Stefanie pressed her lips together.

"It will be waiting for you," he said.

When they were outside the perfumery, Stefanie asked, "At that mansion you showed Nathaniel Dimon?"

A little smile played on his lips. "This one is for my apartment."

"Is it now?" Joyfulness bubbled up in her chest, filling her with contentment.

Maybe it was realizing that moving in with Thomas was going to entail a bigger change in her life than she'd expected. Maybe it was because she hadn't been able to come up with a single definite insight to share with Jeffrey, but Stefanie felt an obscure need to assert herself and took the Tazzari keys from Thomas.

"Text Jeffrey and let him know we're on the way," she said.

As she drove the short distance to Carmichael House, the overheard conversation on the boat still nagged at her. She could swear it was Beryl speaking.

"I find it very suspicious that no one last night on the cruise would admit to being outside the bathroom," Stefanie continued. "They didn't want to admit to being overheard, and why is that, if there was nothing to hide? I'm sure the "him" I overheard refers to Nathaniel. It doesn't make sense for that to be any of the others at Carmichael House. They could all be expected to talk to each other, so why hide it? And why was Nathaniel Dimon so evasive about seeing anyone or talking to them Tuesday at Carmichael House?" she asked. "It's not like we asked him if he peeked in windows."

"Perhaps he knows about the theft and doesn't want to get involved," Thomas said, texting Jeffrey.

"I want to try something when we get to Carmichael House," she said. "Could Nathaniel have seen anyone walk into the buttery if he were in the drive at the front of the house, do you think?"

"Unlikely."

True. They'd seen that for themselves yesterday during their break for water.

"I think it was Beryl's voice I overheard on the boat stairs," she said. "It was low, but emphatic, like her conversations."

When she pulled up to the gate, Jeffrey came from the left side of the house, the direction of the dig. With a wave, he went to the remote on the gate post and let them in.

Stefanie pulled into the drive and parked directly in front of the front door. Out of sight of those at the excavation.

"We've filled in the units and are ready to call it done. The bracelet still hasn't shown up." Jeffrey looked hopefully at them. "Did you find out anything from Nathaniel?"

"He was here Tuesday," she confirmed. "He didn't tell us anything, so you'll have to ask Beryl or Hunter point blank who Nathaniel was talking to. Hunter is the only one who claims to have seen him, but Beryl might have, too." Stefanie glanced toward the side path. "Nathaniel couldn't have seen the buttery from here, the front of the house. But what if he was on that side, checking out the path?"

"There's not much to decide on for landscaping there, but I suppose he could have been," Jeffrey said, looking toward the corner.

"New paths are part of his plan," Stefanie said. "I want to try something. I want the two of you to go to the dig site, and I'll take this side route to the buttery. Tell me when you can see me, and I'll find the point where I can first see the entrance to the buttery. The person I overheard last night might have seen Nathaniel on that side of the house while they were in the buttery."

"In the buttery taking the bracelet," Jeffrey said.

Stefanie nodded.

While the two men humored her and moved off to the excavation area, Stefanie crossed the front of the house to the paved pathway on the side. That area was in need of landscape taming as well. Beyond the rubber tree on the corner, the six-foot tall oleanders that lined the fence were so overgrown they crowded the walkway, making a cozy tunnel between house and street.

One of the blue tarps had blown there, despite Beryl's efforts the afternoon before to hold them down with the buckets. Taking a more focused look at the bundle on the sidewalk, Stefanie stopped. Ten feet along the sidewalk, it wasn't a wind-blown tarp, but a woman, laying on her side. Stefanie's mouth gaped open. Beryl. Collecting herself, Stefanie ran to her and knelt down. Blood from the back of Beryl's head pooled on the pavement.

Chapter Twelve

"Thomas! Jeffrey! Help!" Stefanie called.

She shuddered as she felt Beryl's throat for a pulse. It didn't take long to ascertain there wasn't one. How sad to be experienced at feeling for a pulse and checking for breath, a skill she desperately didn't want.

Pounding footsteps ran up behind her. Thomas, of course. He repeated her actions, checking for life.

"She's gone," he said, getting the same results.

He stood up, but Stefanie stayed on her knees. How could she not have foreseen something like this happening?

Ahead, Marlene stepped out of the kitchen door. "Did she fall?"

When Stefanie shook her head, Marlene ran to her side.

Jeffrey came up behind Stefanie. "I'm calling an ambulance."

"Call the police," Thomas told him.

When Marlene knelt and reached for Beryl's hand, Stefanie saw Daphne peek around the back corner of the house. The girl gasped audibly, but stayed where she was, staring at Beryl.

Stefanie sat back on her heels. In the narrow garden bed sat a chunk of bloody limestone. She glared at the red stain. Beryl's head didn't lay near the rock. Someone had done this deliberately. Heartlessly.

She surveyed the fence line. The same overgrown shrubs that made the narrow garden intimate and cozy blocked any view from the street. No way could anyone in the house on the next corner have seen what happened.

Beryl's body was still warm. Stefanie tried to cement in her mind what happened when they arrived.

Jeffrey had been coming from the excavated area when they drove into the driveway, then he and Thomas went around the house to the left. She hadn't seen anyone else at all. She'd been in front only for a few moments. Maybe long enough to let Beryl's killer slip away, either into the kitchen entrance or to the back. Unless Beryl had been hit before they arrived. It couldn't have been too long before, though.

Touching Beryl's shoulder gently, Stefanie slowly stood up beside Thomas. There was nothing she could do.

"Are you okay?" he asked.

She nodded. "You see the rock?"

"Yes," he said, his mouth set in a grim line.

Lawrence hurried around the corner from the front with Greg Edwards. What was Greg doing at Carmichael House?

Hunter and Ingram followed on their heels. All four men stared at Beryl's body. One of these people had killed Beryl, Stefanie thought.

After a moment, Lawrence asked, "Did she have the bracelet?"

"Lawrence." Marlene's face reddened.

Her husband took no notice. "Was she pushed?"

"Did she hit her head on that rock?" Greg asked, spotting the stained chunk of limestone.

"Beryl's body is in the wrong position for her to have fallen and hit her head on that rock," Thomas said. "What was Beryl doing over here?"

"I don't know." Marlene covered her mouth with her hand. "I was talking to Greg earlier, but didn't see her out here. Did you, Greg?"

Greg, too, studied Beryl's body as he spoke. "No, when I left you, I had a word with Lawrence. Then I took the French doors to the back yard to check out the dig."

"I'm going to get something to cover her up." Marlene hurried into the house.

Stefanie looked upward. The den windows directly faced the sidewalk. She remembered the view from her visit there yesterday.

Seeing her glance, Greg said, "I didn't see anyone walk past the windows when I was in the den with Lawrence."

"Nor did I," Lawrence said.

"Let's check her phone," Jeffrey said. "Maybe it holds a clue." He started toward Beryl, then hesitated.

"Don't touch anything," Thomas said.

Disregarding him, Hunter knelt down and quickly patted Beryl's pockets. "I have gloves on."

Thomas pulled him up by the back of his T-shirt, but not before Hunter pulled Beryl's yellow Rite in the Rain notebook from her shorts pocket.

"No phone," Hunter said. "Just this."

The bulky garden gloves made him fumble as he flipped through the plastic-coated notebook. "Not much written in here. Some pages ripped out."

Daphne hugged her arms across her midsection. "Were you expecting it to say 'Return bracelet today?'" she demanded.

Flushing, Hunter said, "She doesn't have the bracelet on her."

Under Thomas's compelling stare, Hunter started to return the notebook where he'd gotten it, then stopped himself and carefully laid it on the sidewalk beside her.

Stefanie took Thomas's arm, wrapping both her arms around it. The warmth of his body heat helped dispel the horror that chilled her to the bone.

Jeffrey looked sick.

"You were closest to her," she said to him.

He nodded. "We worked together for fifteen years."

They all looked ill, to one degree or another. One of them was pretending.

Marlene returned with a soft blue coverlet, which she gently laid over Beryl's body.

With a tired sigh, she said, "Let's wait in front for the police."

"If Beryl doesn't have the bracelet, who does?" Ingram asked.

Whoever had killed Beryl, Stefanie thought.

Ingram's question met silence as they studied each other, probing to discern guilt behind guarded faces.

The welcome wail of sirens pierced the air, and it wasn't long before several blue, yellow, and white police vehicles and an ambulance pulled up on the street in front of Carmichael House.

When Lawrence met the police and paramedics and escorted them to the crime scene, Marlene went inside. Everyone else clustered on the driveway, watching the police.

"I don't understand how it could have happened," Jeffrey said, his face ashen. "We'd finished with the dig. We were packing up our tools."

"When did you last see her?" Thomas asked. "All of you?"

"Earlier this morning," Jeffrey said. "We've been busy, with a lot of back and forth as we gathered the supplies. I think I saw her take a load to her car earlier, maybe half an hour before you got here."

"That was about nine-fifteen," Thomas said.

"We'd just finished filling in the holes when I got the text that you were stopping by," Jeffrey said. "I met you out here, then we walked back to the site."

Thomas nodded and looked at Hunter. "I didn't see you when I arrived."

The student shrugged. "Since we were finished, I was exploring deeper in the garden. It goes back about fifteen feet."

The area where Nathaniel Dimon planned to add structured paths, Stefanie thought.

"I loaded up some of the supplies in our van shortly before you and Stefanie got here," Ingram said. "I'd gone back for another load. Not sure where anyone else was."

Stefanie eyed Daphne. She'd been in close proximity around the time of Beryl's death.

Daphne raised her chin. "I was in the buttery."

"What were you doing there?" Stefanie asked.

"I wasn't returning the bracelet, if that's what you think." Daphne said. "I just wanted some time alone. We were all sniping at each other this morning. I was tired of it."

"It's true." Ingram shook his head. "We all know what the missing bracelet means. How the news will be received by our superiors. By the college

80

boards."

They had more serious problems than a theft, she thought.

"When did everyone get here this morning?" Thomas asked.

"We were all here by seven-thirty," Jeffrey said. "Myself, Beryl, and Ingram with Daphne and Hunter."

Thomas nodded toward Greg. "And you? When did you get here?"

With a solemn expression, Greg stuck his hands in his front pockets. "About eight-fifteen."

"When did Beryl go to the far side of the house? Who saw her go?" Stefanie asked.

She was met with headshakes, shrugs, and silence.

A forceful woman in a blue skirt and matching suit jacket, business-like with dark hair pulled back into a tiny, no-nonsense bun, finished with Lawrence and walked to the front.

"I'd better talk to her," Stefanie said. "Since I'm the one who found Beryl."

She approached the plainclothes officer, who she took to be in charge.

"I'm the one who found the body," Stefanie said, her stomach in knots.

The woman focused a hard glance on her. "Good morning. I'm Detective Inspector Jenae Franklin-Ross. This is a sad day. A woman has lost her life."

Uh oh, she'd made that cardinal Bermudian error, not starting out with a polite greeting. "I apologize," Stefanie said, starting again. "Good morning, I'm Stefanie Adams." Thomas joined her. "This is Thomas Burkhardt."

"Good morning, officer," Thomas said. "It is a sad day indeed."

The DI's gaze didn't soften. "Did either of you know her?"

Stefanie glanced briefly toward Beryl's body. Mercifully, it was surrounded by crime scene technicians. "We just met her yesterday."

The DI nodded. "I have a few questions for you."

"When did it happen?" Stefanie asked, trying to figure out how soon they'd arrived after the murder.

Light brown eyes zeroed in on hers. "*I* have a few questions for *you*."

Chastised, Stefanie nodded.

"When did you see her last?" the officer asked.

Thomas put his arm around Stefanie. "Last night. On the Glow Worm cruise."

"We met everyone yesterday morning," Stefanie said. "We came here yesterday to help with the dig." Checking to make sure the others were out of hearing, she told the DI exactly how they'd come to be involved. "The emerald bracelet was found Tuesday and had disappeared by that afternoon."

"And it wasn't reported," DI Franklin-Ross stated, thawing slightly with Stefanie's revelation about the stolen bracelet.

Thomas pointed to Jeffrey, who stood near the front steps. "Jeffrey Fitzsimmons suspected it was someone involved in the dig. The owners were willing to give that person time to return the bracelet before they called in the police."

"Jeffrey wanted us to be an extra set of eyes," Stefanie said.

"And to put some pressure on," Thomas added.

The DI gazed steadily at them both. "What time did you get here this morning?"

"About nine-fifteen," Stefanie said.

"Walk me through your movements."

They were suspects, too, Stefanie realized with dismay. She and Thomas recited their exact movements since arriving at Carmichael House.

"The bracelet hadn't shown up," Thomas said.

"Any indication that Beryl Swan had taken this bracelet?" the officer asked.

They had no proof, only suspicion that Beryl might have, based on envy over Stefanie's find, and ambition. Envy and ambition alone weren't enough, and the overheard conversation on the boat hadn't included any mention of the bracelet.

Stefanie shook her head. "She was tense."

"So was everyone else," Thomas said. "We didn't discover which of them had taken it."

"That's why we accepted when Beryl invited us to go on the Glow Worm cruise last night," Stefanie explained. "We thought if they'd had a bit to drink, they'd be more willing to let something slip."

Franklin-Ross followed her team's movements with her eyes. "And did you learn anything?"

"I heard someone on the stairs of the boat," Stefanie said. "I couldn't tell who it was, but what I heard was someone say *I saw you with him.*"

"And this gossip is important, why?"

Stefanie's cheeks grew warm. Maybe it had been meaningless gossip. "No one admitted to it," she said. "That's suspicious, don't you think? With the theft the day before?"

DI Franklin-Ross grunted. "All right. We will see if the theft is connected."

"You might ask Nathaniel Dimon if he saw anything," Thomas said.

"Nathaniel Dimon, the garden designer?" The officer jotted down a note in her notebook.

"Yes," Stefanie said. "He was at the house on the day of the theft."

Dimon hadn't talked to them, but Stefanie had no doubt that DI Franklin-Ross would get everything she needed from him.

"Please give me your cell numbers. I may have questions for you later."

They did.

With an expression that said she had their numbers figuratively as well as literally, DI Franklin-Ross gave Thomas her card. "We will let you know when you have clearance to leave Bermuda."

Definitely on the DI's suspect list.

Each of those at Carmichael House was fingerprinted, then taken inside and searched. When they were released, Stefanie and Thomas went to Jeffrey, who brooded at the gate, staring at the water in the harbor.

"We're heading back to the house now," Stefanie said.

Jeffrey nodded. "Meet me at Greg's in a few?"

Greg pushed away from leaning against his car. "I'll be there too."

Chapter Thirteen

Stefanie and Thomas pulled into Greg's driveway, and Greg drove in right after, parking his Jaguar beside the Tazzari. All three waited outside as Jeffrey drove into his own driveway, then walked over.

Stefanie unlocked the front door, her hands shaking as she inserted the key. Thomas, she noticed, made certain there was no room behind her for Greg to insert himself between them.

Pretending not to notice, she said, "Beryl's death must have had to do with the theft of the bracelet."

"And someone killed her for it." Jeffrey still wore a dazed expression, as if he couldn't believe it had happened.

"Where greed leads, murder follows," Thomas said.

It was an ugly truth, a horrible facet of human nature, one that she would never get used to.

"The question is," Thomas said, "who has the emerald bracelet now?"

"Someone who was at Carmichael House this morning," she said. "The murderer."

Jeffrey crossed to the window. "We're all suspects, you know."

That was another unpleasant truth. No good deed, Stefanie thought. She immediately regretted her attitude. Jeffrey couldn't have foreseen Beryl's murder any more than she or Thomas had.

Greg went to the dining room table. "Coffee will help this discussion. Have a seat."

Thomas sat at the head of the table. He hadn't said anything last night about Greg, which spoke volumes in itself.

"I'll make coffee," Stefanie offered, desperately needing a cup after the shock of finding Beryl. "Or, sorry, that should be you offering," she said to Greg with a little smile.

"No, the house is your place this week," he replied. "Make yourself at home."

She put coffee on, then returned to the dining room and sat down while the coffee brewed. She turned to Jeffrey, whose pallor lingered.

"Between us, maybe we can figure out who did this horrible thing. What exactly went on this morning?" she asked. The archaeologists had been tense yesterday and the Carmichaels angry, but not to the extent that anyone seemed on the verge of committing murder over the theft.

"I was there at seven-fifteen," Jeffrey said. "Ingram drove in with his crew right after, and Beryl arrived closer to seven-thirty. Thomas," he said, with a nod at the German, "told me you planned to visit Nathaniel's office this morning and check with him about whether he'd seen anything Tuesday. I told the rest of the crew that since we were all but done, I'd told you to not bother to return. They understood, you being on vacation and all."

"Did Beryl have an argument with anyone?" Stefanie asked. "Daphne mentioned you were all carping at each other."

"I might have been short with them," he admitted. "I didn't notice Beryl get in it with any of the others. In fact, she was quiet this morning, which was unusual for her." With his finger, Jeffrey traced a square on the polished oak table. "We were busy filling the pits. Hunter and Daphne took care of Unit Three. Neither of them were happy. Kept on about the impact the theft would have on their futures. Beryl and Ingram worked on Two," he said. "I don't know exactly when Beryl walked off. We'd been gathering up the supplies and tools from the yard and the buttery. It wasn't until I got your text that I stopped and noticed I was alone in the backyard. That was about nine o'clock."

"We arrived at nine-fifteen," Thomas said, looking longingly into the kitchen as the aroma of strong coffee filled the air.

Stefanie got up. Gurgling from the machine told her it had nearly finished. "I'll bring coffee in."

In the kitchen, she took four coffee mugs emblazoned with the Riverboat Rum logo from an upper cabinet.

Greg walked in behind her. "Have to advertise where I can, don't I?"

He was dressed more casually today, she noticed, in blue shorts and a tan shirt.

"A shot right now wouldn't go amiss." She tried to manage a smile while she poured, but her mind was on Beryl, finding her dead on the ground. Trying to figure out who had picked up a handy rock and coshed the archaeologist on the head.

Drawing near, Greg put his arm around her and rested his hand lightly on her waist.

"A death is upsetting, especially of someone you know," he said.

Surprised at the intimacy, Stefanie raised her head to tell him that she was fine. Delicately moving out of the subtle embrace, she saw Thomas in the doorway. He focused on Greg's wayward hand. Hurt and surprise registered in his eyes before a shutter came down, masking his emotions.

Crap.

She understood his feelings all too well. In Venice, when his former flame kissed him, Stefanie had vowed that *she'd* never go as far as touching someone else in pursuit of an investigation. Not that they were investigating Greg, or that she'd done the touching. Thomas hadn't been the instigator in Venice, either, but that hadn't prevented her heartache. His was apparent in those grey-blue eyes she loved so much.

Stepping back, she lifted the coffee carafe, holding the pot between her and Greg. "Thomas prefers his coffee black, Greg. How about you?"

Greg moved away. "I thought you'd remember. From our days at the bank, in your office. One sugar," he said, adjusting the position of the sugar bowl on the counter. "Do you miss it, Markham-Briggs? I was disappointed when they assigned me another private banker and told me you weren't coming back."

With the four cups poured, Stefanie picked up a cup for Thomas and one for Jeffrey, and let Greg fix his own. Thomas gave her a significant look when she handed him his cup.

"Just the way I like it," he said.

She smiled warmly, hoping he knew that he didn't have anything to worry about where Greg was concerned.

"Jeffrey?" she asked.

"Black is fine."

She took his cup to the table, then returned to the kitchen for hers.

"Your replacement at the bank isn't nearly as efficient as you," Greg continued, stirring sugar into his dark roast. "Never has any idea where my papers are when I go in."

"I'm sure he enjoys the river in your speedboat," she said lightly. At the table, she pulled her chair slightly closer to Thomas's.

"Jeffrey," she said, her voice a little loud, even to her own ears, "If she was killed for the bracelet, Beryl must have brought it back to return it today."

Thomas rested his forearms on the table. "Who knew she had it?"

"I thought it was her." Jeffrey stared into the black liquid in his cup. "I thought Beryl was the one who'd stolen the emerald bracelet."

She was shocked at his words, though on reflection, she shouldn't have been. Of course he suspected Beryl. That's why he'd asked them to help. He suspected a friend. Thomas didn't seem surprised at all.

"I've heard a lot about this emerald bracelet today," Greg said. "When was it stolen?"

Jeffrey gave the details of finding the bracelet and its subsequent theft. When he finished, he shared the photo on his phone. "I didn't want to think it of Beryl, not of my own employee, a museum employee."

Greg studied the photo closely, enlarging it to take in the details.

"Quite a discovery," he said quietly, handing the phone back to Jeffrey.

"She didn't tell any of us she was returning it, as far as I know," Jeffrey said.

"And you didn't see Beryl from inside the house," Stefanie said, looking at Greg.

"No," he answered. "I got to Carmichael House about eight-fifteen. First I visited with Marlene in the kitchen over a mug of tea, then Lawrence and I talked in his den. He sold his boat building company when he retired a few years ago, and since then, once he gets going about his glory days in the

America's Cup, Lawrence is hard to shut down."

She'd noticed the same thing herself the day before.

"You were with Lawrence until Stefanie called for help?" Thomas asked.

"Actually, I wasn't. I was getting ready to leave. I'd gone into the living room, and was checking out the excavation site from the French doors. I saw you and Jeffrey when you passed the patio."

"Why were you there on a weekday morning? Shouldn't you be at work?" After a glance at Greg's attire, Thomas fixed him with an aggressive stare.

Greg smiled at the challenge. "As Minister of Economy and Labor, Marlene wields a lot of power. I hoped I could persuade her to give me some perks to keep my headquarters in Bermuda."

"At her house," Thomas said.

"That's how deals are done," Greg said. "I know she often works from home since the Pandemic. What is it you do? Teach, I think Jeffrey told me?"

Wanting to forestall any more conversation along those competitive lines, Stefanie said, "The police will find out who killed Beryl and hopefully find the bracelet as well. For your sake, Jeffrey, I hope that's soon."

"More than professional reputations are on the line now," Thomas said.

Stefanie gazed around the table. "The police will be looking at all of us."

"Good thing you wrapped up the project, Jeffrey" Greg said. "That tropical storm has turned north. We're going to be in for heavy rain soon."

Out the broad window, a few clouds dotted the sky above the ocean, but not many, and those were fluffy and white.

Jeffrey turned to Stefanie. Stress had added circles under his eyes that she hadn't noticed the day before. "Nathaniel Dimon wasn't any help?" Jeffrey asked. "He didn't say anything about seeing Beryl Tuesday when the bracelet was stolen?"

"We couldn't get him to admit to seeing anything at Carmichael House," she said. "He was being very discreet. We didn't want to bring up the theft and have him think we were accusing him."

"The surest way to get him to shut down," Thomas agreed.

"I didn't see Dimon Tuesday," Jeffrey said, tapping on the table with his index finger. "But he does have the code."

"The code," Thomas repeated. "The gate security code."

"So Nathaniel Dimon could come and go as he pleased without anyone letting him in," Stefanie said.

Jeffrey shrugged. "He needed it for the landscaping work."

Sipping her coffee, Stefanie considered the implications of Jeffrey's revelation. It would have been logical for Nathaniel Dimon to inspect the dig progress on Tuesday, since the garden renovation was his project, yet no one claimed to have seen him except Hunter. Why not?

She touched Thomas's wrist. "Nathaniel got in the office late today. We need to go back to Carmichael House. I want to talk to the detective inspector."

Chapter Fourteen

Stefanie knew her vague unease over Nathaniel Dimon having the Carmichael House security code was too insubstantial to share with DI Franklin-Ross over the phone. The DI already had a negative attitude toward her. She'd be more receptive in person.

"The detective inspector is probably still at the house," she said.

When she took her coffee cup into the kitchen and placed it next to the sink, Thomas got up and did the same.

Greg took out his car keys. "I'll go with you."

"We have plans afterward," Thomas said.

When Greg protested, Stefanie objected. "Don't be silly, Greg. You just left Carmichael House."

"I'll give you a ride then," Greg said, returning his cup to the kitchen as well.

"We have the Tazzari." Thomas's stare dared Greg to insist.

Greg didn't back down. "Those seats can't be comfortable."

"Remarkably so," Thomas said.

Taking the house key from her purse, Stefanie held it up for the men to see. "If you don't mind, I need to leave. I'd like to lock up. Unless, of course, Greg, there is anything you need to pick up while you're here?"

"No, I'm good. If you change your mind about the car, you have my number," he offered.

"We won't." Thomas held the front door as Greg and Jeffrey exited.

Thomas's gaze followed the Jag as Greg drove off.

With hunched shoulders, Jeffrey lingered in the driveway. "I was certain it was Beryl," he repeated.

"You could have told us," Thomas said. "Why did you suspect her?"

She wished he'd be a little more gentle with Jeffrey, but she was just as aggravated that Jeffrey hadn't shared that suspicion with them. If he had, things might have taken a different turn, and Beryl might still be alive. Opening the passenger door of the Tazzari, she waited for their neighbor's answer.

"Because Beryl didn't back me up when Marlene and Lawrence insisted that we not report the theft," Jeffrey said. "I was certain she would. When she didn't, I gave in to them. I shouldn't have."

"Who do you think knew she had the bracelet on her this morning?" Stefanie asked gently.

Jeffrey shrugged. "I have no idea. I hired her right out of university, you know," he said. "The first real job she ever had."

He trudged over to his own house, and she and Thomas folded themselves into the microcar.

"Remarkably comfy," she said, buckling her seatbelt.

With a self-satisfied smile, Thomas started the engine.

Stefanie turned over the new possibility in her mind, that the garden designer was more involved than they'd thought. "I don't know how Nathaniel would have learned about the bracelet, but we have to let the DI know he has the security code."

"Marlene?" Thomas suggested.

"Maybe. With the way the Carmichaels wanted the finds kept quiet, though, would she tell him?"

"From his clientele and his packed schedule," Thomas said, "Nathaniel Dimon is pressed for time, but not money." Thomas sounded reluctant to accept the landscape designer as a suspect.

"That seems to be the case," she said. "And maybe it is only a coincidence that he was there Tuesday around the time the bracelet was stolen, that he wasn't at his office this morning when Beryl was killed, and that he has access to the property whenever he wants."

Thomas turned onto Cut Road. "I don't like coincidences," he acknowledged with a glance her way.

"Ingram told us Nathaniel Dimon was his roommate during freshman year at college, and that Nathaniel cheated on his exams," she went on. "So he has a history of taking short cuts."

"Beryl said he was ambitious. He was reluctant to talk about her at all."

"But it was clear they knew each other," Stefanie said.

At Carmichael House, Thomas parked at the curb, then they walked up to the gate.

DI Franklin-Ross stood in the drive on the other side. With a maddeningly calm air, she waited for Stefanie to speak.

I'm never going to live that down, Stefanie thought. She pasted on a warm, but not artificially bright, smile for the officer.

"Good afternoon, DI Franklin-Ross. How are you?" she asked.

"Good afternoon," the DI replied. "I'm fine. How are you?"

Why were niceties that she ordinarily used so painful? She didn't have to take that attitude, though. Remembering the lengths she'd gone to at the bank to get along with difficult customers, Stefanie smiled, at both herself and the officer.

Franklin-Ross allowed a shadow of a smile to also show. Thawing. Or being a police officer, perhaps she thought she was reeling Stefanie in. She'd made it clear Stefanie and Thomas were on the suspect list.

"Good afternoon," Thomas said easily.

"We have something to tell you," Stefanie said.

The DI opened the gate. The ambulance had gone, taking Beryl's body with it. Only two uniformed officers remained searching for evidence, and they were in the overgrown garden at the back.

"It's about Nathaniel Dimon," Stefanie continued. "We paid a visit to his office in Hamilton this morning."

The police officer gave her a stern look. "Why?"

"Wanting to find out if he'd seen anything Tuesday morning," Thomas said.

"And you two thought you'd expand playing detective beyond the excavation team? Along with playing archaeologist?"

Stefanie let Thomas handle the officer. He could win her over far easier than Stefanie could.

"Who says the only way to have fun on Bermuda is beaches and rum swizzles?" Thomas asked, giving the DI a charming smile. "We were helping out a friend, we had the time, and we happened to be looking at moving into a new place. So we paid a visit to the garden designer. A legitimate visit."

"Legitimate," Franklin-Ross repeated.

Enough of that.

"We didn't think it had any bearing this morning when we talked to you," Stefanie said, "but you need to know that Nathaniel Dimon arrived late at his office today."

"And you think this is important why?" the DI asked, noting it down in her pad.

"He has the security code for this gate," Thomas said. "He might have known Beryl would be here with the bracelet."

"I see." DI Franklin-Ross added that to her notes. "Thank you for the information. As I said earlier, we'll find out if the missing bracelet had anything to do with Ms. Swan's death and who was involved." She addressed Thomas rather than Stefanie. "We'll be finished canvassing the grounds this afternoon."

"Thank you," Stefanie said, not liking being excluded. "I'll let the Minister and Mr. Carmichael know."

At least they'd given the police all the information they had. Just in case.

The DI eyed them both. "Stick to your archaeology and beaches and rum for the rest of your vacation here on Bermuda."

Did that mean they weren't on the suspect list anymore? It sounded like it, but Stefanie wasn't going to press her luck and ask. She merely smiled.

The DI glanced at her men, who, with heads lowered, held aside shrubs and ivy in their search of the grounds. "It's just as well your archaeological assessment is over." She gave a curt nod at the palm fronds blowing in the breeze. "That tropical storm is heading our way."

When the officer walked across the lawn to her men, Stefanie and Thomas went to the front door.

"So now our pretend storm threat is real?" Stefanie asked.

"Nothing for us to worry about. It will take days to get here," Thomas said. "We'll be gone before then." He rang the bell.

The door was opened immediately by Marlene. "Do the police have news? What did she say?"

A woman of about forty-five, with light brown hair to her shoulders, peered frankly over Marlene's shoulder.

"They'll be finished canvassing the grounds this afternoon," Stefanie said.

The newcomer listened rather than introducing herself. Well, Stefanie thought, extenuating circumstances must affect Bermudians, too.

Marlene turned to the smartly dressed woman. "This is Dr. Fabiola Ortiz, with the Spanish Ministry of Culture."

Oh. The famous Fabiola. She hadn't wasted time.

"I came to see Beryl," Fabiola said after introductions. "You found the medal in the yard? The Military Order of Calatrava?" she asked. "Tonight I will learn who it belonged to."

"You can do that?" Stefanie asked as Lawrence joined the women in the doorway.

Fabiola stepped outside to make room for him.

"The Archives," Thomas said. "The Spanish Archives are famous for their thoroughness."

"Yes." Fabiola's smile turned to a determined stare at Lawrence and Marlene. "Hiding it will not change who the rightful owner is."

As Fabiola descended the front steps, Lawrence pushed a button inside the front door. The whir of a motor sounded, then the driveway gate opened.

When the Spanish researcher turned left on the sidewalk, Marlene pressed two fingers against her forehead and let out an exasperated sigh. "She's accused us of keeping the bracelet. My god, Beryl has been killed over this." She seemed to shrink within herself.

Lawrence took her by the arm and led her inside. Stefanie and Thomas followed them into the small, enclosed entry foyer.

"I'll close the door," Stefanie offered, admiring the small antique table which stood by the front door. The unusually shaped amber vase on it was attractive, too. It made her wonder. Would Thomas like her decorating style once they moved in together? Would she like his?

The Carmichaels led the way into the warm and inviting living room, where Marlene abruptly sat in a cushioned leather chair. The Carmichaels' style was more formal than Greg's, but still comfortable. The tan leather cushions on the easy chairs and sofa were squared off, edged with neat piping for a sophisticated look. She and Thomas sat together on the sofa.

"Fabiola is only throwing out accusations," Lawrence said.

Marlene clasped her hands tightly. "She heard about the bracelet and wanted to see it. She thinks she'll have a better argument for ownership if it looks like we in Bermuda are deliberately hiding something from Spain."

Thomas glanced around the room. "Jeffrey said everyone on the dig team had their bags and vehicles searched Tuesday."

His implication wasn't lost on Marlene. "Do you want to search our house? Get in line. The police have informed us that the house is next when they finish with the grounds."

Lawrence blew out a dismissive breath. "Why would we waste time playing games with the bracelet? I was looking forward to showing it off at the yacht club."

"I wanted to donate it to the National Museum of Bermuda." Marlene gave Lawrence a lost look. "With our names prominently displayed on a plaque."

Marlene's plan would fall apart if she'd been the one who took the bracelet from Beryl, Stefanie thought. The Minister was smart enough to realize that. Had they suspected Beryl, like Jeffrey had?

"Jeffrey suspected Beryl stole the bracelet from the start," Stefanie told them.

"Did either of you?" Thomas asked.

"I didn't suspect anyone in particular," Marlene said. "And I don't have any idea who followed her and did that terrible deed."

"She must have been coming around to the kitchen door," Lawrence said. "To return it to us."

"Any chance you saw Nathaniel Dimon this morning?" Stefanie asked.

"Did he come by?"

"I didn't see him," Lawrence said. "Marlene?"

His wife shook her head. "After Jeffrey and the crew arrived, Greg Edwards stopped in. He was the only one, except for the Museum team. We chatted over tea."

How discreet, not mentioning Greg's purpose.

"We were wondering if Nathaniel knew about the bracelet," Stefanie ventured. "If someone here might have told him about it."

Marlene sat up straighter. "What does that matter?"

Thomas sat forward with his forearms on his knees. "The bracelet was stolen by someone who knew about it. There aren't that many of you."

Marlene's eyes widened at the 'you.'

"Confess, Marlene," Lawrence said. "You told that landscaper, didn't you? After we agreed not to tell anyone."

"He is not a landscaper," Marlene said indignantly. "Nathaniel Dimon is a world-renowned landscape architect. And yes, I told him." Folding her hands together, she addressed Stefanie and Thomas. "He called Tuesday morning wanting an idea of how long the assessment would take. So he'd know when his men could expect to resume work. He has another important project coming up."

"Government House," Stefanie said enthusiastically, in far more comfortable territory working Marlene for information than she'd been with the DI. "I'd like to see that garden when it's done. I'm sure it will be an impressive project."

Marlene smiled her appreciation that Stefanie recognized Nathaniel Dimon's stature. "Yes. Ours will be impressive too, though on a much smaller scale." Inhaling deeply through her nose, she squared her shoulders.

"I understand he and Beryl know each other. Knew each other," Stefanie corrected.

"I suppose they did. But I assure you, Nathaniel Dimon did not murder anyone for a bracelet." Marlene's vulnerability had gone back into hiding, and the Minister of Economy and Labor was back. She stood up. "I'm so sorry you had to experience this tragedy at our house. If you'll excuse me, I have work to catch up on."

She escorted them to the front door.

"Thank you for coming," Lawrence said, as if they'd been visiting guests.

From the keypad near the front door, Marlene opened the driveway gate.

"Change the security code," Thomas said. "If you have to let everyone in and out, you'll know exactly who is on the property."

"Yes, that very efficient detective inspector has already advised us," Marlene said.

Once they were outside the gate, Stefanie turned to Thomas. "I don't know. Do you think Nathaniel Dimon saw Beryl take the bracelet?"

Thomas put his hand on the small of her back. "I think it's time we leave this to the Bermuda police and go snorkeling."

Chapter Fifteen

Grey clouds filled the sky by the time they arrived at Tobacco Bay, but the temperature was warm and balmy when they parked, and the beach was crowded.

Stefanie grabbed her carry-on from the tiny storage compartment in the Tazzari.

"We can't call this a trunk," she said to Thomas. "It's more like a locker."

They walked to the beach, and she stopped for a minute to take it in. Towering rock formations enclosed the bay, making the ocean intimate rather than vast. Protected and isolated.

"This is exactly what I need," she said.

"I thought I was all you needed," Thomas said with a little smile.

She laughed. "This too."

At the little shop, they rented lounge chairs, snorkeling masks, and swim fins, then changed into their swimsuits.

The beauty of nature wasn't enough for her to escape her own recriminations, Stefanie realized as they crossed the sand to the chairs.

If she'd identified the thief, it wouldn't have come to this. Murder. Thomas felt the weight of their failure as deeply as she did. The etched lines at the corners of his mouth seemed permanent.

Catching her perusal of him, Thomas took hold of her hand. "Grab your fins," he said.

She dropped her bag with their towels onto her chaise lounge, then they ran across the warm sand into turquoise water, and at the water's edge they put on their swim fins.

"You're going to walk in and swim on top of the water," he said, "keeping the end of your tube above the surface." He pulled his mask down. "Ready?"

Stefanie adjusted her mask over her eyes and bit the mouthpiece. "Ready."

They duck-stepped further out. The first shock of cool water rising against her body quickly gave way to warmth as she dropped to her shoulders in the lapping water.

"Race you to that rock," she said, pointing to an outcropping on the right. "You're on." Thomas dove forward.

Instead of rushing, they swam leisurely, side by side, observing the tiny fish and the rocky seabed below. Silence surrounded her as she floated, enveloping her in a warm, soothing, living environment.

Despite the serene surroundings, images of Beryl's crumpled form refused to be banished. Stefanie kicked her feet. Why had murder been the solution? For a bracelet. A bracelet! She kicked harder.

Catching up with her, Thomas touched her arm and pointed at the rocks. Bigger fish swam there, beautiful blue fish with yellow tails, thin yellow and white and black striped fish, and large graceful brown ones.

The coral were just as colorful. Purple fan-like structures that reminded her of lace, others with dark fingers that stretched upward, reaching for her, undulating with the ebb and flow of the water as her body did, rocking gently on the surface.

Ahead, the base of one of the rock outcroppings offered a place to stand. Thomas hooked a thumb toward it, and they swam for the formation.

Stepping onto the flat rock, with one hand against the portion that rose above the water, she stood up and pulled off her mask. The sun had broken through the clouds while they were underwater.

Thomas emerged from the sea, taking off his mask, then bending his head back to let the water run off. Droplets and rivulets ran down his chest as well. Her gaze lingered. He could have modeled for a cologne ad.

"Blissful," she said.

"Me, or the water?" he asked, pulling her close against his chest.

"You," she answered, relishing the beat of his heart against her own. Powerful and solid, he was her refuge of calm.

Chatter and shouts of families and couples at the beach carried across to their stony oasis. No one paid them any attention. Their lips met in a kiss, salty and warm, then Stefanie put her hand on his chest and pushed him the slightest bit away. They were at a public beach, after all.

Thomas leaned back against the rock and let the sun warm him. She did the same, nestling close so their arms touched. The sun might be out, but the breeze chilled her wet skin.

Her thoughts returned to Carmichael House. They'd suspected Beryl or Hunter.

"I couldn't tell which one was guilty," she said. "I didn't see any sign of desperation so strong that it would lead to murder."

"I didn't either. Sometimes, we miss things. Beryl's murder isn't on us. It's on the person who killed her."

And they didn't know who that was. She didn't know. Greg had boasted to Jeffrey that she could spot trouble coming, because she'd boasted to him that she could. Her cheeks grew warm with self-recrimination.

"It's peaceful under the water," she said.

"The silence," Thomas agreed. "It takes your stress away."

That's what she needed, to swim until she couldn't see Beryl on the sidewalk anymore.

"Ready to go back in?" Not waiting for him, Stefanie donned her mask and dove forward.

Side by side, they floated. The soft lapping of the water, the physical exertion of kicking her legs, and her measured, steady breathing eased the tightness in her chest and face. Beryl had been killed. There was nothing they could do about it, nothing they could have done to prevent it. As Thomas said, someone else made that cruel choice. Stefanie swam until she was exhausted, then pointed toward the shore.

Thomas nodded and they kicked their way until the seabed was close enough to stand up.

Pulling off her mask, she took deep breaths through her mouth, filling her lungs. "I'm starving."

Thomas removed his mask and ran his hand over his hair, pushing out the seawater. "I'll get lunch."

After squeezing out her dripping hair to the side, she returned their masks and fins, then joined him at the snack shack.

"Two hamburgers," Thomas ordered. "And a beer. One for you, too?" he asked her.

"It's time I tried a rum swizzle," Stefanie said, checking the array of bottles on the shelf behind the server.

When the bartender reached for Goslings, Stefanie said, "Riverboat Rum."

The bartender grinned. "A good choice."

He poured light and dark rums, a bit of orange juice, pineapple juice, and dark red grenadine, then mixed it all with—what else—a swizzle stick. After dropping in a cherry and an orange slice, he presented it to her with a flourish.

"Thanks," she said, rewarding his efforts with a generous tip.

With burgers and drinks in hand, she and Thomas crossed the sand to their chairs.

She settled neatly onto her lounge chair while Thomas stepped astride his, then lowered himself down.

"Those blue fish were beautiful," Stefanie said after she'd taken several bites of her burger.

He consulted his phone. "Princess parrotfish."

"Snorkeling is going in the blog."

Between sips of rum swizzle, she worked on her hamburger.

"I can't help but think that conversation I overheard on the boat is important," she said. Someone has something to hide. If it wasn't Beryl talking, surely it was Daphne."

Having finished his burger, Thomas gave his full attention to enjoying his beer. "Sorry I didn't see anyone come up. Why not one of the men?"

Stefanie gave him a sideways smile. "A matter of delicacy. No one admitted to waiting for the restroom. Now, if it had been the men, they'd have joked about it. Or at least admitted it. That's how men are. But if the men saw either Daphne or Beryl, or both, go down and then return, they'd be more circumspect. They wouldn't want to point out a lady's personal business."

"Who says chivalry is dead?" Thomas raised his beer to her.

Stefanie sipped her cocktail, letting the fruity flavor and the potency of the rum sit on her tongue.

"You heard someone say *I saw you with him*," Thomas said. "But we don't know who the speaker was talking to, or about."

"Daphne knows."

"Logic says the 'him' is Nathaniel Dimon," Thomas said.

"Yes." Stefanie brushed the sand off her feet and ankles, then slipped on her beach sandals. "I think it was her. Daphne, talking to Nathaniel. And for some reason, Beryl had an issue with it. If Daphne was talking to Nathaniel, a person she presumably just met, why hide it? Yet she did. And Jeffrey said Beryl was quiet this morning."

"Hunter might know, if we can get him to talk," Thomas said. "He saw Dimon there on Tuesday."

Watching the gentle waves roll into the shore, she said, "We still don't know how Beryl left with the bracelet on Tuesday."

Thomas didn't have an answer to that.

She looked at him. "Nathaniel Dimon had a perfect opportunity to get the bracelet off the property."

"He wasn't searched," Thomas said. "Beryl could have given it to him."

She nodded, then finished her rum swizzle and sat up. "That would make for a tense conversation, if Daphne saw Beryl."

"Dockyard?" he asked.

"Dockyard."

Chapter Sixteen

After stopping at the house to hang their swimsuits to dry in the lower-level laundry room, Stefanie got the rental house address from Jeffrey. It wasn't actually at the Royal Naval Dockyard, but nearby in Sandys.

"We're going to have to charge the Tazzari if we go that far," Thomas said, entering Ingram's address into the map on his phone.

"Is there a charging station nearby?" she asked.

He checked. "We're in luck. In the Dockyard area. We'll talk to Daphne and Hunter, then go charge our little lightning bug."

At least he could find humor in the small car. She liked it, herself, at least for small trips.

They drove the entire length of Bermuda, from the island of St. George's across the causeway to the main island, to Sandys. All along the way, palm trees blew in the freshening breeze. They rolled up the windows when a light rain started, but the shower didn't last more than ten minutes.

Stefanie watched the scenery go by, the little bus stops, the coves, and the shoreline. Why hadn't either Beryl or Daphne admitted to talking about Nathaniel Dimon on the cruise? The DI categorized the conversation as gossip. Maybe that's all it had been, and the women hadn't responded because it wasn't Stefanie's affair. Instinct and intuition told her those few hissed words were significant, though. And Beryl had been murdered.

Daphne could help.

They pulled up to the pastel-green house just as a second shower started. After dashing together through the rain to the front steps, Thomas knocked.

Allan Ingram opened the door.

His eyes widened in surprise. "News about Beryl?"

"Not yet," Stefanie said, brushing the sprinkle of raindrops off her leather purse.

Stepping back, Ingram let them in.

As she wiped her feet on the mat, she noticed that Ingram had taken off his shoes and socks and was barefoot. The island life. Somehow, that little touch made things easier.

The house wasn't much bigger than Greg's, with easy-to-clean tile floors and furnished in what she could only think of as Grandma castoffs. The dining table and chairs were scuffed and worn, and the living room seats all sagged from years of use. Still, it was perfect for a university rental.

"We'd like to talk to Daphne," Stefanie said.

Vertical creases appeared between Ingram's brows. "She's at the beach."

"In the rain?" Thomas asked.

The professor crossed his arms over his chest. "Walking helps take her mind off things. Beryl's death has knocked us all sideways."

Ingram's camaraderie from the morning and the night before had been replaced with suspicion. Stefanie tried to put him at ease.

"I heard Beryl and Daphne talking on the glow worm tour," she said. "I was hoping to ask her about it. I think their conversation might be important."

He jutted his chin out. "You didn't join us to help. You were there because of the bracelet."

"You're right," Thomas said. "Can we sit down?"

Ingram continued to stare them down. "You can't come in here and badger my students. Or me."

"We don't want to badger anyone. We just want answers. Beryl was killed," Stefanie said. "At a site you were working on."

"Don't you want her murderer caught?" Thomas asked. "We do."

With a huff of resentment, Ingram indicated for them to have a seat in the living room. She and Thomas opted for the brown plaid sofa. Stefanie sat gingerly on the edge, thankful that she'd worn that pair of beach trousers. Like the sofa, which had probably been chosen for its ability to hide stains, they were a forgiving shade of rich brown.

Sitting in a recliner opposite, Ingram gripped the worn armrests. "What do you think Daphne knows?"

Footsteps sounded from a hall on the left, and Hunter appeared. His backpack was slung over one shoulder.

"You're packed," Ingram observed.

"You plan to leave?" Thomas asked him.

Stefanie adjusted the purse on her knees. Hunter would have gotten the same directive to stay from DI Franklin-Ross as they had.

"Haven't you heard?" Hunter said. "A hurricane is coming."

"Now it's a hurricane?" She checked the weather app on her phone. "Projected to be a Category 1. Three days from now." It was Thursday. That meant the hurricane would hit Bermuda on Sunday. She and Thomas were scheduled to fly out on Monday. If all went well, they would, that was. A little tidbit for her travel blog. Always check the weather.

"Cat 1. Seventy-four mile per hour winds. That's not too bad. You're not going to ride it out here?" Thomas asked Hunter.

"Why?" Hunter asked. "I've got to get back to school anyway. My classes have started. Attending online only works for so long. I'm not like Dr. Ingram, who can dictate whether a class is available online or not."

"We're all done at the Dockyard," Ingram said slowly. "Nothing left but the cataloging and reports at this point."

Thomas listened, then looked at Hunter. "The police aren't going to let you leave. Not this early in the investigation."

"Might as well put your things back for now," Ingram told Hunter. "You can't leave Bermuda yet. None of us can. And just so you know, Jeffrey brought them on board to look for the bracelet."

Hunter let his pack slide to the floor, where it rested against the hallway wall.

"You're here because you think we stole the bracelet," he said defiantly.

"We want to ask Daphne some questions," Stefanie repeated. "I heard Beryl talking with her on the boat. I want to know if they were discussing Nathaniel Dimon."

"What's he got to do with anything?" Hunter demanded.

"If Daphne and Beryl were talking about him, I want to know what the big secret is about," she said.

"Nathaniel Dimon could have gotten the bracelet off the property," Thomas said. "He wasn't searched. The bracelet wasn't discovered to be missing until after he left, as far as we can tell."

Ingram acknowledged that with a nod. His fingers loosened their grip on the recliner armrests.

When Hunter didn't respond, Thomas went on. "You are the person we really need to talk to. You're the only one on the archaeology team who admits to seeing Dimon at Carmichael House on Tuesday."

"Where did you see him?" Stefanie asked.

Taking a seat at the battered Formica-topped dining table, Hunter said, "I saw him drive in."

"And?" Thomas settled against the sofa, draping his arm across the back in a deceptively casual move.

The younger man shrugged. "That's it. He didn't come out back at all."

"You can't see the front of the house from the excavation," Thomas pointed out. "On Tuesday, if the three cars were parked in the same places as they were yesterday, Dimon would have parked closer to the front door. Which you wouldn't have been able to see from the site."

Hunter looked at Ingram.

"He's right," the professor said, making no attempt whatever to look only casually interested. "Where were you?"

"I put my backpack in the van," Hunter said. "I'd just finished lunch."

"Where did he go? Who did he talk to?" Stefanie asked. "You must have seen him."

"I didn't watch him. It's none of my business what he does."

"You didn't meet him? Talk with him at the van?" Thomas asked.

Hunter dropped his disinterested act, and defiance showed in his eyes again. "Why would I? Why are you asking me that? I didn't give him the bracelet. I'm the one who found it. That Spanish bracelet was my claim to fame."

Hunter's indignation rang true, and what he said was true as well. Being part of the team that discovered the treasure would gain him recognition and opportunities throughout his career.

Thomas tilted his head. "Your father might have other ideas."

Hunter's left knee began to bounce rhythmically. Noticing it, he planted both feet flat on the floor and clamped his mouth shut.

"Richard Renko," Thomas went on. "Famous shipwreck salvager."

Shaking away the lock of sun-bleached hair that had fallen across his forehead, Hunter said, "So what if he is?"

"Didn't he find a Portuguese ship off the coast of Florida last year?" Thomas asked. "I heard that haul got him nearly a hundred thousand dollars. Laws for salvage and marine archaeology don't apply to land archaeology. Did you think you could scavenge relics from an archaeological site like your father does from shipwrecks?"

"I don't believe I have a right to that emerald bracelet," Hunter insisted.

He looked to Ingram for help.

The professor, stroking his beard, nodded. "I don't have any reason to question Hunter's ethics."

"On Tuesday the whole dig team and the cars were all searched," Stefanie said. "Beryl didn't have the bracelet on her. So where was it?"

The front door opened, and Daphne walked in, pushing back the hood of her lightweight orange windbreaker.

Thomas didn't let her entry stop his questioning of Hunter. "If you have nothing to hide, why won't you tell us who Nathaniel Dimon spoke with Tuesday at Carmichael House?" Thomas sat forward, resting his elbows on his knees. "Was it you?"

Daphne curled her hands into fists and shoved them in her jacket pockets. "Hunter wasn't the one talking to Nathaniel Tuesday at lunch. I was."

Chapter Seventeen

Daphne took off her yellow windbreaker and hung it on a peg beside the front door.

"So you did see Nathaniel Dimon the day of the theft," Stefanie said. "Is that what you and Beryl argued about on the Glow Worm cruise?"

"Yes." Daphne came into the room with her shoulders back and her head held high. "She cornered me about Nathaniel."

"Which you both tried to hide," Stefanie said.

"It wasn't any of your business," Daphne replied.

The girl was quite adamant, Stefanie thought. If Beryl had given Nathaniel Dimon the bracelet on Tuesday, then saw Daphne speaking to him later, Beryl would have been worried, making for an intense conversation.

"These two," Hunter said, jabbing a finger at Stefanie and Thomas, "didn't join the dig to help us. They joined to find out which one of us stole the bracelet."

Pursing her lips, Daphne studied them.

"We know it was Beryl now, don't we?" Ingram said.

Thomas sat back. "We don't know who killed her."

"It wasn't me," Daphne said.

"More importantly," Stefanie said, in case Daphne hadn't grasped the situation, "the police suspect all of us, because we were there when Beryl was killed. Well, Thomas and I weren't, as I'm sure the detective inspector will soon realize. But the three of you were."

"My conversation with Beryl wasn't about the bracelet." Daphne smirked. "Neither was my conversation with Nathaniel Dimon."

"Why would Beryl have an issue with you talking to Nathaniel?" Thomas asked.

Getting a cola from the kitchen refrigerator, Daphne smiled. "He was flirting with me."

"You'd just met. Hadn't you?" Stefanie asked. From what everyone said, Nathaniel had just arrived and hadn't gone back to speak to the team. "From what I overheard on the boat, Beryl sounded pretty intense."

With a pointed grin, Daphne asked Stefanie, "Have you seen Nathaniel Dimon?"

Ah. Stefanie smiled in return. Maybe that conversation had just been about jealousy over an attractive man.

Hunter crossed one ankle over the other with an exaggerated thunk of his heels on the wooden floor. Despite her bravado, Daphne turned red.

Thomas came to Daphne's rescue. "You think Beryl was jealous, is that it?"

The student shrugged her shoulders. "She told me to stay away from him. What am I supposed to think?"

"Good advice," Ingram said.

"Did you see Beryl talk to Nathaniel Dimon?" Stefanie asked her.

Daphne shook her head. "No."

"Nathaniel might have seen Beryl take the bracelet," Stefanie said. "If he was in the side garden, he might have had a view of anyone leaving the buttery."

Daphne smiled again, and this time, she didn't blush. "He wasn't looking at the buttery while I was talking to him."

So had Beryl resented Nathaniel Dimon talking to a pretty young girl, or had she been worried that Daphne saw her give the bracelet to him? The problem was, they didn't know if Nathaniel Dimon was involved at all.

"Why are you worrying about the bracelet when Beryl has been murdered?" Hunter demanded.

Ingram wiped a hand over his beard. "Chances are that they're related," he said. "You can see that."

"Was Beryl back at the buttery while Dimon was at the house, do you know?" Thomas asked, looking from Ingram to the students.

"I never saw Dimon there, so I couldn't say one way or the other," Ingram replied.

Daphne crossed her arms over her chest, thinking. "I didn't see her at the buttery, but I stayed in the front of the house, then went back to the excavation." She checked with Ingram for confirmation.

The professor nodded. "I remember you coming back after you returned your backpack to the van."

"So where was Beryl?" Stefanie asked. "She must have been somewhere where she could see the two of you talking. Since she warned you off."

"Was she with Jeffrey?" Hunter asked. "He went out for lunch."

Great. Just great.

Gritting her teeth, Stefanie exchanged a glance with Thomas. Jeffrey hadn't mentioned that pertinent fact when he went into such detail about the day of the theft. He had more explaining to do.

"Jeffrey went out to lunch before the theft was discovered?" Thomas asked.

"Yes," Ingram said. He grinned maliciously. "Didn't tell you about that, hey?"

Seeing their frustration, he added, "Jeffrey didn't go to the buttery before he left. He went straight to his car."

"Someone who knew Beryl brought the bracelet back this morning killed her," Stefanie said. "Did she say anything this morning to make you think she was going to return it?"

No one ventured an answer.

Stefanie studied Daphne. With the murder and the theft of the emerald bracelet to worry about, the girl had been a little too cheerful in claiming a flirtation with the landscape designer. Stefanie didn't think she was that shallow. Daphne had been worried the day before as well as that morning.

"Nathaniel Dimon could be the one who took the bracelet off the grounds for Beryl on Tuesday," Stefanie said. "If he was involved in the theft, he could also be involved in Beryl's murder."

"I don't expect any of us will see him again," Daphne said.

"Perhaps not." Thomas glanced at Hunter. "We met Fabiola Ortiz today."

Hunter shifted uncomfortably.

110

"No surprise," Ingram said. "She'll be sniffing around. Like you are."

"Until the police find Beryl's killer," Stefanie reminded them, "we're all suspects."

Thomas stood up.

So did Ingram. "It's my turn to cook tonight," he said. "I'm making chili. The best you'll ever taste. Stay. We'll talk this out and have the murder solved by dessert."

Shaking her head, Stefanie picked up her purse. "It's been a rough day. For all of us. We'll leave you alone." Hunter and Daphne weren't going to cooperate, even if they did stay longer. At least Ingram had dropped his resentful attitude, and he had influence over his students.

At the door, Ingram clapped Thomas on the shoulder. "There's a nice little Italian restaurant in Hamilton you'll like. It's a favorite of Nathaniel's."

Thomas nodded his appreciation for the tip, then turned around and looked at the two students.

"If you saw anything Tuesday, or this morning, you are safer if you tell us. Or the police."

Uncertainty washed over Daphne's face, which she tried to hide by taking an intense interest in her fingernails.

Hunter got up from the table and left the room.

With a sigh heavy with disappointment and frustration, Stefanie took Thomas's arm. If Hunter or Daphne knew anything, they weren't willing to share it. Yet.

"We need to find that charging station," Thomas said in a pained tone when they got into the Tazzari. He consulted his phone, then smiled. "It's only a couple of miles away."

He handed her his phone, and she directed him to the cycle shop at the Royal Naval Dockyard.

Thomas parked and set up the charge.

While they waited, Stefanie considered what they'd learned from Ingram and his students. The biggest bombshell hit close to home.

"How could Jeffrey think that his leaving Carmichael House the day of the theft wasn't important for us to know?" she asked.

"I don't like it," Thomas said. "First he didn't tell us he'd suspected Beryl from the start, now this."

Thomas hadn't wanted to take the case from the beginning, and Stefanie was beginning to have her own reservations. But would DI Franklin-Ross seriously look into the celebrated designer if they hadn't shared what they knew? Did she need to?

Thomas leaned against the car. "We've been so focused on the idea that Beryl stole the bracelet, we haven't looked at another possibility."

She waited for him to go on.

"Beryl might have been killed not because she had the bracelet, but because she knew who did."

Chapter Eighteen

On the drive back across the length of Bermuda, Stefanie reflected on Thomas's observation. The same possibility lurked in the back of her mind, as well—that Beryl had been killed because she knew who'd stolen the emerald bracelet, rather than because she was returning it.

"We have to consider the others for the theft." She drummed her fingers against the purse in her lap. "I was right about Daphne and Beryl arguing on the boat."

"Beryl warned her away from Nathaniel," Thomas said.

Certain Daphne knew more than she was telling, Stefanie turned in her seat. "If it was because of jealousy, why the secrecy?"

"Perhaps Daphne knew what Hunter's reaction would be to her flirting with Dimon."

That seemed clear. "I think it's more than that," she said.

"Daphne needs a scholarship for college," Thomas said. "The sale of a bracelet like that would fund her education."

"But where does Nathaniel Dimon come in? Daphne didn't have a prior connection to him, so maybe she was just flirting."

"Ingram does," Thomas said.

"Not a cooperative one," Stefanie said. "Neither did Beryl, apparently. It was in the way she said he was ambitious. And Nathaniel was very reserved when we brought up Beryl. No love lost there."

Thomas slowed for a sharp curve. "Neither of them is likely to have given him a valuable bracelet to hold."

"True."

"I believe we can rule out Dimon sneaking back to the buttery and stealing the bracelet himself," Thomas said. "Even if he did know where the bracelet was kept at that moment, Hunter, Daphne, and Beryl had all seen him. No way would he risk his career. Too many potential witnesses."

"But if someone had given him the bracelet, all he had to do was leave. Which he did," she said. "Is that why Nathaniel didn't check out the garden area on Tuesday? That warrants looking into, don't you think?"

Thomas avoided a motorbike that sped around a corner and whipped in front of them. "It would be logical to check out the damage the archaeologists did, the extent of ground disturbance that his landscapers would have to deal with," he agreed.

"Or, he might have seen who took the bracelet," she said. "When Beryl said Nathaniel was ambitious, did that mean he knew she took the bracelet and was leveraging that knowledge for a share himself?"

"Dimon had the code to the gate," Thomas said. "He could come and go as he pleased."

"And he killed her two days later, at Carmichael House, because he didn't want her to return the bracelet? That seems a stretch." Stefanie blew out a puff of frustration. "What fits what we know? The bracelet was stolen. Jeffrey gave the thief a chance to return it. Beryl is murdered two days later."

She shook her head. "We have to keep Beryl changing her mind and intending to return the bracelet as a possibility."

"That would explain why she was on the far side of the house," Thomas agreed. "To either sneak it into the house by going in the kitchen door, or to slip into the buttery from that side, where she was less likely to be seen by the other archaeologists."

Stefanie cringed inwardly. That last scenario was exactly what she'd been attempting when she found Beryl's body.

"Let's hope we find Nathaniel at the restaurant and that he's more forthcoming with what we know now," she said.

When they pulled up at the house, they both checked Jeffrey's driveway. His car wasn't there.

"We'll talk to him soon enough," Thomas said, climbing out of the Tazzari.

"I don't think Jeffrey took the bracelet," she said. But he had explaining to do. A lot of explaining.

In the bedroom, Stefanie put on the mid-blue velvet dress she'd gotten in Venice, knowing her choice would please Thomas.

As if hearing her thoughts, he came up behind her.

"Let me help," he said, pulling the zipper all the way to the top. When he finished, he slid his hands from her shoulders down the luxuriously soft velvet to the curve of her waist.

She leaned back against him for a moment, then smiling, stepped away and picked up the lapis lazuli necklace he'd given her in Crete. The striking Greek eye was just the counterpoint her solid blue sheath needed.

He took it from her and clasped the gold chain around her neck.

"Perfect match," he said into the mirror.

"Added bonus: it will keep away evil," she said with a playful grin.

"Are you speaking of my intentions?" The gleam in his eye promised the romantic rendezvous they'd come to Bermuda for.

"Never," she said, turning to smooth down the collar of his shirt.

On the way to Hamilton, Thomas took the turns as rapidly as the Bermudians did.

"If I didn't know better," Stefanie said, "I'd think you were enjoying this little Italian Tazzari."

"It will do."

When they entered the restaurant, fragrances of rich marinara, bright lemon, and pungent garlic met them at the door. Stefanie inhaled with hungry anticipation as she scanned the large room for the landscape designer. With any luck, they'd find him wining and dining clients as she had in her banking days.

"I don't see him," Thomas said.

"Good evening," the host said. "Reservation?"

"Thank you. I see our party." Stefanie took Thomas's hand, but he balked when she tried to draw him forward.

He'd seen what she had. Greg Edwards, with Marlene and Lawrence

115

Carmichael.

Thomas pressed his lips together.

"It's just dinner," she said. "We might learn something."

He grumbled something sibilant under his breath.

"What's that?" she asked, knowing exactly which German epithet he'd muttered.

"Nothing."

Greg had just sat down, but he immediately stood up when they approached his table. "Stefanie, Thomas. Join us."

"Would it be an imposition?" she asked Marlene and Lawrence.

"Not at all," Lawrence said.

With a wan smile, Marlene gestured to the empty seat.

Greg raised his hand to attract a nearby waiter, and a chair was brought. He and the Carmichaels scooted together to make room for five.

"Any news?" Thomas asked Marlene and Lawrence after drinks were ordered.

Asking if the police had found the bracelet at Carmichael House would be too blatant. Besides, if it had been found, the Carmichaels would be helping the police with their inquiries rather than dining out.

"No." Marlene put a manicured hand to her forehead. "This ghastly affair."

"It was a beauty," Lawrence said. After glancing around the table, he ducked his head slightly. "The woman's death is a tragedy. Tragedy. I don't mean to take away from that. But the bracelet is the reason for her death."

"If Beryl had the bracelet on her this morning, she might have been on that side of the house to return it." Stefanie looked at Marlene. "Did you notice anything in her manner? Did she say anything to indicate she planned to return it?"

Marlene accepted the tonic and lime she'd ordered and held the glass in both hands. "I didn't see her at all this morning. I'll be honest," she said. "I was angry. I didn't want to speak to any of them. I don't know who took the bracelet, but it had to be one of the archaeologists. Well, the police will find the bracelet now."

"Someone knew Beryl had it," Greg pointed out.

"Which is more than we did," Lawrence said.

"We might as well tell you," Thomas said, turning his pilsner glass round and round on the white tablecloth. "Jeffrey asked us to help identify the person who stole the bracelet."

"Your eagle eye," Greg said to Stefanie. "You quite regaled me with the scrutiny you put bank clients under. Looking for nervousness, people shifting from foot to foot, continuously watching the security guard or keeping their faces turned away from the cameras. Myself included, I assume."

"Everyone," Stefanie emphasized. She picked up her glass of wine. "I didn't realize that sharing those stories with you would lead to being involved in a crime in Bermuda."

"And now Beryl Swan is dead," Lawrence said.

Stefanie's cheeks grew warm. A lot of good her training had done Beryl.

"We don't know that Beryl stole the bracelet," Thomas said.

"Did you see any of those mannerisms in Jeffrey's team?" Marlene asked.

Stefanie took a deep breath. "Everyone was nervous. And fearful. And disappointed." Including you and Lawrence, she thought. Pointing that out would tighten their tongues for certain. She'd learned with Hunter and Daphne her technique needed subtlety.

"So you couldn't narrow it down," Lawrence said. "Shame."

"The police will find the murderer." Greg lifted his glass. "Cheers to that."

They all lifted glasses to that hope.

The waiter brought out a basket of soft white rolls and a plate of butter.

"Let's talk of more pleasant things," Greg said.

"We hear that tropical storm might develop into a hurricane," Thomas said, getting out his phone to check the latest forecast.

"It's just as likely to peter out before it gets here," Lawrence said. "When do you leave?"

"Monday. I hope you're right. It's now predicted to be a Cat 2." Thomas set the phone down between his cutlery and hers. "I wish I could have seen that emerald bracelet."

"I can help with that." Lawrence took his cell phone from his chest pocket and brought up a photo of the bracelet, then passed his phone to Thomas. "Prettiest emeralds you've ever seen."

Thomas put the phone between them so that Stefanie could see, too.

Noting the close proximity of Thomas's phone to Lawrence's, she studied the photo.

Lawrence's photo of the bracelet was clearer than Jeffrey's, which had been taken when the bracelet was exposed in the ground. Lawrence's close up of the cleaned bracelet showed it laid out on the kitchen counter. She recognized the granite pattern.

"They brought it into the kitchen to clean it," Lawrence said.

Delicate gold filigree formed each of nine links, and the rectangular deep green emeralds centered on each sparkled richly, reflecting the flash of the camera.

Leaning over to look, Greg gave a low whistle. "Old mine emeralds."

"Yes." Thomas picked up a roll from the basket and buttered it while he examined the image. "Worth a fortune."

"Quite." Lawrence nodded. "It's a loss, for sure."

"Mind if I have a closer look?" Greg asked.

Thomas finished buttering his roll, wiped his hands on the cloth napkin, and then handed Greg the phone.

Greg leaned back in his chair and stretched one hand out as he looked at the bracelet. "You know, I collect pieces with old mine emeralds. For investment purposes," he said, at their interested looks. "I have several. Beautiful green color. Quality gold work. A necklace and earrings." He smiled at Stefanie. "Perfect for a green-eyed beauty."

She'd just taken a bite of roll. The dough sat in her mouth, dissolving as she stared at Greg. Then she glanced at Thomas. Steam practically blew out of his ears, he glowered so fiercely.

She hurriedly chewed and swallowed. "We talked to Hunter and Daphne this afternoon," she said.

"Were they helpful?" Marlene asked.

"Neither one saw Beryl with the bracelet," Thomas said. "But Nathaniel Dimon was at your house around the time the bracelet was taken. You said

118

you told him about the bracelet."

Marlene dropped her hands into her lap as the waiter set a plate of chicken parmesan in front of her. "Yes, I told him. That was on the phone. He did stop by later."

With her chicken piccata served, Stefanie focused her attention on her plate, avoiding both Greg's and Thomas's eye.

"Nathaniel wanted to see the bracelet," Stefanie guessed. "Did you show it to him?"

"No, he only stopped in briefly," Marlene said. "He wanted to clarify a few details about the moon gate."

So Marlene hadn't shown him the bracelet.

Mercifully, dinner conversation after that centered on Bermuda's attractions.

At the end of the meal, Marlene extended an invitation. "This has been a horrible welcome to Bermuda for you. Please, come have cocktails at the house tomorrow night. About eight should work."

"We'd love to," Stefanie said.

The drive home was quiet. Too quiet.

When Thomas parked, he didn't get out of the Tazzari. Stefanie waited. He'd had enough of Greg, she was sure. To her surprise, instead of complaining about Greg, he took out his phone.

"Let's see who Lawrence has been in contact with," he said.

"You cloned his phone at the table. I suspected that's what you were doing."

He smiled at her, and she leaned over to see if Lawrence's call history would tell them anything interesting.

"No texts," Thomas said.

"That's unusual," she said. "Lawrence must be too old-school for that. He does like to talk. I'll bet he prefers conversations to texts."

Thomas brought up the recent calls list. She scanned the numbers.

"I know that one," she said, cringing inwardly while she pointed.

"Who is it?"

She pulled her hand back. "Greg."

Without looking at her, he gave a single nod. After perusing the other numbers, he blanked his phone.

After getting out, they faced each other over the roof of the car. Tree frogs trilling in the night filled the awkwardness between them.

"Let's move to a hotel," she said.

"No. No need," Thomas replied.

His eyes, when he smiled, held a particularly vindictive light.

Uh oh. Hopefully, Greg would keep his distance.

Chapter Nineteen

"We're at a crossroads," Stefanie said the next morning over breakfast.

Thomas's head shot up from the plate of eggs he'd been salting. A flicker of alarm darkened his eyes.

"Not us." She covered his hand with her own, mentally cursing Greg while she did.

He set down the saltshaker. "Yes?"

"The person who killed Beryl is still out there, walking around. We know it's one of the people we've met. Will we really enjoy a boat ride to watch sea turtles, knowing that the rest of the archaeologists or Marlene and Lawrence could be in danger because they saw something?" she asked. "When we have the skills to help?"

"Franklin-Ross knows what she's doing." Thomas considered the saltshaker, then picked up his fork instead.

"Knowing who stole the bracelet will help identify the murderer," she said. "It's Hunter and Daphne that I'm worried about. They are so young. Fearless, yet still so naïve."

He looked askance. "Daphne, perhaps."

Stefanie buttered her toast. "Beryl's killer is having breakfast with potential witnesses. Sleeping under the same roof. Drinking coffee or rum swizzles with the others. If whoever hit Beryl with that rock thinks they were seen, they're going to feel threatened."

"They've killed once," he agreed. "Once that barrier is broken, it's easier to justify a second time."

"Everyone at Carmichael House that morning is in danger until the murderer is caught," she said. "Someone else could get hurt."

Thomas looked up from his eggs. Their eyes met.

"We won't let that happen," he said.

Her heart swelled with love and pride. Knowing he could help, he hadn't turned away. Even with his plans for their romantic getaway in shreds.

"So no sea turtles today," she said, pouring a second cup of coffee.

"No sea turtles."

The navy sundress she'd chosen for the sea turtle excursion would do just as well for interviewing their fellow suspects. Thomas's Bermuda-length light blue shorts and white cotton shirt would be satisfactory for a visit to Nathaniel Dimon's office, which is what she had in mind since they hadn't found him at the Italian restaurant the evening before.

Stefanie cupped her hands around the Riverboat Rum coffee mug.

"There must be a reason Nathaniel Dimon left without checking the garden on Tuesday. Let's see if we can get him to admit to seeing Beryl or anyone else at the buttery. Maybe even get him to say if he was at Carmichael House yesterday morning."

"After we talk to Jeffrey," Thomas said.

Jeffrey, who hadn't mentioned that he'd left Carmichael House during lunch the day of the theft.

They waited for him in his driveway before he left for the museum. The air was warm and sultry, and the sun bright. Any threat of a hurricane seemed remote.

"Jeffrey," Thomas said, leaning against Jeffrey's blue Ford. "We're still working on finding out who took the Spanish bracelet for you."

"That was Beryl," Jeffrey said, his mouth twisted with bitterness. "It had to be. And she was killed for it."

Dressed for work, he opened the car door and set his lunch cooler in the back.

"How do you know that?" Stefanie asked. "Did you see her when you left for lunch? Ingram and Hunter thought you might have."

Jeffrey's hand rested for a moment on the car door, then he pushed it

122

closed. "No, I didn't see anyone when I went to my car."

Thomas lifted his chin at the cooler on the back seat. "You bring your lunch to work."

Jeffrey looked at it, too, then at them. "I do. I usually do, but in the excitement over the dig, I forgot. I wasn't gone long," he said. "I went down to the beach and got a wahoo sandwich. I forgot all about that when I was telling you about the theft. I was upset about the bracelet. I still am."

Did she believe his lunch outing slipped his mind? He was a nervous wreck over the theft. It was possible, maybe, when he'd first told them about the theft.

"I'm sure you remembered later," Stefanie said. "You didn't think it was important to tell us?"

The circles under Jeffrey's eyes were darker. "I'm sorry. I'm not sleeping and not thinking very clearly."

Giving him the benefit of the doubt, for the moment, since he had enlisted their help to find the bracelet, she said, "We're trying to learn who knew that Beryl took the bracelet. If she did."

"You didn't see Beryl when you left for lunch," Thomas said. "What about Nathaniel Dimon?"

"Hunter told us he drove in during the lunch break." Squinting against the bright sunlight, Stefanie donned her straw fedora to keep the sun out of her eyes.

"Didn't see him. His car wasn't there when I left, or when I got back." Jeffrey opened the driver's side door. Glancing at Stefanie's hat, something clicked in his eyes, and his face flooded with relief. "I remember now. The bracelet was there," he said. "When I left for lunch. Daphne tried it on. She was standing outside the buttery, twisting her wrist so the emeralds and gold caught the light."

Daphne could have damaged the bracelet by trying it on. Thomas wasn't any happier at that news than she was.

Seeing their surprise, Jeffrey shrugged. "The bracelet was in excellent shape, and I knew she'd take good care of it. I knew Ingram wouldn't let it come to harm." He blinked several times. "I thought it would be taken care of."

Thomas settled his stern police stare on Jeffrey. "Did you check on the bracelet after you returned?"

"No, I didn't see any reason to," he said.

"Even after Daphne wore it?" Stefanie asked. Jeffrey made it difficult to extend him the benefit of the doubt.

"You're better off telling us everything," Thomas said. "None of you are safe if the murderer thinks you saw something incriminating."

Jeffrey rubbed his eyes. "I understand. I didn't see the murder. I don't know what happened yesterday morning." Appealing to them with a look, he sat in his car. "I've got to get to the museum. Fabiola Ortiz has an appointment with our Executive Director this morning. Can we talk later?"

When he drove off, Stefanie and Thomas once again folded themselves into their tiny rental.

"I know you're thinking what I'm thinking," Stefanie said. "Jeffrey leaving for lunch during the time the bracelet was stolen is too suspicious to ignore."

"He was irresponsible with that bracelet. We can confirm with Daphne that she tried on the bracelet," Thomas said.

"Here's something else that's been bothering me," she said. "Yesterday, why was Fabiola looking for Beryl at Carmichael House instead of Jeffrey, the boss, if she wanted to discuss new finds?"

Thomas nosed the car out of the driveway. "We should ask her. After we talk to Nathaniel Dimon."

"Stop at Carmichael House on the way to his office," she said. "I'll get Fabiola's phone number from Marlene, or Lawrence, if Marlene has gone to work."

When they drove up to Carmichael House, Stefanie spotted DI Franklin-Ross standing across the street, where the cliff dropped down to St. George's Harbour. Cool and crisp in a khaki skirt and white scoop-necked blouse under a short-sleeved jacket, the detective inspector eyed them as they parked and crossed.

"Good morning, DI Franklin-Ross," Stefanie said. "How are you today?"

A faint tinge of amusement showed in the Inspector's otherwise impassive features. "I'm fine. How are you, Ms. Adams, and you, Herr Burkhardt?"

"We are well, *danke*," Thomas replied.

With the pleasantries taken care of, Stefanie felt she could be bold. "Have you found the emerald bracelet?"

"We are still looking."

So it hadn't turned up among Beryl's things, or at Carmichael House, Stefanie thought. Disappointing, but not unexpected.

"There is something curious that we want to tell you," Stefanie went on. "Yesterday, Dr. Fabiola Ortiz came here to see Beryl."

"Yes?" the DI said, dividing her attention between Stefanie and a uniformed policeman making his way up the steep slope.

"Why did she ask to see Beryl if she wanted to find out about the Spanish artifacts, instead of Jeffrey, Beryl's boss? That's a little odd, don't you think?" Stefanie asked.

A deep voice came over the hand-held radio in the officer's belt. "Detective Inspector, have you made any progress on the Swan case? The Commissioner wants an update."

The DI suppressed an aggravated glance, then answered the call politely. "Searching Cut Road as we speak."

After clicking off and turning down the volume switch on the radio, she gave Stefanie and Thomas a frank look. "A woman who wants to get ahead at work has to be more aggressive than her male counterparts. Fabiola Ortiz is a very astute character. I'm sure she recognized that Beryl Swan was ambitious and hoped to use that to further Spain's case in any way she could."

The uniformed officer made it to the top of the hillside carrying a plastic bag. He held it up. A cell phone was inside.

It had to be Beryl's. Stefanie met the DI's gaze. She couldn't confirm the cell as Beryl's before examining it, but Stefanie knew the detective inspector suspected that as strongly as she did.

"Ma'am," the uniformed officer said.

"Excuse me," Franklin-Ross said, taking the bag from her subordinate.

Dismissed, Stefanie and Thomas looked right, then crossed the street.

"I'll wait in the car while you get Fabiola's number," Thomas said.

The gate was open, and Lawrence greeted her at the door, looking very much the sailor with his light-colored plaid shirt tucked into white belted shorts. As she'd suspected, Marlene had left for work.

While Lawrence found Fabiola's card and copied down the number for her, Stefanie said, "You're retired, aren't you, Lawrence? Were you here all day Tuesday, or out training for your next race?"

He laughed. "My competitive sailing days are over. Now the fun is in backing a winning boat."

Stefanie studied the photos on his shelves. "Think Britain will win next time?"

"Oh yes." He tore the sheet off a small pad and handed it to her.

"When is the next America's Cup?" she asked. "Any chance Thomas and I can catch it while we're here?"

He shook his head. "Not till next year. This is when the boats are being designed and tried out." He came to stand in front of the largest photo. "We almost made it," he said. "Almost made it."

Remembering Greg's comment about the difficulty in derailing Lawrence once he got on the topic of his glory days, Stefanie moved to the door.

"On Tuesday," she said, "did you talk to Nathaniel Dimon? Or see him at all? Maybe out these windows?"

Again he shook his head. "I was here at the computer, looking up those Spanish coins. They are something of a rarity. Did you know that most of the gold *reales* were melted down?"

Disappointed, she smiled. "Interesting. Thanks."

In the car, Thomas tucked his phone into his shirt pocket. "Got it?"

"Fabiola's number is all I got," she said, buckling her seat belt. "Lawrence didn't see Nathaniel on Tuesday."

126

Chapter Twenty

"If Jeffrey's alibi for the theft holds up," Stefanie said, "that Daphne was wearing the bracelet when he left at lunch on Tuesday, then Nathaniel Dimon is the logical choice for getting the bracelet off the property."

"It will hold up," Thomas said. "Too easy to disprove it if Jeffrey is lying. Daphne was in plain view."

Stefanie drummed her fingers on her thigh, feeling the weave of her linen sundress. "What if Daphne damaged the bracelet when she tried it on? She might have taken the bracelet to hide that fact."

"Let's rule out Dimon first," Thomas said. "What we know is that he knew the bracelet had been discovered. Marlene admitted to telling him that when he called her Tuesday morning."

"He and Marlene talked on the telephone, then he came in person to Carmichael House."

"To see the bracelet for himself," Thomas said. "That's a reasonable assumption. But it doesn't make sense that he didn't stay long enough to inspect the garden. Or even to see the bracelet. Something made him cut his visit short."

Stefanie raised her eyebrows. "Maybe learning that Beryl had stolen the bracelet."

"Perhaps. We need to pin down his movements Tuesday at Carmichael House," Thomas said. "Pressure him into telling the truth or catch him in a lie."

"And find out if he went back to Carmichael House yesterday morning," she said.

They caught the landscape designer on the front step of his office just as he was leaving.

"Good morning," Nathaniel said. "Isn't our appointment next Thursday?" He glanced at his wristwatch.

An expensive model, Stefanie noticed. It went well with his linen Bermuda shorts and matching silk tie.

"Morning," she said. "I don't know if it's good or not. You heard about what happened at Carmichael House yesterday? Beryl Swan?"

Nathaniel adjusted his leather portfolio more comfortably under his arm. "Yes. A senseless killing."

He looked like he was about to excuse himself, but Thomas dangled bait.

"We have a dilemma," he said. "The grounds we want you to look at are rather large. About the size of the grounds at Government House here in Bermuda, I believe. Do you have a moment to talk to us about whether renovating the entire landscape is a good option, or if concentrating on a single area that would be a focal point is the way to go?"

The designer's hand tightened on his portfolio, and he glanced again at his watch.

"I want a garden that people will talk about for ages," Stefanie said. "Magazine-worthy. I have connections at Travel & Leisure." Her newly deposited pay attested to that.

After a moment of hesitation, Nathaniel flashed a smile, revealing even white teeth. "I have a consultation scheduled, but I'll tell them I was delayed due to checking plant availability."

In the office, Thomas gave Dimon the address of his property in Germany. While the designer looked it up on his computer, Stefanie pounced.

"You know about the theft of the emerald bracelet they found," she said.

"I saw that on the news," Nathaniel said, studying the German property details.

Thomas stretched his legs out and crossed one ankle over the other. "People say Beryl Swan stole it."

The landscape architect paused for a moment, then resumed his study of the property on the screen. "You're right, this is a large property."

"When we met the first time, you mentioned that you'd spoken to Marlene Tuesday morning," she said. "Did you see Beryl as well?"

"No," he answered. "I was in and out very quickly."

"Long enough to make an impression on Daphne," Stefanie told him. "She's quite taken with you."

Nathaniel glanced up from his computer screen and smiled at some memory. "Was she the young girl? The student?"

"Did Daphne seem okay?" Stefanie asked. "Or like something was bothering her?" If Daphne had damaged the bracelet, she'd be feeling guilty. It would weigh heavily on her mind.

"I saw a couple of the archaeologists on Tuesday, but not really to speak to," Nathaniel said.

"We never did get a chance to see the bracelet," Thomas said with regret. "Did you?"

"No," the designer replied with a curious glance at Thomas. He turned his computer screen toward them. "These woods beyond the lawn are established, and from this photo, the trees are healthy. I wouldn't touch them. But here, closer to the house, are several areas we can play with. A hedge maze, for example, would be in keeping with these great old properties. Another option is a secluded patio, far enough from the house to offer a sense of privacy during a large house party or reception. I'll be doing something along those lines for Marlene. Although on a much smaller scale than you have room for."

"I like the idea of an intimate spot on the grounds," Thomas said, checking with Stefanie for confirmation.

"Yes, I do, too," she said.

"We could surround it with a pleasing array of native plants, combining all the senses," Nathaniel continued. "Juxtapose different flower and leaf colors, a mix of different fragrances, and for sound, the rustling of wind through decorative grasses can't be beat. We can incorporate the softness of edelweiss and lacy chamomile. Or we can go with more formal plantings, a mix of annuals and shrubs." The designer turned off his computer. "Think about those options, and we'll get into more detail on Thursday." He stood up.

"Can we have a moon gate, like Marlene's getting at Carmichael House?" Stefanie asked, tucking her purse under her arm.

"We can do anything under the sun," Nathaniel assured her.

He hadn't given much away at all. "So you didn't see anyone with the bracelet?" she asked.

He stiffened. "With the assessment going on, I didn't stay."

"I'm surprised," Thomas said as they walked out together. "I'd think you'd want to see what damage they'd done and try to rein them in."

"No, I leave that to the archaeologists, then clean up afterward. I only talked to the Minister about a change in plant selection. She keeps busy, you know. As do I."

They could hardly ignore that pointed remark.

On the sidewalk, Stefanie got in one last question. "Yesterday, when you were late to the office, did you run by Carmichael House first?"

He blinked, and his long-lashed eyes zeroed in on hers. Whether there was amusement or resentment behind that gaze, she couldn't tell.

"No," he said. "I wasn't at Carmichael House the day Beryl Swan was killed. I haven't been since Tuesday. And I know you will appreciate that I don't gossip about what goes on at my clients' houses."

Resentment. Definitely resentment.

The designer walked off, clutching the large portfolio under his arm.

Darn.

"That didn't go as well as I would have liked. Too bad he doesn't gossip," Stefanie said.

"What we need," Thomas said, "is fresh air to clear our minds. While we charge the Tazzari. Again."

"The Town of St. George?" Stefanie suggested. "I'll take notes for my travel blog."

They drove back to St. George to the shop where they'd rented the Tazzari.

Thomas pulled into one of the charging spaces. After he took care of the charging, they sauntered down York Street and made a brief stop at St. Peter's Church, a small white church at the top of a brick staircase that seemed nearly the height of the building itself.

The interior was small and intimate, with dark cedar pews lined up on either side of a central aisle, leading to the altar. Timbers of rough-hewn cedar supported the ceiling.

"Parts of this church date back to 1620," Stefanie said, reading the guidebook.

After descending the brick staircase, they made their way to nearby King's Square. The square was small and intimate as well, surrounded by pastel Colonial buildings with their fresh white trim. Stocks and pillories, replicas of those used to publicly humiliate wayward citizens, stood in front of the Town Hall.

"For those who didn't follow their Sunday lessons," Thomas said.

"Or broke the Ten Commandments," Stefanie said, thinking of two in particular. Thou shalt not steal. Thou shalt not kill.

The square fronted the harbor, which was full of docked sailboats.

Nearby was a replica of the *Deliverance*, one of two ships built by the original stranded English colonists and crew to take much-needed supplies to the struggling colony in Jamestown, Virginia. Tourists climbed and clambered over the deck and rigging.

"Tight quarters," Thomas commented of the forty-foot ship.

"They saved the colonists in Jamestown from starving," Stefanie said. "They did the right thing."

"We will, too," Thomas promised.

They chose a restaurant opposite the *Deliverance* and sat at an outdoor table.

Stefanie jotted down notes on the city for her blog, *Travel Tips for the Intrepid Woman*. After filling the last page of her Moleskine notebook, she put it away, ready to give Thomas her full attention.

"Marlene claimed to talk about the moon gate, yet Nathaniel said they discussed plant choices," Thomas observed.

"I don't think anyone is telling the truth. Not the whole truth." Stefanie took a sip of her espresso, which had just been delivered. "Nathaniel is a slippery character. He's vague with his replies and didn't commit to anything."

"Except not being at Carmichael House yesterday," Thomas said.

Frowning out at the ship, she said, "We still don't know whether he knew if Beryl took the bracelet or not."

He looked at her. "We still don't know if Beryl did."

True.

She put down her cup. "Daphne wouldn't have taken the bracelet after wearing it like a royal," Stefanie said, "unless she broke it. I can't see that happening, so let's put that aside until we talk to her. But she hasn't shared everything she knows. Maybe it's nothing. But maybe she saw something. Something that she doesn't realize has a bearing on the theft, or the murder."

Watching the crowd of tourists climbing the *Deliverance*, Thomas agreed.

Lunch came, and they enjoyed wahoo sandwiches and fries. Stefanie speared a fry with her fork.

"Great fries," she said.

"Chips," Thomas said. "We should speak British while we're here." He winked at her.

She smiled. Greg's little comments weren't putting a damper on Thomas's spirits. At least not one that lasted.

"Did Daphne see Beryl while she was flirting with Nathaniel?" Stefanie mused. "Maybe not enough to know at the time that Beryl was taking the bracelet, but enough to put it together afterward?"

"Hunter," Thomas said.

He was fixated on Hunter, and he could be right.

"That whole Hunter and Daphne conversation at the rental house yesterday afternoon felt like we were watching a play," Stefanie said.

"A performance," Thomas agreed. "They are afraid. I've seen it before. One thief at an archaeological site casts suspicion on the innocent, and they are caught in a trap."

"Like what happened to my father, the reason he didn't continue in archaeology." She raised her brows. Thomas had been fixated on Hunter for a reason. "But that's not what you're thinking of, is it?"

"Back in the early part of my career. The earliest," he said.

When he didn't volunteer a further glimpse into his past, she said, "I can see Daphne or Hunter being involved in the theft. Maybe. But in Beryl's death? I just don't believe that."

"They are both hiding something," Thomas said.

Wiping her hands on her napkin, Stefanie said, "They both have their future careers at stake. You'd think they'd share what they know. So why haven't they?"

Thomas pushed his empty plate aside and picked up his glass of local beer. "The bracelet was stolen. Jeffrey gave time for it to be returned. It wasn't. Beryl was killed."

She went over those facts in her mind. The people at Carmichael House. Beryl on the narrow path beside the house that led to the buttery. Hunter and Daphne keeping secrets.

She gasped. "What if the murderer saw someone give the bracelet to Beryl? To turn in?"

His eyes glittered. "And saw it was an opportunity too good to pass by."

Her cell phone rang, and Stefanie dipped into her Kate Spade purse to get it. She groaned inwardly when she saw who it was. Not again.

"It's Greg." Moving to delete the call, she curled her fingers into a loose fist to hold them back. "What if it has to do with the house? I really should answer it."

"Go ahead," Thomas said, planting his forearms on the table as he finished his beer.

"Hello," Stefanie answered.

"Stefanie, it's Jeffrey," Greg said. "The police have arrested him for Beryl's murder."

Chapter Twenty-One

"Jeffrey's been arrested for Beryl's murder," Stefanie said as she put her phone down.

Thomas grunted with satisfaction. "I suspected him from the start."

"Because he didn't report the theft to the museum," she said. But resorting to murder? And a colleague at that? After he'd asked them to help find the thief? Stefanie didn't believe it. "Jeffrey was trying to solve the theft. He wouldn't have killed Beryl."

"He was trying to get the bracelet back." Thomas signaled to the waitress for their check.

"His arrest must have to do with the cell phone the police found this morning," she said, picking up her purse.

"We can safely assume that it was Beryl's phone and that it incriminates Jeffrey."

Tourists climbing on the *Deliverance* laughed and called to each other. She wanted to explore the replica as well, to feel what those long-ago shipwreck survivors felt, to experience their cramped quarters and that feeling of salvation at hand. But Jeffrey needed them. They hadn't learned much in their investigation, but maybe enough to clear him.

"Thomas, I can't believe he would have killed her. Not after bringing us into it," she said. "We've got to find out why he was arrested. He's being held in Hamilton."

Thomas paid for lunch, then wrapped an arm around her shoulders as they returned to the car.

At the police station, their request to see Jeffrey was turned down flat.

"If you aren't family or his lawyers, you can't talk to him," the officer at the desk said.

Through the open door behind him, Stefanie saw DI Franklin-Ross in the hallway.

"Detective Inspector," Stefanie called. "Can we have a word?"

With a long-suffering look, the Inspector came out to meet them. "You heard we made an arrest."

"Jeffrey Fitzsimmons is the one who asked us to help find the emerald bracelet," Stefanie said. "Don't you think Beryl's death is about that bracelet? He wouldn't kill her. He suspected her of taking it."

"Motive," DI Franklin-Ross replied.

"All he had to do was come to you and let you know he thought she was the thief," Stefanie said.

"He did. After he was arrested," the DI told them. "In fact, he's been quite forthcoming since we brought him in."

"This means you've cleared us?" Thomas asked.

Franklin-Ross briefly smiled. "You'll be happy to know your arrival and movements at Carmichael House were corroborated. You are both free to leave whenever you want."

"Thank you," he said.

"Thank you," Stefanie echoed. Not that she thought the DI seriously suspected them.

"Can we talk to Jeffrey? For a few minutes only?" Thomas pulled out his wallet and displayed his police and Interpol IDs. "Nothing official," he said. "But we'll share anything we learn."

Stefanie could see the detective inspector recalculating her judgments of them.

"We were the ones who told you about the emerald bracelet in the first place," she reminded the DI.

"Yes, all right."

"Did you get it? The bracelet?" Thomas asked as Franklin-Ross accompanied them down a long hall.

"Jeffrey denies having it. We'll find it, if he does. We're searching his house." The DI opened the door to a small room, then left them.

In a few minutes, a guard brought Jeffrey in and led him to the small metal table in the center of the room.

When the door closed with the guard on the other side, Stefanie leaned across the table.

"What is this about?" she asked. "Beryl's phone? They found one down the cliff opposite Carmichael House."

Jeffrey raked his hand up over his forehead and through his thinning hair. "I did it," he said.

Involuntarily, Stefanie drew back. Jeffrey was guilty. Her mouth went dry. He'd killed Beryl after asking them to help. They hadn't come through, and he'd resorted to violence. Why hadn't she pushed Beryl harder? She put her hand on Thomas's thigh beneath the table. His strength and warmth steadied her.

"I didn't kill Beryl," Jeffrey exclaimed, seeing her reaction. "Her cell phone. I found it. And I threw it as far as I could."

"Not far enough," Thomas remarked.

Stefanie's jaw tightened. "Why?"

"Because my text was on it." Jeffrey hung his head, staring at the floor rather than them. "I found her when I went to the front to let you in the gate. After I got your text. There was nothing I could do for her. She was already dead."

Stefanie clenched her hands into fists. He'd left Beryl there for someone else to find. For her to find. Pretending nothing had happened.

"And?" she prompted.

"I knew that as soon as the police read my text, they would think I'd killed her. As they do," he pointed out. Not discerning any sympathy on their faces, he went on. "So I searched her pockets, found her cell phone, and threw it across the road, hoping it would land in the harbor and sink."

"Start from the beginning," Thomas said. "Don't play games this time."

Jeffrey shifted in his chair. "Tuesday, at lunchtime, I went to the car for my lunch. There was a folded note on the driver's seat."

A pit burned in Stefanie's stomach. He'd used them from the beginning.

Spun a tale that she'd fallen for.

"Was the car locked?" she asked, determined to stay detached enough to see things clearly and objectively.

"No, and the window was down. The note said, 'Go out for lunch or everyone will know it was your fault.'"

"Signed?" she asked.

Jeffrey shook his head. "Not signed. But I knew who it was."

"What was your fault?" Thomas asked.

"There was an incident when Beryl was first hired," Jeffrey said. "A parcel of land had been sold with a decaying cottage on it. We had to do an archaeological assessment before the hotel developer could build. I'd driven by, and the place was a total loss from the outside, falling down. No one had lived in the cottage for seven or eight years. It was Beryl's first job. We had six other jobs waiting. I told her she could sign off on the property. So the cottage came down."

"I should have checked," he said. "I should have had Beryl double-check before the building was demolished. We drove by later to watch the progress and saw what had been an incredible hand-carved mantel reduced to splinters in the pile of rubbish. Along with fragments of an early stained-glass window. The mantel and window could have been saved. Should have been saved," he said. "I've laid on work stoppages for less. We both knew I screwed up and that she'd get the blame. Neither one of us ever said a word."

That was the real reason Jeffrey had been so afraid for his reputation. Since she'd arrived on the island, she'd heard about the importance of keeping historical artifacts, a duty close to the Bermudian heart. What was the cost of dereliction of duty for an archaeologist in Bermuda? Job loss? A heavy price to pay, especially for a newly minted archaeologist like Beryl had been.

"Beryl made that comment about lost historical items Wednesday at Carmichael House," Stefanie said. "I thought she was referring to the Spanish bracelet."

Jeffrey shook his head. "She was reminding me that she could spill my secret if I revealed she took the bracelet."

Stefanie could guess how Beryl had worked it. With Jeffrey gone, there was one less person to see her slip into the buttery.

"The architectural elements are a loss, but not a tragedy," Thomas said. "Beryl's death is a tragedy."

"You were angry that she didn't return the bracelet," Stefanie said.

"I didn't kill her," Jeffrey said. "I don't know who did. No one was around when I found her."

"Make good on this chance to come clean," Thomas said. "Where is the bracelet?"

Catching on that Thomas was grilling him rather than offering support, Jeffrey said, "I don't have it. Beryl didn't have it on her when I found her."

"Do you still have the note?" Thomas asked.

"I burned it."

Tuesday evening Jeffrey had a fire going in his backyard when he came to talk to them.

"The fire pit," Thomas said.

Jeffrey nodded. "It was a page torn out of her memo book. I should have thrown *that* away instead of her phone."

He'd looked sick when Hunter thumbed through Beryl's memo book after she was found, Stefanie remembered. She'd thought Beryl's death had upset him. He'd been thinking of Beryl's blackmail note.

"I didn't do it," he insisted. "I didn't kill her."

"What did your text say?" Thomas asked. "The one you tried to hide."

"She'd gotten away with stealing the bracelet. I couldn't let it go on." Jeffrey lifted his head long enough to gaze at Stefanie. The disappointment in his eyes wrenched at her conscience. "I texted her yesterday morning. I said, 'I did what you wanted. You can't get away with it.' She never replied."

Beryl's blackmail ploy had cost her life.

"You were angry that Beryl used you," Stefanie said, her jaw tight. "I can understand that."

"Not angry enough to hurt her. I was going to put her on notice if she didn't return it. When I saw that she was dead, I knew the police wouldn't look any further once they found my text." He shrugged a forlorn surrender. "So I threw the phone."

Thomas gave him a look of disgust. "You shouldn't have dragged us into this."

The door to the room opened, and DI Franklin-Ross waited.

Stefanie stood up. "I don't appreciate being lied to."

"If she returned it, I'd never have said anything," Jeffrey said when they reached the door. "Given her a second chance. Like she'd given me."

He sounded sincere, but he'd sounded sincere when he first asked them to look into the theft. Stefanie turned away, too angry to respond.

"Did you hear all that?" Thomas asked the detective inspector in the hallway.

The DI nodded as she escorted them back to the front desk. "Nothing new. He told us all of that earlier."

"With any luck, the bracelet will show up at his house," Stefanie said.

"Yes."

"Until then," Thomas asked, "you'll hold something back from the public?"

"The blackmail note. It goes without saying that you'll do so as well." DI Franklin-Ross held the security door to let them through.

"Right," he said.

On the drive home, Stefanie stared out the window at the grey water and grey clouds.

"I thought it was warm to have a fire going Tuesday evening," Thomas said.

She'd just liked the idea of a fire, without thought to the weather. "If he's lying about killing Beryl," she said, "we don't have to worry about anyone else getting hurt." If.

Thomas reached for her hand. She held on for a moment, then released his fingers as they drew close to the house.

Two police vehicles sat in the drive at Jeffrey's place.

Getting out of the car, she saw Greg standing on Jeffrey's back patio, staring out at the churning Atlantic.

"We can't leave him over there with the police," she said.

"Doesn't he have a headquarters building in Hamilton he can go to?" Thomas asked.

"I'll bet you know everything about it."

He smiled. "I do."

She lifted her eyebrows.

"I did a little reconnaissance on him while you were with Lawrence this morning. Just curious," Thomas said.

"We have to tell him what we found out." She walked over to the dividing wall. "Greg," she called, "Come over."

In the house, she fixed coffee again, and this time when the addition of rum was suggested, all three assented. In pouring a generous dollop into each mug with shaking hands, Stefanie spilled rum on the counter.

"Why would Jeffrey bring us into this at all?" she asked angrily, searching for the dishcloth.

Greg stepped forward and tore a paper towel off the roll beside the sink, then wiped up the spill as Stefanie recapped the bottle of rum.

"How well do you know Jeffrey?" Thomas asked, with a careful eye on Greg's proximity to her.

After tossing the paper towel in the trash, Greg took his mug from Stefanie. "We go back decades. My mother was from Bermuda. She attended Washington University in St. Louis, like you did," he added with a glance at Stefanie. "This was my grandparents' house. Jeffrey's house has been his family home as well. We've been casual friends for a very long time, long enough that I don't think he'd commit murder."

"He had reason," Stefanie said.

"Beryl stole the emerald bracelet, and Jeffrey knew." Thomas didn't show his police credentials to Greg, she noticed.

Greg tapped on the rim of his coffee cup. "The police didn't release Jeffrey, did they?"

"No," Stefanie said. "Why?"

"Someone was in the house this morning," he said. "Before the police arrived. My suitcase had been opened and gone through."

"Could it have been Jeffrey himself?" Stefanie asked.

"No," Greg said. "He was at work this morning, at the museum. That's where he was arrested."

"Did they take anything?" Thomas asked.

"Nothing of mine," Greg said. "I don't know about Jeffrey's things."

"Local news has broken the story of the emerald bracelet," she said. "Maybe a thief thought he'd find the bracelet at Jeffrey's house, since he was in charge of the dig."

"Or someone closer to the situation," Thomas suggested. "Hunter Renko."

"We suspected Hunter originally, along with Beryl," Stefanie said for Greg's benefit.

"What did Jeffrey have to say?" Greg asked.

As Stefanie related Jeffrey's tale, leaving out the blackmail note, the burning in her stomach grew stronger.

"He said the bracelet was stolen at lunch time. He didn't mention that he'd left at lunch, just that everyone at Carmichael House had been in and out of the buttery, checking out the finds. He flattered me," she said, her cheeks burning as well as her stomach. "He said he wanted my help because I was discreet. What he really wanted was someone to point the finger at Beryl and who wouldn't share the crime with police."

"He underestimated you," Greg said.

"Something I've learned to not do," Thomas said.

Stefanie picked up her coffee mug. "Without the full picture, we didn't know what we were looking at."

That aggravating truth made her pause. Jeffrey had told them the truth at the beginning. Just not the whole truth. Had he finally told them everything? He admitted to knowing Beryl took the bracelet, but not to killing her to get it back. And why would he kill her?

She turned to Greg. "Jeffrey said he knew Beryl had stolen the bracelet. She was involved in a botched archaeological assessment in the past. A hotel that went up. About ten years ago."

"The government has gotten strict about those," Greg said. "Construction delays cost businesses thousands of dollars. I was lucky. When I established Riverboat Rum headquarters here, I chose an existing building. Every improvement had to be approved by a committee, but I could open without delay."

"Time is money." Thomas looked at his watch, then at Greg.

"I'm good," Greg answered.

"Jeffrey let his emotions get the better of him," she said, bringing the subject back to Jeffrey's arrest. His pleading expression as they left the interrogation room stuck with her. He'd been desperate for them to believe that he'd tried to give Beryl a second chance.

"At least we know Beryl took the bracelet." Stefanie went to the front door and checked Jeffrey's driveway. "The police are gone. Thomas, call the DI and ask her if they found the bracelet. You have better luck with her than I do."

He called.

"It wasn't there," Thomas said as he clicked off. "Not at Beryl's place, either. And you," he said with a pointed look at Greg, "are free to return to Jeffrey's house."

Greg's brows drew together. "They haven't found the bracelet," he mused, making no sign of leaving.

Doubt dampened the edges of Stefanie's suspicion. Jeffrey's guilt didn't fit with what they knew of his personality. He seemed mild-mannered and more apt to passively let things happen, than to kill a friend in anger.

"What if Jeffrey is finally telling the whole truth?" she asked. "If he was honest about wanting to give Beryl a second chance, and he didn't kill her in anger, who did?"

None of them had an answer to that, or even a strong guess.

"Alright," Stefanie said. "Why was she killed?"

"For the emeralds," Greg said.

"If Jeffrey's text gave her second thoughts," Thomas said, "Beryl would have been returning the bracelet."

She could picture Beryl slipping around the house to the kitchen door, or slipping into the buttery and leaving the bracelet there for Marlene or Lawrence to find at some future time. Maybe Beryl would have even suggested the dig team search the buttery one more time for good measure.

"If Jeffrey is innocent," Greg said, "who else would know Beryl had the bracelet on her Thursday?"

She and Thomas looked at each other.

"Fabiola," they said in unison.

Chapter Twenty-Two

"Fabiola?" Greg's brows drew together. "Dr. Fabiola Ortiz? The Spanish researcher?"

"Does everyone on Bermuda know everyone else?" Stefanie asked.

"I met her through my trusteeship at NMB—the National Museum of Bermuda," Greg said.

"Fabiola heard about the Spanish bracelet," Stefanie told him. "Probably after Jeffrey reported its find to his director at the Museum. She went to Carmichael House yesterday looking for Beryl."

"Nathaniel Dimon might also have known," Thomas said. "I didn't like his vague answers when we talked to him."

"Perhaps he objected to your polite curiosity," Greg said with a smirk.

Thomas smiled at Greg's dig, but his eyes darkened. "Perhaps."

She had to deflect that trouble before it got worse. "I have Fabiola's number. I'm going to call and ask if she'll meet. I'll tell her we want to hear about anything she discovered about the owner of that Spanish medal I found."

"We have two suspects," Greg said. "Why don't I go with you, Stefanie, since I know Fabiola and Thomas here can interrogate Nathaniel Dimon."

Thomas pushed back from the table. "I think not. You collect old mine emeralds."

Greg laughed out loud. "Yes, I do." He smiled at Stefanie, but thankfully didn't bring up again how well he thought they would suit her. Rising, he said, "I'll leave you to your investigations. Give Fabiola my regards."

Stefanie called Fabiola, who agreed to meet.

"Do you know Bermuda well?" Fabiola asked.

"We haven't been able to see much with all that's going on," Stefanie said.

"Then let's meet at Fort Hamilton. The rain is holding off, and we can walk through the moat garden while I tell you all about Don Reynaldo."

Another site for her travel blog.

"It's a date," Stefanie said.

They met Fabiola at the wooden bridge at the fort's entrance. Her light brown hair was pulled back in a ponytail, Stefanie noticed, held by an ornate metal barrette, one that reminded Stefanie of the filigree links on the bracelet. It seemed Spanish taste in adornment followed a common thread through the ages.

"You found the medal of a hero," Fabiola said after greeting them.

"So the bracelet and gold coins weren't buried pirate treasure," Stefanie said with a smile at Thomas.

"No," Fabiola said. "Most certainly not."

They crossed the bridge to the stone staircase which led down into the moat garden, then Fabiola stopped at the top of the steps.

"Let me show you what Don Reynaldo de Cordoba looked like." Bringing up a photo on her cell phone, Fabiola showed it to Stefanie and Thomas. "He received the Military Order of Calatrava for his service to King Philip II. He was lost on his third trip to the New World."

The painted portrait featured a dark-haired man with mustache and neat beard, wearing a black beret with white feather, a small high ruff, and a black coat with gold buttons. Younger than Stefanie expected, he looked to be about her own age, thirty-five. The artist had captured shadows beneath his eyes and Don Reynaldo's weighty expression.

"So this is the man who buried his valuables beneath the chest," Stefanie said.

"Yes," Fabiola answered. "I would like to know why he did."

"He must have had a reason," Thomas said.

They descended the stone stairs from the daylight above to the shadowed garden below.

Searching for another photo on her phone, Fabiola nearly stumbled on the last step.

Thomas sprang forward.

"*Alles gut?*" he asked, holding her by the arm as she descended the last step.

"Yes, thank you, I'm fine," Fabiola said with a smile of thanks.

Between palm trees that grew to the height of the moat and stretched their fronds wide and rampant philodendrons that climbed the walls and blocked out the sunlight, Stefanie felt as if she'd gone from daytime to nighttime. The humidity was oppressive, causing the skirt of her smart linen sundress to wilt. Perfect for the ferns and tropical plants living there, not so much for her.

Fabiola held out her phone again. "Here is what I also want to show you."

The second picture was a portrait of a young woman, serene and pretty, pink-cheeked in a white-yoked black dress from the same time period as Don Reynaldo. She had blond hair parted in the center, capped by a gold and pearl jeweled hair net. On the ring finger of her left hand, she wore a ruby ring.

"This is Maria-Theresa. Don Reynaldo de Cordoba's wife." Fabiola peered into their faces as Stefanie and Thomas stood close to view it. "The emerald bracelet was meant for her."

And Maria-Theresa never got it, Stefanie thought.

"Do you know what happened to him?" she asked as they strolled past the giant ferns, palmettos, and bromeliads that filled the lushly planted moat floor. Above their heads, wispy Spanish moss hung from tree branches.

"Oh yes." Fabiola tucked her phone into her shoulder bag. "Don Reynaldo was on the *Santa Ana*, part of the New Spain fleet, which ran into a terrible storm off Bermuda in the fall of 1588. His ship capsized. All but two of the crew were lost. Don Reynaldo and his shipmaster Alfonso Nunez made it to the shore of Bermuda. One month later, a ship saw the wreckage of the *Santa Ana* on the reefs and rescued Nunez. Don Reynaldo succumbed to injuries from the shipwreck and died on the island. We know this from an account written by Alfonso Nunez."

So that was how Don Reynaldo had come to be stranded on the uninhabited island. He'd died without recovering the emerald bracelet or returning to Spain.

"Unusual that Don Reynaldo would have been wearing his medal," Thomas commented.

Fabiola looked him up and down. "He must have thought he would die in the storm, don't you think? He wore it to show his pride in who he was."

Thomas smiled. "Yes, I see that."

"It's amazing that you can learn that information from such meager evidence," Stefanie said. "Is that what you went to Carmichael House to share with Beryl yesterday?"

"It isn't amazing. It is organization," Fabiola said. "We have archived the letters and reports and ship manifests from all of the fleet voyages. Bermuda was known as 'the island of devils' because of the treacherous reefs. There were frequent shipwrecks. Many, many sailors' lives were lost."

Fabiola, she noticed, hadn't answered her question about Beryl.

"And Beryl?" Stefanie prompted as they walked past a patch of red, orange, and green crotons backed by vines that climbed the twenty-foot walls, reaching for the sunlight.

Fabiola smiled at the bromeliads further along the moat floor. "Beryl knew everything that happened as soon as it happened," she said. "She was also a very practical person. Once I heard that a Spanish bracelet had been found, one made of gold and embellished with emeralds, I knew that I could make her see the rightness of returning the bracelet to Spain."

"Did she call you?" Stefanie asked.

Fabiola adjusted her purse as they strolled. "I called her Wednesday evening. She agreed to meet."

"You agreed to meet Thursday at Carmichael House," Thomas said. "To exchange the bracelet for...?"

Fabiola gave him a sly smile. "She did not say she had the bracelet." Her expression turned grave. "Unfortunately, our meeting never happened." She crossed herself.

"Beryl was supposed to be done at the site by the afternoon," Stefanie said.

Fabiola's mouth turned down. "I did not know that. Perhaps if I had gone in the morning, things would have been different for her."

"Perhaps," Thomas said.

Yesterday, Fabiola had expressed strong opinions about who she thought had stolen the bracelet.

"You insinuated the Carmichaels kept the bracelet," Stefanie said, pausing in front of a massive fern to gauge the woman's facial expressions. "Do you have a reason to think they did?"

Thomas and Fabiola paused as well.

While Thomas bent to inspect windows low in the inner wall of the moat, Fabiola lifted her shoulders up in a delicate shrug. "I say what I can to get what belongs to Spain. If the Carmichaels think they are suspect, they will work hard to avoid the wrath of the police."

So Fabiola didn't actually believe the Carmichaels had hidden the bracelet for reasons of their own. She'd been bluffing in hopes of bringing the bracelet to light.

Stefanie took out her cell phone and aimed the camera down the moat path, capturing the stone wall, the oversized philodendrons and the colorful crotons. Getting a nice shot, she shifted the camera slightly and took another photo, that time capturing Fabiola's profile.

"The police didn't find the bracelet at their house. It was searched yesterday," Thomas said.

"The Carmichaels did not resort to murder to get back what they think is theirs," Fabiola replied. "She is a government minister. He is a retired businessman. They have influence. They will pressure the police to find out which of the archaeologists took the bracelet."

"We know Beryl stole the bracelet," Stefanie said.

"She did?" Fabiola asked.

"Jeffrey Fitzsimmons knew she stole it." Should she reveal that Jeffrey had been arrested? Knowing the police had someone in custody would take pressure off Fabiola, if she were involved. They didn't want that. On the other hand, she'd learn it soon enough from other sources if she hadn't heard about it already.

"Jeffrey's been arrested for her murder," Stefanie went on. "But he denies it, and he doesn't have the bracelet."

Absorbing that information with wide eyes, Fabiola said, "The police will find out who has it."

"And you will try to get it from that person, even if they resorted to murder," Thomas said, standing up after inspecting the curiously placed windows.

Fabiola shrugged. "Whoever has the bracelet."

"Even if that is Hunter Renko," Thomas said.

Stefanie was surprised he chose that tactic, but it was effective.

The Spanish woman's jaw dropped. "Hunter Renko did not kill Beryl." She swallowed and looked at Stefanie, as if hoping for support. "What makes you say that?"

"He's lying to us," Stefanie said. "About where he was when the bracelet was stolen. He might have seen Beryl take it. And he has no alibi for when she was killed."

Fabiola's jaw clenched. "I have known him since he was a boy. He would not steal. He could not have killed anyone," she said, her tone arrogantly confident.

Spotting the stone staircase, Fabiola pulled her purse close under her arm. "I see we are at the end of the garden, and I have other people I must meet." Her gaze rested on Stefanie. "I hope you have enjoyed learning whose medal you discovered."

As Fabiola ascended the stairs that would take her out of the moat, Stefanie saw the fear in her eyes.

"That was an interesting tale Fabiola told about Don Reynaldo and his shipmaster," Stefanie remarked as the Spanish researcher disappeared into the leaves and greenery at the top of the moat garden. "The way Don Reynaldo buried his treasure tells a different story. Did he really die of injuries from the shipwreck, as Alfonso reported, or did he meet his fate at Alfonso's hands, a man he did not trust?"

Thomas nodded. "The survivor tells the story."

Chapter Twenty-Three

"No matter what Fabiola says about Hunter's character, she's worried that he's involved," Stefanie said, climbing the moat stairs. "If Jeffrey is telling the truth, that he didn't kill Beryl for the bracelet, our suspicion of Hunter is right on the mark."

"He neglected to share his friendship with Fabiola with us, and she wants the bracelet," Thomas said. "But I am just as interested in knowing Greg's history with Fabiola."

"That's because you don't like Greg," Stefanie said.

"Partially true," he replied as they got in the car. "I want to get to Hunter before Fabiola does."

"After we confirm Jeffrey's alibi for the theft with Daphne, we can find out if Hunter knew Beryl brought the bracelet back Thursday morning."

"I want to search his room," Thomas said.

"And the same with Daphne," Stefanie said, as much as she didn't want to believe Daphne could be the cause of Beryl's death.

The dark smudge of worry she'd been holding at bay blossomed. Whoever had killed Beryl must be feeling threatened. If it was Daphne, they'd soon find out. But if it was Hunter, Daphne could be in danger. She knew more about what happened than she'd admitted to. The same was true of Hunter.

"Hurry up," Stefanie told Thomas, though loath to have him drive any faster along the narrow winding roads.

He accepted the challenge with enthusiasm.

Anywhere else, a twenty-two mile-an-hour speed limit would be a snail's pace. On Bermuda's narrow and winding roads, thirty-five felt like an amusement park ride, whipping and zipping around curves and corners.

When they arrived at the green rental house, the van was parked outside. With any luck, all three would be inside. They hurried up to the door, and Thomas knocked. It was more of a pounding, really, and Ingram frowned when he answered.

"What's the emergency?" the professor demanded. Alarmed, he immediately looked past them.

"Where is Hunter?" Thomas asked.

Walking into the house, Stefanie looked around. No one was in the living room, but a stack of books and papers were on the table.

Daphne crept out of the short hall. "Hunter went out earlier."

Relieved to see her, Stefanie asked, "Do you know where he is?"

"He didn't say." Daphne dropped into one of the sagging, overstuffed chairs.

Stefanie and Thomas exchanged glances. If Hunter was meeting with Fabiola, they were too late.

"We have news," Thomas said, taking a seat on the sofa. "Jeffrey has been arrested for Beryl's murder."

"Well, thank God for that." Ingram rubbed behind his right ear. "I wouldn't have thought it, though."

Daphne smiled, then quickly wiped the expression off her face. "It's just good to know," she said.

Sitting carefully on the sofa next to Thomas, Stefanie said, "Jeffrey told us that he knew Beryl took the bracelet. We're not sure we should believe him."

"Jeffrey has an alibi for the theft." Thomas looked at Daphne. "That is, if you can confirm it."

Her eyes widening, Daphne sat up. "Me?"

"He saw you wearing the bracelet near the buttery while he walked to his car for lunch," Stefanie said.

Daphne opened her mouth, then closed it again. "Yes, I did," she finally said. She looked at Ingram. "The bracelet was in good shape, the emeralds were well-attached. You said that, and I checked myself. I just tried it on for a minute. Then I put it back on the table in the buttery. I swear it."

Ingram nodded. "She asked if she could try it on. I told her yes. A find like that only happens once in a lifetime, you know?" he said.

Thomas nodded. "I can understand."

Stefanie understood, too. She would have liked to have held the medal of Calatrava longer, to examine it closely and at leisure. But the medal wasn't fragile like the bracelet was.

"And that was when Jeffrey went to his car?" she asked.

"Yes." Daphne nodded, pulling her curls back into a ponytail. Taking a band off her wrist, she wrapped it several times around her thick hair and finished by pulling two halves of the ponytail to tighten it.

"So Jeffrey's alibi for the theft holds true," Stefanie said. "That's good. We can believe him when he says he knows Beryl took the bracelet." She clutched the handbag in her lap, kneading its supple leather for support before tackling the next subject. If Daphne had damaged the bracelet when she tried it on, the girl might have taken steps to prevent that knowledge from getting out.

"Old jewelry can be delicate," Stefanie said. "I know. I have a few pieces that are about a hundred years old. Sometimes a link in one of the chains breaks, and I have to fix it. Sometimes the stones come loose because a claw mount breaks. Those things are all fixable with the right tools."

A slow flush rose from Daphne's neckline to her forehead as she listened.

"The bracelet is so much older," Stefanie continued. "Almost four hundred and fifty years old. We just talked to Fabiola Ortiz, and she knows which ship the bracelet was on. It went down in 1588. Did the bracelet break when you tried it on, Daphne? Did you try to prevent Beryl from giving it back before you could fix it? Argue with her about it?"

The girl shook her head vigorously. "No. The bracelet was fine. I was very careful." Tears filled her eyes. "I know that if anything happened to the bracelet, it could be repaired. Last summer I interned at a museum and shadowed a restoration expert."

Stefanie nodded. That could be checked. Daphne wasn't guarded as she'd been when she talked about Nathaniel Dimon. But she had one more question to ask the girl.

"When I found Beryl's body," Stefanie said, "while I was still kneeling beside her, you came around the back corner of the house."

"I was in the buttery," Daphne said. "But I didn't hurt her, and I didn't know she'd taken the bracelet."

"Did you see anyone on the sidewalk? It's important," Stefanie said.

"No. I wish I did. I really wish I did," Daphne said. "I didn't come out until I heard you shout."

Thomas sat forward. "Jeffrey tried to get Beryl to return the bracelet. He swears he didn't kill her."

"Well, he would, wouldn't he?" Ingram said.

"The problem is that the police didn't find the bracelet at his house when they arrested him," Thomas said. "So we believe he's telling the truth about that as well."

"He could have given it to Fabiola Ortiz," Ingram said. "She'd pay a pretty price for it, I'd say."

"If Jeffrey wasn't the one who coshed Beryl, someone else must have known Beryl took the bracelet." Stefanie focused on Daphne again. "On Tuesday, when did you see Nathaniel Dimon drive in?"

Daphne shrugged. "A few minutes after I took the bracelet off? I went to the van to get my lunch. Hunter was getting his, and Nathaniel had just gotten out of his car."

"Where did Hunter go?"

Daphne looked down at her short fingernails. They had a fresh coat of sheer pink, something that hadn't been there Wednesday when she worked at Carmichael House.

"I assumed he went back to the garden," Daphne said. "Like I told you, I flirted with Nathaniel, and then I took my lunch back to the site. It's shady in the trees. Beryl was sitting back there, but she left when I came up."

"Where did she go?" Thomas asked. "To the buttery?"

"I didn't pay attention," Daphne said. "Didn't she talk to you?" she asked Ingram.

"I'd started working again by then," he said. "We joked about our chances of finding anything else, then she walked off. Sorry, I didn't notice where she went."

"Which door did Nathaniel go in?" Thomas asked.

Daphne looked at him quizzically.

"When you parted ways, did he walk to the front door and knock, or did he go around the side to the kitchen door?" Thomas's manner was gentle with her.

Her fingers twisted tightly in her lap. "I didn't see. I really didn't see."

Narrowing his eyes, Ingram said, "Dimon could have gone round the east side of the house and seen Beryl. There's a clear line of sight from there to the buttery."

"That must be when she stole the bracelet," Daphne said.

"Did you see them together on Tuesday? Or Thursday morning? Beryl and Nathaniel Dimon?" Thomas asked.

"No." Daphne looked at Ingram.

He shook his head. "I didn't either."

"Whoever killed Beryl knew she was returning the bracelet yesterday. Yesterday morning, did either of you notice if Fabiola Ortiz came to Carmichael House?" Stefanie asked. "Here is her photo." She held it out for both to see.

"I didn't see her there," Ingram said.

Daphne studied the photo. Pressing her lips in a tight line, she shook her head. "I didn't either." Her expression said she'd liked to have.

Stefanie tucked the phone back in her purse. Not a single person had mentioned Fabiola being there in the morning, but they'd had to check. Fine. Fabiola was not the person who'd hit Beryl over the head with a handy rock.

"The other possibility is Hunter," Thomas said. "He could have seen Beryl take the bracelet Tuesday, or known she brought it back Thursday."

"He would have said something if he did," Daphne insisted.

"Did he tell you that he knows Fabiola Ortiz?" Stefanie asked.

"No," Daphne said.

Ingram was taken aback. "What?"

"They've been friends for a long time," Stefanie said. "He knows she'd like to get her hands on the bracelet."

Thomas lifted his chin at Ingram. "Have you searched Hunter's room? His things?"

"We were searched yesterday by the police," Ingram said.

"Yes, so were we," Thomas said. "Can we look in Hunter's room?"

Ingram gestured in the direction of the hall. "Go ahead."

Daphne stood up, crossing her arms. "You might as well search my room, too."

Stefanie was happy to oblige. She searched every inch of the room and went through every pocket, shoe, and makeup container, but didn't find the bracelet, broken or intact. It was a relief.

Thomas searched Hunter's meager belongings with the same vigor. When they were done without finding anything, Ingram leaned against Hunter's door frame.

"Want to search my room, too?" he asked.

Thomas shot him a grim smile as he passed. "No need. You have too much to lose."

"You're right. I do." Ingram followed him back to the living room, his face drawn. "So you don't think it was Jeffrey?" His voice was almost pleading.

She understood. If Jeffrey murdered Beryl, the rest of them were in the clear.

"I don't think he killed her," Stefanie said. "And if he didn't, that means someone else at Carmichael House Thursday morning did, and the rest of you are potential witnesses. You could be in danger." Her eyes went to Daphne.

"If you saw anything, it is safer to report it," Thomas warned her again. "Don't think you can use that information. Blackmail is a deadly game to play."

"Blackmail?" Daphne asked. "Why did you bring that up?"

Thomas looked into her eyes. "Because you know more than you are telling."

Daphne sat back, clasping her hands together tightly.

Ingram escorted Stefanie and Thomas to the door.

"Keep an eye on Hunter?" Thomas requested.

"Sure," the professor said, stroking his beard thoughtfully.

When they left the house, Daphne ran after them, her arms wrapped tightly around her stomach.

"Yes?" Stefanie asked.

A look of dread spread across Daphne's features. She swallowed.

"I don't think Hunter saw Beryl take the bracelet. On Tuesday, at lunch, I was flirting with the landscape designer. Hunter saw me. I made sure he did. I was trying to make him jealous. I did it because—" she took a deep breath. "I did it because I saw him having drinks with a woman Monday night. Hunter and I have been working together all summer. There was something between us. At least, I thought there was. Until he went out Monday night without me and met up with someone else at one of the bars on the beach."

"You said everyone had been sniping at each other yesterday morning. Did Hunter and Beryl argue?" Stefanie asked.

Daphne shook her head. "Not that I saw." She turned on her heel and went into the house.

Chapter Twenty-Four

"Think Daphne's telling the truth?" Stefanie asked when they got in the Tazzari.

Thomas took out his phone. "Not about knowing where Hunter went today."

She agreed.

"We didn't find Hunter," she said, buckling her seatbelt, "but at least Daphne finally told us what went on at lunchtime when the bracelet was stolen. She kept her eye on Hunter." Stefanie watched scissor-tailed birds fly by, thinking it through. "Hunter has been aggravated at her interest in Nathaniel Dimon, so Daphne's probably right that Hunter didn't see Beryl take the bracelet because he was too focused on her. We're back to Nathaniel Dimon." The garden designer still hadn't accounted for his whereabouts Thursday morning.

"He's not going anywhere," Thomas said. "Those two students had a relationship. Daphne might cover for Hunter."

"After learning Hunter has a roving eye?" she asked.

"Perhaps not," Thomas said, bringing up one of the apps on his phone.

"He has a relationship with Fabiola, too," she said. "I wish we'd put a GPS tracker on them all when we were there Wednesday." She touched the Greek eye necklace at her throat. Thomas had tracked targets before.

His crafty smile made her think of the way he'd agreed to stay on at Greg's house.

"We might not know where Hunter is, but we can find Fabiola," Thomas said. "I put a tracker in her purse."

When he'd helped Fabiola at the bottom of the moat stairs. Stefanie smiled. Thomas always thought ahead.

He checked the tracking app for Fabiola's blue dot. "She's just a few miles away," he said. "At the museum. The National Museum of Bermuda."

"Could we be lucky enough to find Fabiola and Hunter inside turning in the bracelet?" she asked.

"Not likely." Thomas handed his phone to Stefanie. "Tell me where to go," he said with a wink. "Hunter might have learned Beryl had the bracelet yesterday and took it to give to Fabiola."

"And struggled with her?" Stefanie suggested. "Hit Beryl harder than he realized?" She wanted to believe that if Hunter killed Beryl, it had been unintentional. But no one picks up a large rock by accident.

Following the pin, she directed Thomas to another old fort. This one was on the hilltop above the buildings of the Dockyard. The Keep, she learned from the Bermuda website. Thomas parked, then they entered the Keep through an arch in the wall.

"Fabiola didn't have the bracelet earlier, or she'd have left for Spain," he said. "But she might have it by now."

Zooming in on the pin, Stefanie saw that Fabiola wasn't inside any of the buildings. "She's on the grounds."

Thomas paid the entrance fee.

"You're free to walk around inside and out. Lots to see," the elderly ticket seller said. "Exhibition halls are to the right, the museum is to the left."

"Just came for a walk in the fresh air today," Thomas said, taking his phone from Stefanie. He oriented himself to their quarry.

"Mind the sheep dung," the old man called.

They took the path to the left, which led uphill to a set of buildings, the most impressive of which was a large three-story structure with covered verandas along the exterior of the upper floors. The museum itself. The path led along a wall of battlements, dotted with cannons and benches. Fabiola wasn't in sight.

"I think she's around the bend," Stefanie said.

Would they find Hunter with the Spanish woman? Had she brought him there, remorseful over Beryl's death, to turn in the bracelet?

They followed the path as it hugged the coastline in a curve and discovered the sheep grazing in the grass. Stefanie stopped Thomas with a hand on his arm.

Fabiola stood at the wall, staring out at the water. It wasn't Hunter at her side, but Greg. He saw them and must have said something to Fabiola, because she turned in their direction.

"Hello again," Fabiola said when they drew close.

She'd lost her worried look.

"Hello," Stefanie said. "I'm surprised to see the two of you together, Greg."

Grinning, Greg casually stuck his hands in his pockets. "Fabiola's been telling me about Don Reynaldo and the medal that you found at Carmichael House."

After studying the cannon stationed at the ramparts, Thomas gave the couple a sharp glance. "We're looking for Hunter."

"I don't know where he is," Fabiola said. "He hasn't answered my phone calls."

"Did you call him for information on the bracelet?" Thomas asked.

"I don't need Hunter for that," she said. "I expect to be told of its whereabouts by the Museum."

"You called Beryl Wednesday night. Now you've lost your contact," Stefanie said.

"There is also the director. I make a point of establishing relationships where they matter." The wind whipped strands of Fabiola's hair around her face, and she calmly removed her hair clip, pulled her hair back, and refastened it.

It really was a pretty barrette, heavy and metal, more ornate than what Stefanie could find at department stores. In other circumstances, she'd ask Fabiola for an online Spanish shopping recommendation. But not today.

Because the wind blew so strongly, Stefanie had left her fedora in the car. She tucked her hair behind her ears for what that was worth. She was certain the woman had an idea of where Hunter was, and Greg needed to see Fabiola clearly, to accept that she might have conspired with Hunter to get the bracelet.

"Hunter is the one who found the bracelet," Stefanie said, hoping to soften Fabiola's defenses. "I know how he must have felt. When I found the medal, the Military Order of Calatrava, and lifted it out of the dirt, I was so proud," she said. "What a find. I almost didn't want anyone else to hold it. It almost felt like it belonged to me. Hunter probably felt that about Don Reynaldo's bracelet."

Fabiola lit a cigarette. After taking a deep drag, she flicked the ash. "Hunter isn't taking the same route to historical artifacts as his father is. He wants to find them for posterity. He even hopes he can talk his father around to seeing things his way." She raised her eyebrows. "I don't think he'll be successful there."

"We're just trying to find out who knew Beryl had the bracelet on Thursday," Stefanie said.

"What about that Nathaniel Dimon?" Greg asked. "He had the security code for the gate. Did you question him yet?"

"We're going to pin him down next," Thomas said.

Stefanie tried the tactic Thomas used on Daphne. "You know, someone might have tried to blackmail Beryl," she said. "To get her to give up the bracelet."

"A struggle that ended in her death," Thomas said.

"Hunter," Stefanie suggested. "Trying to get the bracelet for you."

Fabiola turned to Greg. "If the police question Hunter, will you help him? Can he count on you to connect him to the right people?"

"Of course he can," Greg assured her.

"Why is that?" Thomas asked. "Dr. Ortiz, have you ever sold any Spanish gold to Greg Edwards?"

She scoffed. "I am in the business of retrieving pieces that belong to Spain. Not in selling them."

"Fabiola isn't my source for old mine emeralds," Greg said.

Stefanie searched his face. She didn't like the way he sided with Fabiola and agreed so readily to step in if Hunter needed legal help, but he wasn't flustered or angry. His posture was open and relaxed. He didn't look like he had anything to hide. But then, she thought, Greg knew exactly the type of tells she was looking for.

Thomas fixed Greg with a steely gaze. "I didn't think Fabiola was," he said. He took Stefanie by the arm, and they worked their way through the flock of woolly sheep toward the exit.

"It's time we found out exactly why Nathaniel Dimon left Carmichael House so abruptly on Tuesday," he said.

Chapter Twenty-Five

"I don't understand why Greg would agree so readily to help Hunter," Stefanie said on the walk back to the car.

Thomas shot her a glance. "I suspect he purchased his Spanish Colonial jewelry from Hunter's father, Richard Renko." He scowled. "I feel like we're being made fools of. I want to get to the bottom of this."

Stefanie studied his profile. Even wearing a scowl, she couldn't help but notice how handsome he was, with sharp eyes that took in everything and his determined mouth. Was he only aggravated that they hadn't made progress, or did Greg's presence make matters worse?

"Daphne flirting with Nathaniel Dimon to make Hunter jealous rings true," she said, moving to a less contentious topic. "But that doesn't mean Nathaniel didn't meet up with Beryl after Daphne returned to the excavation."

"With her information, we can pressure him into revealing exactly why he left without seeing the bracelet or checking on the garden," Thomas said.

In the car, he telephoned the landscape designer's office.

"You will love this," he said when he clicked off. "Nathaniel is at Carmichael House."

"The scene of the crime," she said. "It's supposed to start raining again tonight. After we talk to Nathaniel, let's go back to the house and have a quiet dinner before cocktails at Carmichael House. You, me, a cold beer and a glass of wine."

He smiled. "That's worth waiting for, Schatzi."

A glow of happiness warmed her heart at his endearment. "I'll even let you pick what to eat."

At Carmichael House, Thomas parked along the street, and he and Stefanie walked up to the gate.

Nathaniel, Marlene, and Lawrence all stood on the front terrace by the drive. Lawrence and Nathaniel both sported colorful shorts and knee socks. She couldn't imagine Thomas ever branching out like that. He was quite content with his jeans or khakis and button-up shirts in a limited array of colors.

"Good afternoon," Stefanie called.

Marlene went to the gate post and tapped in the code, opening the driveway gate.

Greetings were quickly gotten out of the way.

"Have you found out anything at all?" Marlene asked Stefanie.

"I was going to ask you the same thing," she said. "You heard Jeffrey has been arrested for Beryl's murder?"

"Yes, the police called us," Marlene said.

"He told them Beryl stole the bracelet," Stefanie said. "But the police didn't find it at his house."

"He has to have hidden it somewhere," Marlene insisted.

"They didn't find it at Beryl's either," Thomas added.

Lawrence frowned. "You don't think Jeffrey took it? That he and Beryl fought over it?"

Thomas shrugged. "Until it's been found, we're trying to keep an open mind."

"You two have taken quite an interest in the Spanish bracelet," Nathaniel Dimon said, giving them the once over.

"Jeffrey asked us to help find out who took the bracelet. Now that he's been arrested, we feel obligated to help," Stefanie said.

"Then get him to tell you where it is," Marlene said with a sniff.

If only it were that simple, Stefanie thought.

"We learned something interesting today," Thomas remarked. "Hunter Renko knows Fabiola Ortiz."

"And she was here yesterday afternoon, accusing us." Marlene's face was pinched with indignation. "How does an archaeology student know Fabiola Ortiz?"

"Hunter's father is a shipwreck salvager," Thomas said. "I imagine Richard Renko comes across Spanish artifacts fairly often."

Marlene lifted her chin. "I see."

"What?" Lawrence said. "How could this Hunter be allowed to work on our sites, then? Marlene, you're a trustee of the museum. Are you going to talk to them?"

"We discussed Fabiola at the museum board meeting Monday night. Greg probably told you that," Marlene said to Stefanie. "He was there."

It took Stefanie a moment to digest that news. Greg had been in Bermuda Monday night. Was it odd that he hadn't mentioned it?

"When we discovered the brass chest, or rather when Nathaniel's men did," Marlene went on, flashing a brief smile at the designer, "we knew Fabiola would come calling. I didn't expect her at the house, though."

Lawrence huffed. "I suppose Jeffrey Fitzsimmons and this Beryl are the ones to blame for that."

"Greg Edwards is friendly with Fabiola Ortiz as well," Thomas said.

"Doesn't surprise me," Lawrence said. "Greg collects those Colonial emeralds."

"Are the police watching Hunter Renko, do you know?" Marlene asked, resting a hand on the gatepost.

"They are, and it's a good thing," Thomas said. "If it wasn't Jeffrey who murdered Beryl, someone else did."

"Surely they have the right man," Lawrence said.

Marlene's brows furrowed.

Taking advantage of the pause, Stefanie said, "I did have one question for you, Nathaniel." It would be harder for him to evade questions with Marlene and Lawrence there.

"Yes?" he asked.

"Did you see Beryl near the buttery when you came here Tuesday at noon?" They'd asked a similar question that morning, and he'd answered in generalities. Hopefully, this time he'd be more specific.

164

Marlene and Lawrence listened for his answer as intently as she and Thomas did.

Nathaniel chuffed, then laughed and looked at the Carmichaels. "I expected a question about the garden. No," he said, "I wasn't here long on Tuesday."

Stefanie checked Marlene and Lawrence, but neither added anything to his answer. She nodded her thanks. "We're trying to pin down anyone that might have seen her at the buttery."

"In particular," Thomas said, "we want to know who knew she'd brought the bracelet back on Thursday."

"Other than Jeffrey, you mean," Marlene said.

"Beryl should have turned it over as soon as she got here yesterday," Lawrence said.

Nathaniel cleared his throat. "I think we covered everything that I needed earlier. I'll say my goodbyes and see you bright and early Monday morning."

"If the storm has passed," Lawrence said, watching the palm fronds blow in the breeze.

Thomas put his hand on the small of Stefanie's back. "We'll say goodbye as well. You must be getting ready for dinner."

"I never cook," Marlene said. "We dine out. Except, I think, with Beryl and Jeffrey, maybe we shouldn't." She looked to Lawrence. "I could fix sandwiches."

"No, let's go out," he said. "We need to face the public. We don't have anything to be embarrassed about."

"Cocktails at eight," Marlene reminded them.

"We'll be here," Stefanie assured her.

When Lawrence opened the gate, Stefanie and Thomas walked out with Nathaniel.

On the sidewalk, Stefanie said to him, "Be honest with us. On Tuesday, where did you go, and who did you talk to?"

"You and Marlene didn't get your stories straight," Thomas said. "And we talked to Daphne again."

Nathaniel glanced back at Carmichael House. Both Marlene and Lawrence had gone inside. Still, he moved further down the sidewalk to where a thick stand of orange bougainvillea blocked the view from the house.

"Helping Jeffrey, are you?" he asked. "What is this about?"

"Why did you leave so quickly Tuesday without checking on the garden or even the Spanish bracelet?" Thomas asked.

"I did talk to the girl, Daphne, for a few minutes," Nathaniel said. "She flirted with me. She was much too young, and I was diplomatic about it. She went back to their excavation. It was all proper and above board, whether she's claimed anything to the contrary or not," he said, his eyes registering growing alarm.

Daphne hadn't said anything of the sort, but Stefanie let it hang in the air, and so did Thomas.

When they didn't confirm or deny his fears, Nathaniel went on. "I wanted to have a word with Marlene, and my mind was on that."

"About?" Stefanie asked.

"Why not tell the truth, unless you have something to hide?" Thomas said. "If you saw anything, you might be in danger."

Nathaniel ran a hand over his mouth. "All right. Marlene called and mentioned that the emerald bracelet and a dozen Spanish coins had been found in the garden. With that exciting news, I knew she would be at the house, away from Ministry business, and so it was the perfect time to come and get an installment on our project. She stays busy and can be hard to get hold of." He looked at them frankly. "To put it crassly, I was here to get paid."

"And did you?" Thomas asked.

"Yes. I picked up a check." Nathaniel's mouth pressed in a tight line. "And then I left. Beryl had seen me with the girl. She can be difficult. I knew I'd get a chance to see the bracelet later. At least, I assumed I would."

"One more question," Stefanie said. "You and Beryl seemed to be at odds with each other. Thursday morning. Where were you when Beryl was killed? You were late to your office."

"You have the security code. The police know that," Thomas added.

The landscape designer gave them a tight smile. "Beryl is my ex. We avoid each other when we can. As for Thursday morning, I was enjoying a leisurely breakfast with a lady friend. DI Franklin-Ross has her number and has already confirmed that I was nowhere near Carmichael House when Beryl was killed."

So Nathaniel Dimon was in the clear.

"Thank you," Stefanie said.

With a fed-up look, Nathaniel got into his car.

Chapter Twenty-Six

At the house, Stefanie opened a bottle of Bermuda Amigo beer for Thomas and poured herself a glass of pinot grigio.

"It's a good thing we don't really need Nathaniel Dimon's services," she said.

"His fee just went up," Thomas joked.

"He's in the clear." He'd been the outlier, the only suspect not directly involved with the excavation, but there at the right time and with the right contacts.

"We can count on that, since the DI confirmed his Thursday morning alibi," Thomas said.

They were planning a quiet dinner at home. Home. Greg's home. Greg, who'd been in Bermuda since Monday, but showed up Wednesday night as if he'd just arrived. She shook her head. Why should Greg tell her his plans? He wasn't any more obligated to tell her his whereabouts than she'd been to let him know the friend she was bringing was male.

"I guess getting paid was too crass for Nathaniel or Marlene to mention—if they had, it would have saved us time and trouble," she said.

"Dimon is doing well, with high-end clients. So he doesn't need the money." Thomas checked the cabinets for something they could fix for dinner. Finding little, he then opened the refrigerator. "How do you feel about an omelet?"

"You're going to cook for me?" Stefanie asked. "An omelet sounds perfect."

She smiled, relishing the image of Thomas cooking for her each morning. Well, maybe not every morning. Once a week, on Saturdays. She could make him waffles on Sundays.

He took the carton of eggs to the sink. "Dimon doesn't need the money, but what does his special trip to get paid say about the Carmichaels' finances?"

Stefanie took two plates from the cabinet, then handed him a large bowl to mix the eggs in, enjoying their domestic moment in the kitchen.

"They owned the bracelet in the first place. But we should look at them anyway," she agreed.

The couple stealing their own bracelet wasn't logical, but if nothing else, looking into them would help with the big picture.

"Drinks there tonight will give us a feel for their financial situation," Thomas said as he whipped the eggs with a whisk.

"Try to get a peek into their safe," Stefanie said. "You haven't seen the Spanish chest yet, or the gold coins. Let's use that to see if they have anything to hide."

Thomas paused his whisking and looked at her. "Everyone has something to hide."

"Is that a reminder from my boss to keep an open mind?" she asked, leaning against the counter.

He smiled. "Someone knew Beryl had the bracelet on her yesterday morning. Who?"

"We've cleared Daphne, Fabiola, and Nathaniel Dimon. Other than looking into the Carmichaels, that leaves Jeffrey and Hunter," she said. "And Greg." He'd been at Carmichael House Thursday morning.

Thomas took a swig of beer. "And Greg."

"I think Jeffrey is telling the truth, that he didn't hit Beryl on the head with that rock."

"His choices are questionable, but I believe that also," Thomas said. "Jeffrey didn't have the bracelet. He would have turned it in."

He scrutinized the eggs and scraped at the pan with a spatula. "It'll be scrambled eggs instead of omelets."

Resting her chin on his shoulder, Stefanie surveyed the contents of the frying pan. "Add a little cheese and chopped tomato to them, and they'll be fine."

She washed and chopped a tomato, divided it between their two plates after he split the eggs between them, then took a block of cheddar from the fridge and shredded just enough to top them off. It was a moment of domestic bliss. The first of many, she hoped. Thomas hadn't brought up the subject of their living arrangements. Because he was afraid to? But then, neither had she. Monday they would fly out. His ticket was to Munich, hers to Saint Louis. But that could be changed. The truth was, she was savoring the anticipation. Every moment with Thomas was an adventure.

They carried their drinks and plates to the table.

"What about Ingram?" Stefanie asked. "Do you think we looked closely enough at him?"

She didn't think the college professor had done in Beryl, but she wanted to make sure Thomas agreed.

"He was loading up the van at the crucial time," Thomas said. "Hunter and Daphne would have looked to him for direction, so he couldn't count on not being missed. Plus, he was searched."

The doorbell rang, and they looked at each other.

Thomas groaned. "We never have enough time alone."

Together they went together to the door, which Thomas opened. Greg stood outside, wet from the drizzle which had started again. His Jag was behind him in the driveway.

"Come in," Stefanie said, despite Thomas's noncommittal silence.

Stepping inside, Greg wiped the rain off his face.

"I just came by to pick up some extra shirts," he said. "Mind if I grab a towel in the bathroom to dry off?"

While they waited, Thomas stayed near the entryway, making it clear he didn't want Greg to sit down and get comfortable.

Greg came out of the master bedroom, toweling off his hair and hands. "I see you still wear Fresh Water." He went into the kitchen and tossed the towel into the washing machine. "I knew it suited you."

Damn.

Stefanie avoided looking at Thomas, but felt him stiffen at her side. She hadn't wanted him to know that Greg was the one who'd introduced her to

Lili Bermuda perfume.

"So you've been here in Bermuda since Monday?" she asked Greg, debating whether to take Thomas's arm or not.

How silly. So what if Thomas was disappointed? He knew she wasn't interested in Greg. She slipped her arm through his and held it close, hoping he wouldn't try to pull away.

"Yes," Greg said. "Got in Monday afternoon. I should have picked up more laundry then. Want to grab a bite to eat before heading over to Carmichael House?" he asked, checking with them both.

"We're good," Thomas said.

"Right then," Greg said, seeing their plates at the table. "I'll grab my shirts and see you later this evening."

He came out with a garment bag from the master bedroom, then left with a friendly wave.

Sitting at the table, Stefanie did her best to pick up their conversation from before.

"It was a surprise that Hunter was such good friends with Fabiola," she said.

"Think so?" Thomas asked. "I think Fabiola and Hunter's father must run into each other often."

Stefanie let his smugness pass and ate her eggs. "Could Hunter have planned it with Fabiola?"

"Yes."

"Fabiola called Beryl Wednesday night." She finished her eggs, then carried both their plates into the kitchen. "It must have been before or after the glow worm cruise. She didn't get a call on the boat."

Thomas picked up their glasses and took them to the kitchen, then helped load up the dishwasher.

"She called Beryl because Beryl knows everything," he said. "She knows who does what, when, and with whom."

Stefanie smiled. "Your English is better than mine."

"I studied."

She laughed, happy that he'd unbent a little. After drying her hands on a dish towel, she handed him the towel.

"Ready for another beer?" she asked. "We've got an hour until Marlene is expecting us."

"Always." His smile didn't have the warmth of the ones he'd given her before Greg made that comment about her cologne.

She gave him another Bermuda Amigo and poured just a splash of wine in her glass.

With refilled drinks, they moved to the living room. The rain outside poured down steadily. Stefanie opened the curtains, then looked around for candles. A little mood lighting would help dispel the awkwardness between them. No luck there. It was too much to hope that a bachelor would have any candles as decor. Instead, she turned on the small lamp on the end table beside the sofa, then turned off the overhead lights.

Thomas watched her from his perch on the comfortable sofa. She brought her glass of wine over and curled up beside him.

Should she bring up the cologne? He'd probably deny that he was bothered. Least said, soonest mended was the way to go.

"So we're back to Hunter, taking the bracelet to give to Fabiola," she said.

Thomas shifted and pulled his phone out of his rear pocket. "Right now, Dr. Ortiz is in Hamilton." He tapped on the map to zoom in. "At the Port O' Call restaurant."

"I wonder if Hunter is with her. That's one thing," Stefanie said. "If Fabiola is still here in Bermuda, I'll bet she doesn't have the bracelet. Which means that Hunter hasn't given it to her."

"The question is, why hasn't he?" Thomas asked. "Because he didn't take it from Beryl? Because he did, but has hidden it somewhere on Carmichael House property, so he wouldn't get caught with it after Beryl's death?"

Stefanie stretched her legs out on the leather ottoman that doubled as a coffee table, hoping Thomas would put his feet up and relax, too.

"Where was Hunter today?" she asked. "Maybe he left Bermuda. With his father's connections, I'm sure he knows plenty of sailboat captains."

"Not many that would be out in these seas," Thomas said, taking her hand and holding it in both of his. His right hand was cold where the beer had left its thermal impression.

She set her wine glass down and warmed his hand with her own, thankful that his irritation over Greg had passed.

"I expected to find Hunter with Fabiola. Daphne was worried about him, too," she said.

Thomas nodded. "Hunter's affinity for Spanish relics is motivation, and there is his friendship with Fabiola."

"And what about Jeffrey's house being broken into this morning?" she asked, resting her head contentedly against his strong shoulder.

"Someone who thinks Jeffrey is guilty and wants the bracelet," Thomas said.

"We've ruled out Fabiola," Stefanie said. She couldn't picture the neat, composed Spanish woman breaking into Jeffrey's house in her quest to take possession of the emerald bracelet.

"Fabiola's role on the Spanish Cultural ministry team is like ours," Thomas said. "A version of Interpol's Cultural Heritage division." He turned his head to look at her. "Her job is remarkably similar to ours at ART."

"We don't want the bracelet to end up on a Most Wanted Works of Art poster," Stefanie said.

Fabiola wouldn't want that either. How far would she go to make sure Don Reynaldo's emerald bracelet was returned to Spain?

"We're getting nowhere," Stefanie said.

"It was one of the people at Carmichael House that morning," Thomas said.

He entwined his fingers with hers, then held up their hands. "This is what we know." He lifted her index finger. "Jeffrey was blackmailed by Beryl." Middle finger. "Beryl steals the bracelet."

She raised her ring finger. "Beryl killed." Thinking about it, she lifted her little finger and wiggled it. "Are we looking at the crimes wrong?"

Thomas lowered their hands. "Ideas?"

"Our first premise is that Beryl was killed for the bracelet, which Jeffrey had allowed her to steal and which Beryl brought back to return. We can't find any answer that fits, except for Hunter. I know he looks guilty, but we don't have any evidence for it."

"We have very little evidence at all," he said.

"We have to start over."

"All right. What do the suspects have to gain by taking the bracelet?" Thomas asked. "Are those gains worth the risks?"

"Marlene and Lawrence own it. What do they gain if they pretend it's been stolen?" she asked. "Do they need the money that would come from selling it?"

"They don't appear to," Thomas said. "She's a government minister. Steady income, with the promise of lucrative endeavors when she leaves office."

"Agreed," Stefanie said. "Lawrence sold his business when he retired, which would provide a nice nest egg."

"The bracelet wasn't insured," Thomas said.

"And they lose out on the prestige that comes with owning it. In particular," she said, "the prestige of donating the bracelet to NMB, where a large plaque with their names would preserve their generosity for posterity. The Carmichaels would risk their prestige and standing in the community if they pulled a hoax like this," she concluded. "That is something they both value highly."

"If the Carmichaels wanted to sell the bracelet, there is no reason for them to go through the farce of pretending it's been stolen. That wastes time and damages their credibility. Not to mention going to prison for Beryl's murder," Thomas said. "All right, we rule them out. Jeffrey next."

Jeffrey. He'd kept the truth from them from the beginning.

Thomas ran his hand through her hair, drawing the strands through his fingers. "Jeffrey gains money if he sells it. Risks his career, jail time, and his reputation. Which he is experiencing right now. Not worth it."

"The same could be said of Beryl. But she did risk all those things and took the bracelet anyway. She must have really been fed up being Jeffrey's assistant for all these years." Stefanie stared across the room at the rain pelting the window. "What if Beryl stole it, fully intending to return it, just so that she could be seen as a hero when she 'found' the bracelet?"

Thomas considered that idea. "It doesn't get us any further. We know she

174

stole it."

"We need to find out who knew she had the bracelet Thursday," Stefanie said. They kept coming back to that sticking point. No one on the dig team admitted to knowing Beryl's plans, and the Carmichaels hadn't spoken to her at all on Thursday.

"On to Ingram. He is someone I can relate to," Thomas said. "He's working hard in a job he loves, finds a spectacular artifact. What does he do? Would he keep it, so he can gloat over it privately? At the same time enduring the shame, insults and disparagement from his colleagues?"

"Is that what you faced?" she asked, hoping to get past Thomas's unspoken disappointment at Greg's revelation earlier.

"Somewhat," Thomas replied. He didn't go into detail. "Plus, Ingram was searched."

The sticking point for every suspect. Where was that bracelet?

Stefanie checked her phone for the time. They would have to leave for Carmichael House soon. They'd spent an hour going through motives and risks, and had gotten no further. An awkward hour, and discouraging.

"We are at a dead end," Thomas said, frowning.

"Enough of this. Marlene will be expecting us. Maybe we'll get them to shed some light on it." Raising her lips to his, she kissed him.

His response wasn't as enthusiastic as she wished.

Stefanie turned on the overhead light, the official end of their romantic evening.

Chapter Twenty-Seven

It was raining heavily when they drove up to the gate at Carmichael House. Peering through the darkness, Stefanie saw a strip of bright light at the open front door.

"Marlene's waiting for us," she said, hoping that focusing on the Carmichaels would take Thomas's mind off Greg and her Fresh Water cologne.

"We need to pressure them about why they didn't want the theft reported," Thomas said. "Get them talking, and they will reveal their secrets."

If that was a tiny arrow aimed her way, she'd let it pass. Greg wasn't worth any trouble between them.

They waited, but when no one appeared to open the gate, Thomas tapped the horn.

Marlene looked out, clinging to the door frame. When Stefanie lowered her window and waved, the gate slid open.

"Greg's not here yet. He can park behind us," Thomas said, pulling up directly in front of the door.

"Did you see him?" Marlene called as Stefanie exited the car.

After dashing for the shelter of the front steps under the overhanging upper martini deck, she turned around and looked toward the gate, the direction in which Marlene was staring.

"Greg won't be long, I'm sure," Stefanie said. What she wished was that he wouldn't show up at all.

"Not Greg," Marlene cried. "A burglar—he just knocked me down."

Thomas ran up the steps, out of the rain. Putting a hand on Stefanie's shoulder, he scanned the front yard.

Stefanie did, too, her heart pounding. She couldn't see any darker shadows against the backdrop of shrubbery. Nothing moved except leaves bouncing under the assault of the rain.

"I didn't notice anyone. Did you?" she asked Thomas.

Taking a last survey of the yard, he shook his head and propelled her and Marlene into the house. "If anyone was lurking, he might have slipped out after we drove in, when the gate opened."

Marlene swiftly closed and locked the front door, then entered the code to close the driveway gate.

Stefanie stared at the scene in the small foyer. The antique table that had stood by the front door was overturned, and the vase she'd admired the day before lay shattered at Lawrence's feet.

Lawrence held a hand to his bleeding forehead. "We surprised him," he said. "He shoved past us when I opened the front door."

Marlene helped Lawrence to the kitchen and into a chair.

"Did you see who it was?" Thomas asked as they followed the couple.

"We hadn't turned the lights on yet, it was that quick," Marlene said. "He shoved past me, and I fell into the table by the front door. I didn't get a good look. Dark sweatpants and a dark hoodie, was my impression."

"I see how he got in," Stefanie said.

She crossed to the kitchen door. A pane of glass had been broken just above the door handle. The broken shards were scattered over the floor.

Marlene's face fell. "I have to clean that up."

"No," Thomas said. "The police will want to see everything as it is. I'll call them."

Marlene left the room, then quickly returned with towels and a first aid kit. She was cleaning Lawrence's wound when a honk outside caught their attention.

"That'll be Greg," Stefanie said.

While she stayed with Lawrence, Marlene went to let Greg in.

Greg followed her into the kitchen, far wetter than they'd gotten in their short sprint to the door. He wiped a hand over his hair, slinging drops onto the floor.

Thomas, she noticed, wore a smirk at Greg's rain-dampened appearance.

"Break-in?" he asked, surveying the damage.

"This is why I didn't want the gold and the bracelet reported to the news media," Marlene said tersely. "Now everyone knows what we found."

It seemed Marlene's argument against reporting the items was sound.

A forceful knock at the front door announced the arrival of the police and paramedics. While Marlene explained what happened, Stefanie took Lawrence by the arm.

"Let's go into the living room where we'll be more comfortable," she said.

In the cozy living room, Lawrence settled in one of the sleek leather armchairs, then let the paramedics examine him. After recleaning the wound, one of them taped a square of gauze over the two-inch cut.

"You might have a mild concussion," he said. "Watch yourself for the next week or so. If you get dizzy or nauseous, see your doctor."

When they left, one of the two uniformed police officers walked in.

"What happened?" he asked Lawrence.

"We came home from the restaurant, and as soon as I walked in the front door, some bloody bastard hit me on the head," Lawrence said.

The officer eyed the bandage. "Feeling alright?"

"Eh, it's not too bad. Nothing cracked. My skull is thicker than that." Lawrence rested his arms along the armrests.

Marlene frowned at a small circle of blood that oozed through the gauze. "The paramedic said you'd have to watch yourself for a few days."

"I'm fine," Lawrence insisted. "Just angry."

"Let's take a look around, see what's been taken," the officer said.

"My office," Lawrence said, getting up.

He led the way, and Stefanie and Thomas followed the police officer, with Greg behind. From the office doorway, Stefanie saw that two of the desk drawers were partially open.

"I know I closed these before we left for the restaurant," Lawrence said. "He was in here." Opening the drawers further, he studied the contents, then shook his head. "Nothing's been taken."

"Have a safe, a strong box?" the officer asked.

Lawrence crossed to his wall of built-in shelves. "Our gold coins are in the safe."

At least he'd taken that precaution, Stefanie thought.

Moving one of the photos that stood on a chest-high shelf, Lawrence pushed on the back of the bookshelf, and a panel sprung open. When he glanced their way, Stefanie and Greg moved into the doorway. Thomas stayed in the room against a side wall.

Opening the safe, Lawrence pulled out a short stack of papers, looked through them, then replaced them. He reached in again and brought out the folded blue flannel bundle. Setting it on a lower shelf, he unfolded the cloth.

"That's right," the officer said at the sight of the gold coins. "You're the ones who discovered buried treasure in your backyard."

Lawrence counted them, then looked up. "All here."

After locking the coins in the safe, he closed the back panel and recentered the photo on the shelf.

"So nothing has been taken?" the uniformed officer asked.

Stefanie stepped back as Marlene appeared in the doorway.

"I've checked my jewelry," Marlene said. "It's all there."

"We'll dust for fingerprints, but it looks like you surprised this burglar before he could get to anything," the officer said.

"You'll search for him?" Marlene's question was more of a directive.

"Do you have a description, ma'am?"

"I think dark pants and a dark hoodie," Marlene said, "but that was just an impression. It happened so fast, I hardly had time to notice. I couldn't even tell if the person was a man or a woman."

"Given that word of this treasure has gone out, we'll patrol regularly, let our presence be seen," he assured them. "Make sure to patch that window pane in the kitchen door tonight."

"I'll take care of the glass," Lawrence said.

In short order, the two officers finished with fingerprints and photographs. When the police left, everyone pitched in to sweep up broken glass, tape the window, and dry the wet footprints that remained on the dark wood floor.

"Cocktails," Marlene exclaimed when things had been set to rights. "In the living room. I'm sure we can all use a drink after that."

"Let me," Greg said. "You sit down." Going to a buffet against the wall, he opened the doors and pulled out bottles, glasses and an ice bucket. He took the latter to the kitchen.

"You two have been looking into this theft," Lawrence said, addressing Stefanie and Thomas. "What do you think?"

"It's curious that someone would search your house for the bracelet," Thomas said. "Why is that, do you think?"

Returning from the kitchen with ice and tongs, Greg listened while he poured drinks.

"I'll tell you what I think." Lawrence's glance took in them all. "It's Hunter Renko, that archaeologist kid. After the gold coins."

"Oh?" Stefanie asked. She wondered if it had been Hunter as well.

Greg looked up from the buffet. "Tonic and lime for you, Marlene?"

"Yes, please."

"I'll have that, too," Stefanie said.

"Whiskey for us?" Greg asked with a glance at Lawrence and Thomas.

Both men agreed. Greg finished pouring, then said, "Jeffrey's house was broken into today. This morning, before the police searched it."

Marlene looked thoughtful. "So it wasn't just our house. I was right. They heard about the emerald bracelet on the news and are looking for treasure." Taking her glass from Greg, she said, "I hope whoever broke in didn't find the bracelet at Jeffrey's."

Stefanie hoped that, too. "Jeffrey swears he didn't take it," she said.

"Mark my words. It was that shipwreck salvager, Hunter Renko," Lawrence said, touching the bandage on his forehead lightly. He winced and dropped his hand.

"Maybe so," Marlene acknowledged. "Or Fabiola Ortiz."

Fabiola's accusation had really gotten to Marlene. Stefanie tried to reassure them on that point. "Does it help to know she doesn't really think you have it?"

Marlene swirled her tonic and lime. "What do you mean by that? She

180

accused us."

"It was her ploy to get you to pressure the police," Stefanie said. "She told us."

"Hm." Marlene sipped her drink as she took that in.

"There's the professor that helped Jeffrey," Lawrence said. "Dr. Ingram. He was not happy about the theft. Seemed to blame us for it."

Thomas leaned back. "Have there been any other odd occurrences related to archaeological finds where he's concerned? You'd know, Marlene, being a museum trustee."

"No, I can't say there has been," Marlene said. "There hasn't been any trouble on his project. He's turned in everything that's been found." She met Thomas's gaze. "As far as I know."

Discussion went back and forth about the possible burglars.

"It was someone who heard about the bracelet on the news," Marlene said again. "Not smart enough to realize the bracelet was stolen from us."

"It is safe to say that whoever broke into Jeffrey's house didn't find the bracelet there, if that same person broke in here." Thomas stood up.

Stefanie got up too, glad to see that Lawrence wasn't hurt too badly, and Marlene was calmer.

In the car, Stefanie said, "The Carmichaels did have a good reason for not reporting the theft. There was no way news outlets wouldn't carry the story. Now we've seen the consequences. Their house was broken into. Like Jeffrey's."

Thomas was quiet on the ride home, without much to contribute.

At the house, Stefanie dropped her purse on the table. "What are your real thoughts about the break-ins?"

"Someone thinks the Carmichaels have the bracelet," he answered. "It could be like Marlene suggested, a local burglar who hoped to get lucky. Or it could be someone more closely involved. Hunter. Or Ingram."

With a subdued glance at her, he went to the back. Stefanie lingered in the kitchen to see if he'd like another beer or a glass of wine, something to recapture their mood from earlier. She prepared coffee for the morning and emptied the dishwasher. Five minutes passed. He wasn't coming back out.

Disappointed, she switched off the living room lamp, then slowly walked down the dim hall.

What could she say to reassure him there had never been anything between her and Greg? Nothing except a friendly business relationship. It didn't help that Greg didn't appear to see it that way.

The light in the bathroom was on, and the door open. Stefanie walked to the door and leaned against the doorframe.

Thomas stood at the sink, his fingers on her bottle of Fresh Water cologne.

Her heart sank at his solemn expression. She longed to reach out to him, to brush her fingertips across that shadow of beard on his cheeks. Anything to take that look of deep sadness off his face.

They had to talk about it sooner or later.

"Yes," she said quietly. "Greg gave me my first bottle. I use it because I like the fragrance, the freshness. Not because it reminds me of Greg."

Her muscles tensed, waiting for his reply. He picked up the bottle.

He'd had one shipped to his apartment in Germany. That would be another reminder waiting. A reminder of this disastrous romantic rendezvous.

"You want to throw it away?" she asked. "I don't mind. Really I don't."

Thomas pushed the nozzle and let the cologne spray on his finger. He set the bottle on the counter, then turned to her. His eyes were dark, smoldering with an unknown emotion. His gaze dropped, and Stefanie stepped closer, aching for him to tell her he didn't mind, that it didn't matter.

"It smells like you," he said.

He touched his finger to her clavicle, where it was exposed beside the wide strap of her dress, then slid his finger slowly to the hollow of her throat.

She shivered.

"No," he said, his voice deep and husky. "I'm not going to throw your cologne away." He bent his head to hers, and she felt the whisper of his breath against her skin. His lips pressed a feathery kiss on the soft flesh where her shoulder met her throat. "I'm going to make sure that when you wear it, you never think of any man but me."

Chapter Twenty-Eight

Stefanie hummed to herself as she dropped two slices of bread into the toaster the next morning. When Thomas walked in, fresh from his shower, she looked up.

"What do we make of them?" she asked. "The break-ins at Carmichael House and Jeffrey's?"

Thomas poured himself coffee. He'd dressed in a pale blue light cotton shirt over khaki shorts. The long sleeves of the shirt were rolled up, exposing his muscular forearms. Unable to resist, she wrapped her arms around his waist and kissed him.

He smiled. "Good morning."

Satisfied, she stepped back against the counter. Brushing down the fitted sleeveless top she wore, she hoped he approved of how well its deep peach color went with her coral and white striped loose trousers.

"We came to a dead-end last night," he said. "With these break-ins, we have to look at the situation differently."

In their discussion the evening before, she hadn't had any specific new direction in mind. The toast popped up and she dropped the hot slices onto a plate.

Thomas frowned. After adding more bread to the toaster, he took his coffee to the table and sat down. "We're missing something."

Biting into her toast, she tried to clear her mind, discarding what they thought they knew. One possibility stood out.

"What if Beryl wasn't the one blackmailing Jeffrey?" she asked.

Thomas set his cup on the table, his eyes bright. "Then Beryl knew who did."

"The note wasn't signed," she said. "It was written on the same notepaper that everyone had."

"Perhaps Jeffrey didn't realize Beryl hadn't written it. Who besides Beryl would know enough about Jeffrey to blackmail him?" Thomas asked.

"Almost everyone," she said. "Really, it seems as if everybody in Bermuda knows everyone else's business. Their secrets."

"Secrets," Thomas repeated. "Ingram knowing about Dimon's poor choices in college."

"Beryl knowing that Marlene comes from a poor background," she said.

"Beryl might not have realized at the time what she was seeing," Thomas said. "That would explain why she didn't say anything. Perhaps she saw someone drop the note in Jeffrey's car and later wondered if it was the bracelet that had been dropped."

"And by Thursday, she realized it was important." Stefanie finished her toast and took her plate to the kitchen. "Jeffrey said she was quiet that morning. Was Beryl even the type to blackmail? We know she kept Jeffrey's secret for years. So why resort to blackmail now? Last night we talked about motives. Envy or ambition is hardly motivation to blackmail your boss and steal a priceless gold bracelet, especially when that bracelet can help your career."

"I know how we can find out." Thomas held up his phone.

He called Nathaniel Dimon.

Checking the time, Stefanie saw that it was just eight o'clock. On a Saturday. Hopefully Nathaniel was an early riser.

"No, it's not about the garden plans," Thomas said when the landscape designer answered. He put the phone on speaker. "You know we're helping out with the Carmichael inquiry. I have a delicate question to ask about your ex."

An impatient sigh was released. "What about Beryl?"

Giving Stefanie a thumbs up, Thomas asked, "You were together a long time?"

"Three years," Nathaniel said.

Long enough to know Beryl's personality inside and out, Stefanie thought.

"Was Beryl the conniving type?" Thomas asked. "Did she work knowledge to her advantage?"

Nathaniel's loud guffaw rang out. "With me, perhaps." He composed himself, then in a serious tone, said, "No, I can't say that was her style. She liked gossip. That was Beryl. But she wasn't hurtful. She was a good woman."

Giving his condolences, Thomas clicked off.

"Beryl wasn't the type to resort to blackmail," he said. "Keeping Jeffrey's secret affirms that."

Stefanie leaned against the counter, enjoying her third cup of coffee. Or she would have, if they'd gotten any closer to discovering who'd killed Beryl. "Does this mean we have to start from scratch?"

"No, but we need to be careful," Thomas said. "Last night, it seemed likely that local thieves had broken into Jeffrey's and Carmichael House. Now, I'm not sure. It might have been one of the dig team. That person is still willing to use violence."

That sobering thought gave her pause. Lawrence had been attacked. He could have been hurt worse.

"Ingram," she suggested. "Marlene thought their burglar might have been Ingram."

"The blackmailer wouldn't break in. He wouldn't need to," Thomas said.

He finished his toast, then got up and looked in the refrigerator. "We need fruit. Tangerines or oranges. Let's go to the store and decide what step to take next."

"Mind going by yourself?" she asked. "I'd like to get started on my blog on Bermuda. We haven't had the downtime I expected."

He looked at her sideways. "Whose idea was it to drag us into this?"

She gave him a wry smile.

"I'll go. I won't be long."

As he left, Thomas said, "Lock this door behind me."

She did, then took her laptop out of her suitcase and went to the living room window. Nothing but grey clouds as far as she could see and a constant drizzle. No sitting on that covered patio with an ocean view and sunshine, despite the 80-degree temperature.

With a sigh, she settled down on the sofa. She'd hesitated to bring the laptop on their getaway, but since starting the travel blog, she knew she ought to. Seven steps ahead, she thought, laughing at herself. Writing a commentary on the computer would be far easier than on her phone with its tiny screen, or in her Moleskine notebook, which wasn't a whole lot bigger.

Shifting her position, she opened a blank document. Her mind was supposed to be on extolling the virtues of a trip to Bermuda and what women traveling alone might like or need. Instead, her thoughts returned to Beryl and the emeralds and the break-ins.

Had the break-ins been thieves who'd heard about the find on the news, like Marlene suggested? Or had it been one of the people they knew, desperate to get their hands on the Spanish emeralds? Hunter, or Ingram. They still didn't know who killed Beryl.

She forced her attention back on her essay. What to include? Courteous greetings, without a doubt, looking right when crossing streets, The Town of St. George and the glow worm tour would all make it. Reminded by that of Daphne, she added situational awareness. She'd mentioned it on the blog before, but as a tip for women traveling alone, it was worth repeating.

A click at the front door caught her attention. She recognized the sound, the turning of the doorknob. Thomas was back. She closed her laptop and set it to the side.

In the entryway, she stopped. Through the slim sidelight she saw the edge of a sleeve. Not the pale blue shirt Thomas put on that morning. The sleeve was dark, a jacket sleeve. When it was 80 degrees out? The doorknob twisted again, sounding abnormally loud in the silence while she held her breath.

Stefanie swallowed, every nerve in her body taut. Glancing around for protection, she spied the lamp on the end table and unplugged it. She wasn't going to be a victim. Not like Lawrence and not like Beryl.

I'm overreacting, she thought. It was daylight, and she was nervous after the Carmichaels' break-in. Greg was next door. She could call for him if she needed to.

Striding forward silently, she yanked the door open as abruptly as she could.

With one hand extended, Lawrence fell forward, then caught himself by grabbing the doorframe. He stared at her in surprise.

Stefanie stared back, just as surprised to see the white-bearded man as he was to see her. He wore a navy blue windbreaker against the drizzle.

"I was looking for Greg." Lawrence stepped back and confirmed the house number. "Yes," he said. "I'm at the right house."

She checked his hands. He wasn't holding a key. But then, he wasn't holding a lockpick, screwdriver or credit card, either. Keeping a firm hold on the door with one hand, her other gripped the lamp out of Lawrence's sight.

"We're staying here this week," she said. "Greg let us use the house for our vacation. He didn't plan on being in Bermuda."

"Oh." Lawrence touched his forehead.

He'd taken off the gauze bandage, and she could see last night's wound, which had the addition of a bruise. Still, she didn't want to let him in. Not with Thomas gone.

Lawrence wiped a hand across his brow. His complexion was ruddier than usual. "It's this Spanish bracelet. We've got to find it. I thought Greg might have an idea where it was. Since the police didn't find it in Beryl Swan's house." He gazed at her intently, as if searching for any knowledge she had about the bracelet.

"Greg is staying at Jeffrey's while we're here," Stefanie said.

"I see. He isn't there now," Lawrence said, looking over at Jeffrey's driveway. "Any idea where he went?"

"No." Her hand had begun to cramp around the lamp stick. Her muscles tightened, ready to slam the door and lock it if Lawrence advanced on her. Not that he would. But still.

"Maybe Greg went to see Hunter Renko," Lawrence said. He took a step back, then turned and walked to his car. "I'll find him later. I'm on my way home from the market. Better get this cake to Marlene, or she'll be upset. Can't have that." He waved and got in the car.

187

As she closed and locked the door, Stefanie's shoulders slumped. Thank goodness she'd locked the door after Thomas left.

She plugged in the lamp, but before she could open her laptop again, her phone rang. Stefanie picked it up. An unfamiliar number. Spam? It might be Fabiola. No, it was a US number, and besides, she'd entered Fabiola into her contacts.

She swiped up and answered. "Hello?"

"Stefanie, it's Daphne." The girl spoke rapidly.

"Daphne," Stefanie said, returning to the door and checking through the sidelight to make sure Lawrence had driven away. "Is everything alright?"

"Yes. I need to tell you something."

"Okay," Stefanie said, settling onto the couch with one leg curled beneath her. "I'm listening."

"It's about Monday, when I saw Hunter at the beach bar," Daphne said. "Yes?"

Stefanie heard a big intake of breath on the other end of the call.

"The woman he was with," Daphne said. "It was Fabiola Ortiz."

"Fabiola," Stefanie repeated. Fabiola met with Hunter on Monday night. "Did you ask him about it? Is he there with you?"

"No, he's out," Daphne said. "Ingram is at the store stocking up on groceries because he thinks we could be stuck here in Bermuda through this hurricane." Her voice rose. "I was supposed to go home today."

Daphne wouldn't be leaving without official approval, no matter what the weather was like.

"Did you hear from the police, releasing you?" Stefanie asked, making a mental note to check the weather app.

"Not yet."

"Don't worry, these houses are sturdy, and when the police allow you to leave, the airlines will make sure your flight is changed," Stefanie told her. "Was Hunter back at the house for dinner yesterday?"

"I don't know. I didn't want to see him," Daphne said. "I went to a restaurant at the Dockyard by myself."

"So you don't know if Ingram was at the house either," Stefanie said, discouraged.

"No, I'm sorry."

"Until the bracelet is found, I want you to be careful. Don't go out by yourself anymore, and be aware of your surroundings, of the people around you and what they're doing," Stefanie advised. "Okay?"

"Okay," Daphne said.

Stefanie shifted her Moleskin notebook to get the yellow memo book beneath it, as well as a pen. "Can I get Ingram's number? And Hunter's?"

Daphne gave them to her, and she wrote both down.

"What was the restaurant you were at last night?" she asked.

"Did something happen?" Daphne asked, her voice a little higher again.

How much should she share? She didn't want to scare the girl, but knowledge was power.

"Carmichael House was broken into," Stefanie said.

Daphne was silent.

"He didn't do it. It wasn't Hunter," she finally said.

"If you know anything else about the theft or Beryl's murder, you need to tell us. It will keep you safer," Stefanie said.

"I will." Daphne ended the call.

Stefanie sat with her phone in one hand and the memo book in the other. Hunter met with Fabiola Monday night. What did that mean?

Chapter Twenty-Nine

A heavy knock on the door startled Stefanie out of her suspicions. She got up and let Thomas in.

"Hunter met with Fabiola Monday night," she said.

"Monday night," Thomas repeated, setting the bag of groceries on the kitchen counter. "Hunter met with Fabiola Monday night."

"Are they working together? Did they plan it all along?" Stefanie went to the window in the dining room and watched the grey rain sweep by.

She didn't want to believe Hunter and Fabiola had planned it out, that Hunter might have stolen the bracelet Tuesday, found out Beryl knew, then killed her.

"The idea is that Hunter blackmailed Jeffrey?" Thomas asked. He took a mandarin orange from the bag and peeled it.

The bright, sweet fragrance of the orange filled her nostrils. It grounded her, and she took a deep breath. "Hunter didn't need to actually have anything on Jeffrey. That note was vague, wasn't it?" she said. "Hunter might be wily enough to figure a vague note had a chance of getting Jeffrey out of the way. Give the same note to ten different people, they'd feel caught in ten different secrets."

"Everyone has something to hide," Thomas said.

She thought of the secrets she'd learned in her years at the bank, the little confidences in the privacy of the safety-deposit box vault. Confessions about family trouble when adding unexpected beneficiaries to CDs, or leaving errant spouses off.

"We have to look at whether Hunter and Fabiola planned this," she said.

190

"They knew the Spanish chest had been found."

"They're friends." Thomas found a bowl in one of the upper cabinets and poured the bag of tangerines into it. "Hunter knows Fabiola wants all Spanish artifacts from the treasure fleets. They could have made plans for any potential finds. If Hunter blackmailed Jeffrey and took the bracelet, where could he have hidden it?"

She'd gone through the art supplies in Hunter's backpack Wednesday. None of them were capable of storing the bracelet, and Tuesday, the backpack itself had been searched.

Hunter had two women on his side.

"He might have used Daphne," Stefanie said.

"After she caught him with another woman the night before?" Thomas asked. "I don't think that's likely."

But Stefanie wasn't so sure. Fabiola had given her inspiration for a way the bracelet could have gone undetected.

"What's your idea?" he asked.

"Almost too outlandish to mention," she said. She'd used a similar trick in Crete to search Thomas's room. When they'd searched each other Tuesday, would Beryl have thought to search Daphne's hair?

"Daphne didn't wear her hair up on Thursday," Stefanie said, "but maybe she did on Tuesday when the bracelet was stolen. Marlene can help there."

"Call her," he said.

Stefanie did. "Marlene, how are you today? I saw Lawrence earlier."

"You did?" Marlene asked.

"He was looking for Greg. He didn't realize Thomas and I had co-opted Greg's house," Stefanie said. "I have a question for you. On Tuesday, when you were talking to Daphne, did you notice, was she wearing her hair up in a ponytail? Do you remember?"

Marlene paused before answering. "I think her hair was down. Yes, she did wear it down on Tuesday. With a red headband," Marlene said. "Very pretty. Why?"

"A headband, not a folded scarf, like a rolled bandana?" Stefanie asked.

"It was a headband. Leather. She took it off and slid it back on while we

191

talked."

Darn.

Stefanie could hear the unasked question in the air.

She gave a little laugh. "It occurred to me that it would have been a way to get the bracelet off the property. Tucked into a ponytail, or rolled inside a bandana."

"I thought Beryl stole the bracelet," Marlene said.

Stefanie looked at Thomas. "We aren't so sure anymore."

After thanking Marlene, she ended the call.

"So Daphne didn't get the bracelet off the property, either on her own or for Hunter," Thomas said.

"I didn't think she was involved, but we needed to check, right?"

Stefanie still thought Daphne was vulnerable. On Tuesday, she'd been in the buttery, in front of the house with Nathaniel Dimon, then back in the overgrown garden by the excavations. In short, all over the yard when the bracelet was stolen. And all the while, she'd been wrapped up in making Hunter jealous, oblivious to what was going on around her. Most worrisome of all, she'd been at the buttery when Beryl was killed.

"I'm afraid that Daphne might be in just as much danger as Beryl was," Stefanie said.

Thomas nodded. "We need to corner Hunter."

"I got his number from Daphne." Stefanie entered the numbers Daphne had given her into her cell phone, then called Hunter.

He didn't answer.

"Call Fabiola," Thomas said. "We'll have better luck getting her to meet us than we will Hunter."

"Hurricane Lina is on the way," Stefanie said, consulting the weather app.

Thomas leaned forward to read the report. "It's not going to hit Bermuda until tomorrow morning. We'll be back at the house before the weather gets too bad," he said. "Safe and snug."

Reluctantly, Stefanie gave in.

Fabiola agreed to meet in Hamilton at Flanagan's Irish Pub on Front Street and promised to bring Hunter.

"If we're going to corner them into giving away the truth, we have to let them walk into a trap," Thomas said. "Hunter could have taken the bracelet Tuesday on his own, or Thursday from Beryl. First we'll pressure Hunter, and if that doesn't work, we go after Fabiola."

No one had seen Fabiola at Carmichael House Thursday morning, but they needed to compel Fabiola and Hunter into revealing if they'd been involved in the theft. Or the murder. Or at least to share what they'd seen.

The rain was heavier, blown at an angle by the wind. After parking across the street by the water, Stefanie and Thomas crossed at the light, then hurried to the Irish pub.

Inside the entryway, Stefanie hesitated, nervous about blowing it. Someone who'd killed once to hide a secret would kill again. She didn't want to be the reason Daphne came under added danger.

Thomas gently tucked a wind-blown strand of her hair behind her ear. "We can do this."

With a nervous smile, she followed him upstairs, where they were supposed to meet. Fabiola and Hunter were at a table in the back. Standing up, Hunter stared at them defiantly.

"So you told Hunter all about our Don Reynaldo de Cordoba?" Stefanie asked Fabiola.

"I knew about the *Santa Ana*," Hunter said. "I told you the Spanish Colonial era was my field of study."

The waitress brought four menus. It was eleven o'clock, but Stefanie's nerves were in no shape to tolerate lunch. She opted for coffee while the others ordered breakfast items.

"Is that what you were discussing Monday night when you met?" Thomas asked, pulling out a chair and making himself comfortable.

Fabiola and Hunter exchanged glances.

"Among other things," Fabiola admitted. "We knew the small sea chest had been found."

"An exciting find for everyone," Stefanie said when the waitress had gone. "But Hunter, you met Fabiola alone, instead of bringing Daphne and Ingram."

"Surely it was of interest to all of you," Thomas said.

"We're old friends. We hadn't seen each other in a while. I wanted to catch up."

She could see that. Fabiola was maternal toward Hunter. Older by about fifteen years, Fabiola was also attractive enough that if Daphne hadn't been close enough to hear their conversation, she would have reason to believe the relationship could be romantic.

"Catch up, or make plans?" Thomas asked.

"We didn't need to make any plans," Fabiola said. "We were both excited about what might be found. After all, anything that rightfully belongs to Spain will come back to us." She fixed Thomas with a confident stare.

Nearly as fanatical as a collector, Stefanie thought. Maybe sympathizing with Hunter would get further.

"I know how you felt when you found the bracelet," Stefanie said to him. "I feel the same about the medal. Like I'm part of its history now. That, in some way, it belongs to me, too."

Hunter nodded with understanding. "I felt that way, a little. But I didn't want to keep the bracelet. I'm not my father." He turned to the Spanish woman. "Tell them. Tell them what my goal is."

"She already did," Stefanie said. "She's been a good friend to you."

"The question is, have you been a good friend to her?" Thomas asked.

Hunter's reply was forestalled by the waitress returning with plates of pancakes, waffles, bacon, and eggs.

As the only one not eating, Stefanie continued the conversation.

"It occurred to us that someone might have wanted to take the bracelet from Beryl on Fabiola's behalf," she said, "seeing how determined she is that the bracelet be returned to Spain." Stefanie waited until Hunter looked up from his plate. "Did Beryl tell you she found the bracelet and was returning it?"

"No," Hunter said emphatically.

He wasn't going to admit to anything.

With eyes narrowed, Thomas turned to Fabiola. "Did Beryl tell *you* she had the bracelet and was returning it Thursday?"

Hunter's eyes widened, and as the implications dawned on him, he turned

194

to Fabiola with a look of dread.

Chapter Thirty

"Fabiola, yesterday you told us that if you'd met with Beryl Thursday morning, things might have been different," Stefanie said. "Maybe you did meet her at Carmichael House. Maybe you knew she was returning the bracelet to the Carmichaels, and you had to stop her."

Hunter gripped his fork, waiting for Fabiola to answer before he took a bite of waffle.

Reassuring him with a smile, Fabiola rested her hands on the table. "I have an alibi."

"Which is?" Thomas asked.

"Unimpeachable," Fabiola said, proceeding to cut into her pancake. "I was at early mass at St. Theresa's. We can go there after our meal and talk to the Padre if you don't believe me. It isn't far from here. He'll remember me. I talked to him after mass."

She had to agree. Fabiola's alibi was unimpeachable. Stefanie sipped her coffee while the others ate. Their interview wasn't going well. Hunter looked like a scared kid, but he wasn't admitting to seeing anything, much less to blackmailing Jeffrey. Maybe he hadn't. But maybe he had. Another push might be all it took for him to open up. Stefanie gave Thomas a sidelong glance.

Thomas took the lead. "We no longer believe the bracelet was at Carmichael House on Thursday. We don't even know if Beryl took it." He leveled his gaze on Hunter. "We only have your word the bracelet was missing when you went into the buttery Tuesday after lunch."

"It was missing," Hunter insisted.

He wasn't reacting when threatened himself, but he'd shown he had a weak point.

"Maybe Daphne took the bracelet," Stefanie said.

Hunter leaned across the table. "Daphne didn't take it. I thought Jeffrey saw Beryl take it?"

"Daphne was the last one with it, Hunter," Thomas said. "She tried it on. Jeffrey saw her, and so did Ingram. As far as we can tell, you were the next one who went into the buttery, and you claimed it was missing. That looks suspicious, don't you agree? Jeffrey thinks so."

Hunter scowled at his plate. "The bracelet was gone. I searched everywhere before I told Jeffrey about it."

Nothing in Hunter's reaction indicated that he'd left the blackmail note. They weren't going to break his story.

Holding her coffee cup in both hands, Fabiola asked, "Do you think if Hunter had given me the bracelet, I would still be in Bermuda? Hurricane Lina is going to hit tomorrow. I would have flown home."

Exactly what they'd thought themselves. Hunter had been their strongest suspect.

Disappointed that they still hadn't made progress, Stefanie said, "We think it's more likely that Beryl saw something she shouldn't have, and that's why she was killed. Hunter, you claimed you were in the back garden when Beryl died."

"I was," Hunter said. "Daphne and I had a fight. About my meeting Fabiola Monday night at the bar. I didn't tell her it was Fabiola, just an old friend. She didn't believe me. She thinks I took the bracelet. I just wanted to lose myself in that jungle and not have to talk to her again until it was time to get in the van."

His story meshed with what little they knew. Little by little, they were getting to the truth.

"Thank you for being honest," she said.

"There have been new incidents," Thomas said, having polished off his pancakes. "Break-ins at both Jeffrey's house and Carmichael House."

Hunter finished his cola and studied the remains of his waffle, trying very hard to look uninterested.

"When were these break-ins?" Fabiola asked with cool detachment.

Fixing his gaze on Hunter, Thomas said, "Jeffrey's house was broken into yesterday around lunchtime before the police arrived to search it. Carmichael House was targeted last night just before eight. That was more serious. Lawrence was hit with a vase. He has a concussion."

"He was—" Fabiola started.

Thomas held up his palm, stopping her. "I want Hunter to tell us where he was."

"Last night I had dinner with Fabiola," Hunter said. "Here in Hamilton."

"Which restaurant?" Stefanie asked.

"The Port O' Call," Hunter answered right away.

They knew from Thomas's tracker that Fabiola herself had been there.

"And Friday, around lunchtime?" Stefanie asked.

Playing with his fork, Hunter stared down at his plate. "I was walking around, thinking about the bracelet, and Beryl, and how my life was ruined."

"Ruined how?" Stefanie asked.

Hunter looked up. "By suspicion. And rumors. You know that. I won't get a job as an archaeologist when people learn what happened here. If the bracelet isn't found, I might as well change my major now. And Beryl's murder—if her murderer isn't arrested, what do you think people will say about us? All of us?"

Fabiola put her hand on Hunter's arm. "I think you can tell them the truth."

"I have," he said.

Looking at Stefanie, Fabiola raised her eyebrows.

Stefanie leaned forward on the table. "You're right. It's in everyone's best interest to find the emerald bracelet," she said. "The trouble is, if someone isn't being honest, we have to suspect they're guilty. That's the way the police will look at it."

With a sigh that was more protest than resignation, Hunter said, "I went to Jeffrey's house yesterday to look for the bracelet."

"How did you get in?" Thomas asked.

Hunter grinned. "You learn all kinds of ways to manipulate locks in the salvage world."

Thomas pursed his lips but didn't remark on that talent. "What did you find?"

"Nothing," Hunter said. "He lives a sad life. Has the smallest TV I've ever seen."

Fabiola appealed to Stefanie and Thomas. "So, you won't report that to the police, will you? He had a lot at stake. He didn't take anything. He was only looking for the one thing that could save his reputation. The thing we are all looking for."

She'd leave that for Thomas to decide.

"The police searched Jeffrey's house after you were there," Stefanie told Hunter. "If you left your fingerprints, they found them."

Visibly more relaxed, Hunter grinned again and shook his head. "I didn't."

Thomas raised his hand to catch the waitress's attention. "Looks like we're finished here."

Fabiola eyed Thomas, still waiting for him to give assurances.

"If Beryl's killer is identified," Thomas said, "and the bracelet found, I don't see why we'd have to bring up the break-in at Jeffrey's. As long as Hunter isn't involved in either of those crimes."

"I'm not," Hunter muttered. "Thanks."

"Thank you," Fabiola said.

Thomas paid the bill, then he and Stefanie walked out onto Front Street, into more rain and wind. They rushed down the sidewalk and across the street.

"Hunter's break-in shows that he wasn't the thief, and Fabiola has her unimpeachable alibi," she said once they were in the shelter of the microcar. "Two more cleared. Where do we go from here?"

"Back to the house, out of this weather," Thomas answered. "You said Lawrence came to the house this morning?"

In her alarm over learning that Hunter and Fabiola met on Monday, she'd forgotten to fill Thomas in on the details of Lawrence's visit.

"Looking for Greg. He was trying to come in without knocking. I thought it was you," she told him. "He scared me."

Thomas started the engine. "It's time we checked those numbers on Lawrence's phone."

Chapter Thirty-One

The wind had picked up, buffeting the Tazzari as they crossed the causeway to St. George's. Spray from the churning sea splashed over the guard rail with alarming regularity.

Though it was just past noon, clouds darkened the skies. At the house, Thomas walked around the living room, turning on lights.

Stefanie took a bottle of sparkling water from the refrigerator and poured them each a glass.

"No coffee?" Thomas asked, sitting at the dining table.

"After Lawrence's appearance here and our conversation with Hunter and Fabiola, I'm wound up enough." She watched the wind whip the trees in Jeffrey's yard. Greg didn't have any trees. Less trouble during the months he was back in the States, she guessed. "I don't know why Lawrence made me nervous," she said. "It wasn't as if he were holding a lockpick or credit card in his hand, trying to break in."

"It's because we don't know who is behind the crimes. We've eliminated Daphne, Nathaniel Dimon, Hunter, and Fabiola. Come help me research these numbers," Thomas said. "See if they give us any new leads."

She sat beside him and looked at the list on his phone.

"We're only interested in the ones since Monday," he said. "That's when the chest was found."

Greg's number was there, as she'd pointed out before. "This one is Greg's. It's to be expected, since they're friends." There were five calls between Lawrence and Greg.

Thomas growled low in his throat.

Stefanie waited until he looked up. "He wasn't at Carmichael House Tuesday, so he didn't blackmail Jeffrey."

"He's been here on Bermuda since Monday. And he collects the jewelry." She let it go, then studied the other numbers.

"This one is familiar," she said of another US number. "When Daphne called earlier, she gave me Hunter and Ingram's numbers." She took her phone from her purse and opened her contacts list.

Comparing the two phones, they found the answer.

"Ingram." Stefanie sat back. "Why would Ingram call Lawrence? Wouldn't his contact be Jeffrey, or the museum?"

Thomas studied the call log. "The call was made Tuesday afternoon. At one-fifteen."

"When the bracelet was stolen. Or after the bracelet was stolen." She drummed her fingertips on the oak table. "Why would Ingram call Lawrence when they were at the same house?"

"Following up on the blackmail note?" Thomas suggested. "The call wasn't picked up, and he didn't leave a voicemail." With his brows drawn together, he scanned the ten or so other numbers that registered on Lawrence's call list between Monday and Thursday night, when he'd cloned Lawrence's phone. "Only the one call."

"Check the other numbers," she said, trying to come up with a plausible reason for the professor to call a man he could just as easily talk to. She knew he hadn't texted photos of the find. Lawrence hadn't had any texts at all on his phone.

One by one, Thomas called each number except for those belonging to Ingram and Greg. He put the phone on speaker so Stefanie could hear as well. Most were local businesses. A financial advisor. A liquor store, and a yacht club that Lawrence was a member of. A local boat builder.

"All perfectly reasonable," Stefanie said. "To be expected, with Lawrence's interests."

"All except Ingram." Thomas looked at her. "That could have been me, if I hadn't changed careers. Professor of archaeology, working diligently, year after year, on one site or another."

He went to tap Ingram's number, but she stopped him with a hand on his wrist. "What are we going to say? Let's think this through before we accuse him."

He considered Ingram's motive. "Ingram could have called Lawrence out to the buttery to ask where the bracelet was."

"Or to tell him it was missing." That made sense. "Then maybe Lawrence came outside, and Ingram ended the call because he saw Lawrence and spoke to him in person."

Thomas nodded.

They didn't need to jump to conclusions. But what if they weren't?

"What if our instincts are right, and there is something fishy about this call?" she asked. "If Ingram stole the bracelet, why call Lawrence, the man he'd stolen from?"

"A good question. One answer is that Ingram is the blackmailer, and he was holding the bracelet for ransom."

She pictured it in her mind, Ingram writing out the note, dropping it into Jeffrey's car, then waiting for his moment to hit the buttery when Hunter and Daphne were safely in front with Nathaniel Dimon, and Beryl was sitting in the back in the shade of the trees, maybe out of sight.

"Why would he, though?" Stefanie asked. "Last night, we dismissed Ingram as a suspect because we didn't think he'd risk the shame and censure of his colleagues. Did he decide tenure wasn't enough after working for years at a job he's good at, as far as we can see? Maybe seeing Nathaniel Dimon's success pushed him over the edge to try cheating himself?"

"Perhaps."

She used their ultimate reason for eliminating anyone as a suspect. "He was searched."

Thomas raised his eyebrows.

"I know," she said. "The bracelet hasn't been found. We just haven't figured out how it was hidden."

"I don't want to believe it either." Thomas held up his phone. "We know Ingram called Lawrence. Let's find out what he has to say."

She pressed her lips together.

Thomas hit the number and put the phone on speaker.

"Hello?"

"Ingram, it's Burkhardt. Stefanie is here with me."

"I hope you are out of the rain. It's storming out there."

"We are," Stefanie leaned forward on her elbows so he could hear her. "We have a question for you. About Lawrence."

"Yeah. What about him? Think he did it?" In the background they heard utensils on metal pans.

"Why did you call him Tuesday?" she asked. "Was it about the bracelet?"

A lid dropped on the counter at the other end. "I didn't call Lawrence. Not on Tuesday, or any day."

No way would they tell Ingram how they knew he'd called. Thomas's cloning of Lawrence's phone surely violated at least one law, if not more.

"We know you did," Thomas said. "There was a call from this number to Lawrence's phone. On Tuesday, around the time Hunter discovered the bracelet was gone."

"Look, guys, I know you want to find the bracelet and maybe even who killed poor Beryl. Don't try to pin this on me. I didn't have anything to do with it, and I didn't call Lawrence. Ask him." The clatter of cooking utensils quieted as Ingram listened for their response.

"We know Hunter and Daphne didn't take the bracelet," Stefanie said quickly. "The police do, too." Or they would, as soon as she called the DI with what they'd learned that morning. She tried a different approach. "Were you at Carmichael House last night?"

"What? No, I was here. Watching TV."

"Stop playing around, Ingram," Thomas said. "Denying the call won't work. The police will see just as clearly as we can that you called Lawrence Carmichael on Tuesday. We want to eliminate you as a suspect."

If you didn't do anything wrong, Stefanie thought.

"What about Nathaniel Dimon? Weren't you checking on him?"

"His dishonesty these days appears to be restricted to fibbing on time commitments to his garden design clients," Thomas said. "He has an alibi."

"You're trying to railroad me because you want to clear Jeffrey. It won't work. Leave me out of it." Ingram clicked off.

With a solemn expression, Thomas turned his phone over on the table.

"Neither Daphne nor Hunter can verify that he was at home last night. They both went out," Stefanie said.

He ran a hand through his hair. "We should have searched his room when we searched Hunter's and Daphne's. I shouldn't have let my personal feelings guide me."

It wasn't like Thomas to take things personally.

Daphne and Hunter shared the same house as Ingram, and that had her worried.

"I'm going to call Hunter," she said. "Either there is a simple explanation for that call, or at least he and Daphne will be warned about Ingram. Call the DI and tell her what we've learned."

"Ja, I will."

When Thomas started mixing German in with his English, she knew things weighed heavily on his mind. While he made his call in the open living area, she walked to the front door to call. Hunter answered on the first ring.

"Hunter, are you at the house?" Stefanie asked, peering through the sidelights at a palm tree in Jeffrey's yard whose trunk swayed with the force of the wind. "Don't let Ingram know it's me on the phone."

"Yeah, we're sitting out the storm, Mom," Hunter said.

Smart, she thought. "Ingram called Lawrence shortly after the bracelet was stolen, at one-fifteen," she said. "He denied it when we asked him about it."

She heard footsteps, then a door closing.

"You think it's Ingram?" Hunter asked in a whisper.

"Were you with him when he made that call Tuesday? Maybe there's an innocent explanation," she said.

"I don't remember him calling anybody."

There had to be some reason there was a call from Ingram to Lawrence's phone.

"Maybe it was when you were all searched. Walk me through how that worked," she said.

"Jeffrey frisked me and Ingram, Ingram frisked Jeffrey, and Beryl and Daphne searched each other," Hunter told her. "The Carmichaels let Jeffrey and Beryl search themselves and the house. Jeffrey told us they opened their safe and all their drawers for him and Beryl to see in. Jeffrey insisted on it, and Mrs. Carmichael agreed."

"But you didn't see Ingram use his phone?" Stefanie asked.

"I can search his room," Hunter said.

"No, we don't want you to do anything dangerous," Stefanie said. "Just be on your toes. You and Daphne."

"Got it."

Stefanie hung up and returned to the living area. Thomas had finished his call as well.

"Hunter didn't see Ingram make the call," she said. "I asked him about when they were searched, and he didn't notice a call then, either. Another dead end."

"Not a dead end," Thomas said. "An unanswered question."

As if they needed any more of those.

"If Ingram had ransomed the bracelet to Lawrence, what would Lawrence do?" Thomas asked. "He'd pay and get the bracelet back."

"You know," she said to Thomas, "if Ingram ransomed the bracelet, he wouldn't have any need to search for it elsewhere."

"I know," he said with a scowl. "We got it wrong. Again."

"And now we've made Ingram mad at us." Stefanie walked to the picture window. "What does the weather app say?"

Consulting his cell phone, Thomas said, "Lina is still projected to hit Bermuda in the early morning tomorrow as a Cat 1."

So much for their week in the sun. "We aren't going anywhere in this storm," she said. "I'll fix rum swizzles. I'm sure the ingredients are all here."

She took her phone into the kitchen and looked up the rum swizzle recipe on the Riverboat Rum website. Light and dark rum. Check. Orange juice. No, but she did have tangerines she could squeeze. Pineapple juice. Check. Grenadine. Check. Angostura bitters. Check.

Finding all the bar tools she needed, she used her rusty barista skills and mixed the cocktails. When she was done, she brought both to the sofa and got comfortable.

"What did the formidable DI say?" she asked, handing Thomas his glass.

"She thanked me for giving her Fabiola and Hunter's alibis, and that was it." He sank onto the sofa and took a drink. "Not bad."

"What happened early in your career, that you wanted to believe Ingram and Jeffrey, against all of your police instincts?"

Before he could answer, Stefanie's phone rang. She held it out to Thomas. It was Hunter, calling back.

"Hello," she said, tapping the speaker icon.

"Hey, Mom," Hunter said.

What had been smart the first time was annoying the second. Stefanie made a face at Thomas. She was only thirty-five.

"I searched his room," Hunter said. "The bracelet isn't there. I was thorough. He doesn't have a lot of stuff, mostly books."

That was promising.

"But that's not all," Hunter said. "Thursday, when we came home from Carmichael House, Ingram had me check the mileage on the rental van because he plans to turn it in tomorrow. I checked just now, and it's only gone up by two miles. So he didn't break into Carmichael House last night."

Two miles was far too short for Ingram to have driven the length of Bermuda.

"Thanks, Hunter," she said. "Still be careful, though, and stay close to Daphne."

Thomas bent towards Stefanie's phone. "You might make a good archaeologist after all."

Hunter laughed.

At Stefanie's questioning smile, Thomas shrugged. "Digging for information. Archaeology and investigation go hand in hand."

"Does this mean I'm off the hook?" Hunter asked.

"Yes," Stefanie said. "Ingram probably started to call Lawrence, realized he didn't need to, and forgot all about it."

Thanking him, she ended the call.

She sipped her rum swizzle. "You were going to tell me about something early in your career."

Thomas stared into the amber liquid in his glass. "I was working the site of Stavrodromi in Greece. On Crete," he said with a smile for her.

She smiled back. Crete would always hold a special place in their hearts.

"I was at University, my last year. I had my plans made. I was going to be a great archaeologist. Up there with Evans and Carter." He laughed, but his self-deprecating smile faded. "Then an obnoxious man joined our team and artifacts were stolen. Suspicion fell on me."

She touched his arm in sympathy.

"That was it," he said. "I decided I wanted to be the one investigating, and not the one investigated. No, that's not the entire reason," he said with a genuine smile. "I wanted to stop the theft of artifacts. That is why I joined the police, and work with Interpol."

His reflective mood dissipated as quickly as it had come on, and once more, he was the confident and cocky man she knew. Only now she knew a little more.

"And now you are the head of your own Artifact Retrieval Team," she said, smiling into those grey-blue eyes. "With a perfect record."

"Almost," he reminded her.

She wasn't about to bring up the one that got away.

"We don't want Don Reynaldo's emerald bracelet to show up on Interpol's Most Wanted Works of Art Poster," she said again. The Interpol tool was where most of ART's cases were gleaned from.

Thomas angled his head to the side, searching her face. "That means not dismissing Greg as a suspect for the same reasons we shouldn't have dismissed Ingram."

She nodded.

"I want to know how avid Greg is to increase his collection of old mine emeralds," Thomas said.

She knew that look. Prey was in his sights.

Chapter Thirty-Two

"There were five calls between Lawrence and Greg," Thomas said. "Between the new discovery and Greg being a collector, it is a safe bet the topic was the emerald bracelet."

If Greg was the thief and killer, she hadn't seen it.

"How would Greg have gotten the bracelet in the first place?" Stefanie asked.

"He was at Carmichael House when Beryl was murdered," Thomas said.

"If Beryl was the blackmailer, and if she brought the bracelet back to Carmichael House Thursday to return it, Greg could have found the bracelet, maybe picked it up after she was hit," Stefanie admitted.

"That sounds a little farfetched," Thomas said. "It's more likely that if Beryl had the bracelet on her, the killer took it."

She couldn't believe Greg murdered Beryl just to add to his collection. He might have known Beryl the same way he did Fabiola, through being a museum trustee, but he wouldn't have known she'd have the bracelet on her.

Remembering Lawrence's red-faced agitation when she found him trying to get in that morning, doubt edged her certainty. She had to keep an open mind. Their investigation had gotten them nowhere, and she couldn't deny Greg's collection was a sound reason for him to have an interest.

"Lawrence might not think it's farfetched that Greg has the bracelet." She set her glass on the ottoman. "Lawrence didn't expect us to be here this morning. He didn't expect anyone to be here. Greg's Jag wasn't in the driveway, and neither was the Tazzari."

They looked at each other.

"The only time Greg was out of our sight last night was when he went into the bedroom," Thomas said.

It was so little to go on, but every other theory they'd had led up blind alleys.

"We're as desperate as Lawrence," she said. "Greg wouldn't have brought it here. Would he?"

"Wouldn't he?" Thomas asked. "Lawrence seemed to think he would."

And Lawrence knew Greg well, Stefanie thought. She stood up. "Where would he hide it?"

"He went in the bedroom for his shirts."

They rushed down the hall.

"Let's check both bedrooms," Stefanie said. They hadn't monitored Greg's movements.

Thomas nodded. "I'll take the master, you take the spare."

She was good with that. The master bedroom was more likely to have a safe or lockbox of some kind in it. Thomas had experience searching rooms. But she'd be thorough.

The guest room had a bed, a single nightstand, and a small desk in it. She searched the closet first, though. It was disappointingly easy to do. A quilted grey comforter lay folded on the closet shelf, and snorkel and tennis equipment were stored on the floor.

"Any luck?" she called.

"Not yet."

She quickly went through the desk and nightstand drawers, half expecting to find a Gideon bible in the nightstand drawer, the room was so void of personal items. Instead, she discovered a box of wooden matches and candle tapers. Hm. So, he did have candles. For power outages, she realized. Good to know if the storm got worse. Glancing at the rain-spattered window, she remembered the forecast and corrected herself. When the storm got worse.

Finished, she walked into the master bedroom. Thomas stood in front of the closet with a lockbox.

"It's locked," he said.

She grinned. "Allow me." Crossing to her suitcase, she took out the battery operated lockpick Thomas had given her. Finally, a chance to use it. She inserted the pick into the key slot and in seconds the box was open. A little giddy, she slipped the lockpick into her pocket, then sat on the bed.

"Let's see what he has in here."

Thomas sat on the other side of the box.

She lifted the lid. Old photographs were stacked inside. Family photos from the look of them. Her giddiness at her first time officially using the lockpick quickly dropped to guilt. She was prying into the private life of a friend.

She carefully removed the photos without going through them. A gold wedding band was at the bottom. The ring was loose, not in a ring box.

"Greg must have been married before. I didn't know," Stefanie said. Then she realized her mistake as Thomas picked up the only other item in the steel box, an older model watch.

"These are his parents' things," she said.

He laid the watch back in carefully. "There's nothing here for us."

She replaced the ring and photos, and with her lockpick, relocked the box. "I feel awful," she said.

"Don't," Thomas replied. "One of these people killed Beryl for the bracelet." He returned the steel box to the closet shelf.

"Greg got a towel to dry off with," Stefanie said. "Let's check the master bath."

She started at one side of the sink and Thomas the other, searching through the shelves beneath. Thomas pulled out cleaning supplies and personal care items.

Sitting on her hip, Stefanie removed and unfolded each towel, one at a time. She'd gone through six bath towels, as many hand towels, and then a short stack of washcloths that looked like they'd never been used.

"Nothing here," she said.

Thomas closed the lid of a plastic tub of hair pomade. "Nothing here, either. Kitchen next."

That would take the most time. Reluctantly, she stood up.

"Greg has his parents' dishes, too," she said, thinking of the stacks of dinnerware.

In the living area, Thomas stopped, hands on hips.

"There is a problem with our logic," he said. "If Greg 'found' the bracelet Thursday and chose this house, his home, to hide it where the police wouldn't search, he would have hidden it Thursday, when he came here to talk about Beryl's death."

She saw where he was going. "And if that was the case, last night if he did anything here, he would have picked up the bracelet from its hiding place." Stefanie rubbed her hands over her face. "We're overthinking this. Greg wouldn't stash the bracelet at Jeffrey's if he had it. The police are liable to search Jeffrey's house again at anytime."

"We need to step back," Thomas said. "To think clearly."

Greg was friendly with Marlene and Lawrence. And he was a collector. She knew well enough to what lengths collectors would go in order to snag a coveted item. Illegal collecting happened often enough that Thomas had his own team who worked full time combating that sort of artifact theft. And there were all the calls. Surely five calls were excessive for even a close male friendship.

"Greg knows more than he's telling. Five calls between him and Lawrence from Monday to Thursday?" she said. "Doesn't that seem excessive for two men? Unless they are planning something."

Thomas smiled. "Are you saying if those calls were between two women, there would be nothing unusual?"

She pressed her lips together. "You know I'm right."

"You are," he agreed. "I don't think Greg murdered Beryl. But he is a collector, and I didn't find a safe in the bedroom. He's connected to Marlene, Lawrence, Fabiola, and Hunter Renko. He might know something. Let's pressure him about his emerald collection. Maybe he'll give something away."

Rapid knocking on the door interrupted their conversation.

"He's back," Thomas said. "We won't have to go find him."

Stefanie went to the door and checked through the sidelight. Thomas was

212

right. Greg waited outside, a worried look on his face. She let him in.

"I want to walk you through hurricane prep," Greg said.

"I'll make a pot of coffee," Stefanie said, knowing Thomas would grill Greg as soon as he could. Coffee would get all of them through it.

"The house is sturdy," Thomas said.

"So is the roof," Greg replied. "Let's get these shutters closed." He started in the living area. Opening the windows, he battled the wind and pulled the wooden shutters from each side into the center, latched them, then closed the window.

"Wind's strong," Thomas said, tackling the window next to him.

"This is nothing. Wait until the hurricane hits." Greg moved to the single window in the kitchen.

He didn't look like he thought it was nothing. He looked like it weighed on his mind. Or something did.

"I've been through hurricanes before," Greg said, noticing her scrutiny. "It'll be okay, as long as you're prepared. Which you can be. Unlike our tornadoes in Missouri, hurricanes give plenty of notice."

That was true enough, Stefanie thought. They'd been warned it was coming for days.

"The worst that will happen here is the power going out or a few trees going down," Greg said.

The men went from room to room until the house was snug.

When they returned to the kitchen, enough coffee had brewed for three cups. Stefanie lifted the pot, making sure the automatic cutoff engaged. She poured, then handed them each a cup.

"Candles are in all the nightstand drawers, in the kitchen drawer by the stove, and in the drawer of the buffet in the corner here," Greg said. He sat at the table. "How is the search going? Find it yet?"

For a moment, Stefanie stared, and then she sat down. He couldn't possibly know they'd searched his house.

"We've answered some questions, but come up with more," she said.

"One is," Thomas said, "what were you doing yesterday with Fabiola Ortiz?"

"I told you I know her from being a trustee on the museum board," Greg answered with a wary smile.

"That is what you said. Why did she ask you to help Hunter Renko?"

Greg shrugged. "Fabiola must think I can help put the kid in touch with a lawyer."

"He isn't a kid. He's twenty years old. Renko," Thomas emphasized. "I think you know his father."

Light dawned in Greg's eyes. "Ah. Richard Renko's son. Yes, if Hunter needs help, I'll make sure he gets it." He lifted his chin. "Does he need help? Does it look like he did it? That he has the bracelet?"

Should they tell him or not? Despite Greg being a collector and on scene at Beryl's death, they had no evidence he was involved. Thomas gave her a nod.

"Hunter has been cleared in the theft and murder," she said. She wasn't about to reveal that he was the one who'd gone through Greg's suitcase at Jeffrey's house. "Besides, I'm sure if Hunter had stolen the bracelet, he would have given it to Fabiola. She's still here, not on a plane to Madrid."

Thomas had taken a seat at the end of the table. He casually put his phone on his lap. After a quick check of the tracker, he said, "Fabiola is still at her hotel in Hamilton. As far as we know."

"Jeffrey didn't have it either," Greg said. "The police left his house in a mess after they searched it. I've been straightening up since yesterday."

"Doing their job," Thomas said.

"They could be neater about it."

A muscle flexed in Thomas's jaw, but he didn't comment.

Thomas taking exception to Greg's comments wouldn't help them.

"Thomas," she said, "I want to work on my blog later, and I'm having a little trouble with my laptop. Would you mind looking at it for me?"

His chair scraped back as he got up.

"Be back in a sec," she said to Greg.

In the bedroom, she closed the door, unsure how Thomas would take what she had to propose.

She clasped her hands. "I can get more out of him than you can."

It was the exact argument he'd made in Venice, and she hadn't liked it. Not one bit. And she'd made sure he knew how much she didn't like it. But now, she saw the advantages of working a suspect with a little individual attention. She searched his eyes, afraid of seeing anger, or even worse, hurt in them.

She needn't have worried. They glittered and narrowed the slightest bit. He remembered that moment in Venice, as well.

"I know," she said. "I see it now."

A slow smile lit his face.

Her muscles relaxed in relief. He wasn't mad.

Still smiling, he said, "You are right. Put the screws to him."

Thomas not only wasn't angry, he was enjoying her embarrassment at the situation. Fine. Let him have his fun. One point to him.

"I will stay here and fix your computer." He sat at the desk and took out his phone.

With a last sidelong glance at him, Stefanie left the room, leaving the door open.

She went straight to the kitchen for another cup of coffee. Between the closed shutters and rain pounding against them, it felt more like a gloomy winter afternoon than mid-September.

"Another cup?" she asked Greg, holding up the pot.

"No thanks," he said. "So, what is the story about you and Thomas?"

"I'm sure he told you enough about us. I want to hear about your old mine emeralds." Should she bat her eyes at him? No, he was aware enough to know she didn't mean it. "I never knew you collected old jewelry."

He stretched his legs out and clasped his hands behind his head. "Just the necklace and pair of earrings. A little later than Don Reynaldo's bracelet."

"Any chance I could see them? I have a few pieces of vintage jewelry," she said hurriedly, so he wouldn't think she was asking because he'd joked about giving them to her.

He smiled. "We'd have to go back to St. Louis for that. I keep them in my safe deposit box at Markham-Briggs."

The bank where she'd been working when they met. Well, she hadn't been up for VP of customer service for nothing.

Going into the kitchen, she pulled another glass out of the cabinet. The ones she and Thomas had used earlier were still on the counter.

"I made rum swizzles today for the first time," she said. "Using your Riverboat Rum recipe. The one on the website."

Greg joined her in the kitchen. "Glad to hear that. How did you like it?"

"Delicious. You can get the pineapple juice out of the fridge, if you will. It's five o'clock somewhere."

After getting the bottle out, he leaned against the counter and crossed his arms while he surveyed her technique.

"Where did you get your Spanish pieces from?" she asked, measuring the rum and dividing it between the three glasses. "They aren't something that shows up in the local antique shop."

"Thomas will want to hear this," Greg said.

She finished adding the other ingredients, then picked up Thomas's glass and went to the hall. "Thomas, I've got another rum swizzle for you."

"Payment for my computer services?" Thomas asked as he left the bedroom.

"You'll want to know this as well, I suspect," Greg said. "I did purchase the Spanish Colonial jewelry that I have from Richard Renko. It was a few years ago, all above board. Thought I'd come clean with all the interest now and Hunter being involved."

"Have you?" Thomas asked with a steady gaze at Greg. "Come clean?"

"I don't have the bracelet, if that's what you're suggesting," Greg said. "I could hardly benefit from owning stolen property. Couldn't sell it at auction."

Thomas nodded and took a drink.

Another dead end, Stefanie thought.

"Greg, you told us your mother was from Bermuda," she said. Being nice to him about his family eased her guilt at sifting through his personal things. "Those lovely dishes must have belonged to your parents."

Greg flashed her a flirtatious smile. "You know, it's easy to get married in Bermuda. Cash is all you need."

Thomas studied the concoction in his hand. "She only needs her passport and birth certificate to get married in Germany."

Greg winked at Stefanie, then took a healthy drink.

Shaking her head, she headed for the sofa and her writing supplies. They were going to be fine.

"I have a travel blog to write, so I'll leave you gentlemen to figure out where the Spanish bracelet is."

"We may never find it," Greg said. "Like Tucker's Cross. Do you know that story?"

"Yes," both Stefanie and Thomas answered at once.

After picking up her laptop and notebooks from the leather ottoman where she'd left them that morning, Stefanie went back to the guest room. Working on the blog was exactly what she needed to clear her mind.

She settled in at the desk and turned on her computer, then flipped through the Moleskine notebook. Finding her place, she got back to the blog: snorkeling in Tobacco Bay, the wind and seas dictating so much of everyday life.

Where had she added the details about the moat garden? Remembering that she'd filled the Moleskine notebook, she picked up the yellow memo book and flipped through it, musing on whether she'd added notes to it since her Moleskine was full.

A gap between two pages near the back stopped her. Had she written on a random page? That wasn't like her. But her mind had been wrapped up in a tangle of theft and murder since the day she'd arrived in Bermuda.

She opened the memo book at the gap. She hadn't written on a random page. Instead, there was a slim remnant of paper near the spine where a page had been torn out. Marking the page with her finger, she held the book in her lap. The memo book had been new when Jeffrey got it from the stack in the buttery. She'd barely opened it. She hadn't torn a page out.

Opening the memo book again, she studied the telltale strip. She hadn't torn a page out, but someone had.

Chapter Thirty-Three

The realization hit Stefanie with almost physical force. She drew in a deep breath, staring at the small yellow notebook in her hands. The source of the blackmail note. The theft of the emerald bracelet had been planned from the very beginning.

The blackmailer was someone with ready access to the buttery where the spare memo books were stashed. But not one of the archaeologists, who each had their own notebooks and wouldn't have needed to use one from the buttery. Someone who wanted to frame the dig team for blackmail and theft.

The Carmichaels. One of them could have torn out the incriminating sheet of paper at any time they were alone in the buttery after the bracelet had been found. Once they'd dropped the blackmail note into Jeffrey's car, all they had to do was wait for the remaining archaeologists to be occupied, then walk out the kitchen door. When the coast was clear, slip into the buttery and take the bracelet.

Eagerly, Stefanie stood up and held the open pages under the light of the overhead fixture, looking for the indentations that would prove her right. She angled the book back and forth, but try as she might, she couldn't see any letters pressed into the paper. The righthand page was as smooth as could be. That made sense. Tear the page out quickly, without being seen, then write the note in private.

Fingerprints. The rush of excitement gave way to alarm. She dropped the notebook on the bed. How could she be so careless?

Before she did anything else, DI Franklin-Ross needed to know.

Stefanie picked up her phone and called the detective inspector's number.

How many sheets were torn out of Beryl's memo book? The police would be able to tell. Beryl had written the name of the cruise boat for her on one page and torn it out. She'd bet anything that only one sheet was missing from Beryl's notebook.

The phone call went to voicemail.

Damn.

"I've discovered something," Stefanie said after the voicemail prompt. "It wasn't one of the archaeological team who wrote the blackmail note. I have the notebook it came out of. The Carmichaels are trying to frame Beryl."

Hanging up, she walked down the hall. The men were at the table, deep in conversation.

Thomas saw her and looked up. "What is it?"

"Come here a minute," she said.

He got up while Greg stayed at the table, looking curious.

"Greg, do you have any plastic bags, like sandwich bags or something for leftovers?"

He glanced toward the kitchen. "Sorry, no. Will anything else do?"

"That's alright. I'll just grab a paper towel. My necklace broke, and I want to keep the pieces together," she said. She tore one off the roll and returned to the bedroom with Thomas.

As soon as they entered, she closed the door.

"I know where the blackmail note came from." She pointed to the yellow Rite in the Rain memo book on the bed. "Someone tore a sheet out of that one."

"Jeffrey burned the note, but there might be fingerprints on it," Thomas said.

Stefanie handed him the paper towel. As Thomas wrapped the notebook, she filled him in on her theory.

"It's got to be one of the Carmichaels. Marlene or Lawrence." She watched him put the package in his leather duffle beneath a stack of folded pressed shirts, wardrobe items that he always traveled with, from what she had seen. "I've called the DI. Do we tell Greg?" she asked. "He could have worked with them."

Thomas nodded. "We can't bring up the blackmail note," he said. "The police held it back, and anyone with the foresight to take the note from the archaeologists' supplies is intelligent enough to use anything he's given."

Thomas zipped and locked his bag while Stefanie returned to the living room.

"We know it was someone at Carmichael House that stole the bracelet," Stefanie said.

Greg sipped his cocktail. "Of course, that's where the bracelet was found."

"That's not what she means," Thomas said, following her and picking up his glass, which held the last vestiges of rum.

Greg raised his head in an expectant nod.

"It was Marlene or Lawrence," she said.

Thomas rubbed a finger along his upper lip. "We don't know why they would, but it's one of them."

"Greg," Stefanie said, "you've been pretty close to the Carmichaels since you've been in Bermuda this week."

"I have. I did go see Marlene about that favor," Greg said cautiously. "And, of course, I wanted to see what they found."

"What was the favor?" Thomas asked.

"Still suspect I'm involved?" Greg asked. "All right, I'll tell you. I wanted a concession from Marlene on taxes, and threatened to move my headquarters if she didn't concede. I was offered a sweet deal by the state of Missouri, and I wanted her to match it. She made a few calls and took care of it. Riverboat Rum HQ will stay here."

Greg had more than that going on with the Carmichaels.

"Then why did Lawrence come by this morning?" she asked.

Greg paled beneath his golden tan. "He did?"

"He said he was looking for you," she said. "I thought he was trying to come in without knocking. I thought he was trying to get in."

He set his glass down. "He didn't bother you, did he?"

"To be honest, he frightened me." No question, Greg was upset. It was the right moment to put pressure on. "Did he want the bracelet back?" she asked.

Swiping a hand over his forehead, Greg said, "There is no reason for him to think I have it."

"Did Marlene promise you the emerald bracelet if you kept your headquarters here in Bermuda? Is that why you came here last night?" Thomas asked. "Did you hide the bracelet here, in your house, while we're staying here? Putting Stefanie in danger?"

Greg shook his head. "I would never do that," he said earnestly. "I don't have the bracelet, and Lawrence knows that."

"How would he know?" Stefanie lifted her rum swizzle for emphasis. If Greg wanted them to believe him, he'd have to share more than that.

Greg looked at her, then at Thomas. "I was at Carmichael House Thursday because Lawrence asked me to come. He wanted me to buy in with him on a prototype for the America's Cup."

"Did you?" she asked.

"No," Greg said. "I'd already loaned him a tidy sum for his previous buy-in. I told him if he wanted me to invest more money in his plans, I wanted collateral."

Stefanie blinked, not wanting to voice, even to herself, what Greg's admission meant.

Chapter Thirty-Four

"Y̲ou wanted collateral." Stefanie's hands went cold suddenly, and she rubbed them together, trying to warm them. Trying to keep the ugly truth at bay. "The emerald bracelet."

Thomas's jaw tightened as the realization struck him as well.

Greg looked stricken. "Lawrence didn't come here to search for the Spanish bracelet. He came here to give it to me."

Stefanie closed her eyes. Beryl had been killed so Lawrence could fund a prototype for the America's Cup race.

"Why didn't you report him?" Thomas demanded.

"He insisted the bracelet had been stolen." Shaking his head, Greg held his hands out, palms up. "I didn't have any reason to doubt that. Not until he showed up here today."

Stefanie felt his anguish. Greg, with no intention of harm, had been the unwitting catalyst for unintended consequences. Tragic consequences.

"But why did Beryl have to die?" she asked. "Did she hear you and Lawrence discussing the bracelet Thursday?"

"I didn't notice," Greg said. "But we were in his office, and the window was open. Lawrence told me about the bracelet on Tuesday. He called again Wednesday, asking for another loan and promising he could pay."

The phone call she'd heard when she stood outside Lawrence's den.

"You didn't see Beryl outside the window when you talked to him Thursday," Thomas asked.

"We had our conversation at his bookshelves. No, I didn't see Beryl walk by. Or anyone else," he said before they could double-check his story again.

"When you were negotiating with Marlene, where were you?" Stefanie asked.

"In the kitchen. It was over tea." Anticipating why she asked, he said, "Didn't see anything outside then, either. My back was to the side window. As I told DI Franklin-Ross."

"If Lawrence stole the bracelet," Thomas said, "who broke into Carmichael House last night? You?"

Greg had been rain-soaked the night before, far wetter than they'd gotten.

He didn't quail beneath Thomas's thunderous gaze. "I had dinner in Hamilton and didn't get a close parking spot." He started to go on, then changed his mind.

"With Fabiola," Thomas guessed.

Greg lifted his empty glass in salute. "I won't ask how you know that. I can see you both have a knack for finding out things."

Thomas gave a quick smile, which just as quickly flattened. "Which restaurant?"

"Port O' Call," Greg said. "Great place. The two of you would like it."

"What were you discussing?" Thomas asked.

Greg's confidence had returned. Stretching his legs out, he hooked an elbow over the back of his chair. "She made me an offer. A very generous offer."

"For Don Reynaldo's bracelet?" Stefanie asked.

He shook his head. "No. For the Spanish jewelry that I already own."

"The Spanish government wouldn't have a lot of money to pay for them," Thomas said.

"She knows individuals who are willing to pay big bucks to have the items returned to Spain," Greg said. "It was a very generous offer," he added.

What would be the commission for an exchange like that?

Greg hadn't broken into Carmichael House, and neither had Hunter or Ingram. Someone else had.

The crime had been well thought out. Lawrence had taken steps to ensure he wouldn't get caught and that blame would fall elsewhere.

"That gash on Lawrence's forehead," Stefanie said. "He didn't have the gauze over it this morning when he came by. It was superficial, not a deep cut." She looked at the men. "He could have done it himself. He could have staged the break-in and somehow inflicted that injury on himself to throw off suspicion."

She had their full attention.

"Marlene said it happened right as they entered the house," she reminded them, "before they'd turned the lights on. With the clouds and rain, it was darker than normal, and they'd be rushing to get in the door. Marlene said as soon as the door opened, she was shoved into the hall stand. What if it was Lawrence who shoved her?"

"It happened just before we got there, and we didn't see anyone running away," Thomas mused.

"What about Hunter Renko or Dr. Ingram?" Greg asked.

"We know it wasn't Ingram or any of the university team that broke in," Thomas said. "Hunter checked the mileage on the van, and only two miles were added between Thursday afternoon when he checked and this morning when he talked to Stefanie."

Greg nodded. "I buy that. You don't take the bus, ferry or a ride share if you're going to break into a house."

Stefanie pictured the scenario in her mind. "The Carmichaels are at the front door," she said. "As they step inside, Marlene is blindsided by being shoved against furniture in the dark hall, and Lawrence yells as he falls to the ground, supposedly hit. Taken by surprise like that, it would be natural for Marlene to assume a third party shoved her to the side rather than her husband."

"The glass in the kitchen door was broken," Greg said. "And the broken vase—we saw that for ourselves."

"Lawrence could have grabbed the vase as he entered. It was on the table right beside the front door," she said.

Thomas crossed his arms over his chest. "Nothing was taken. The police didn't give the break-in much attention other than promising to drive past more often."

Something else about the break-in nagged at the back of her mind, but

Stefanie couldn't quite grasp it.

"I see what you're getting at," Greg said. "But why? Why would he pretend that his own property was stolen?"

"So he wouldn't have to share it," Stefanie said. "So that he could sell it to you."

Grimacing, Greg nodded.

"But what about Ingram's call to Lawrence? How do we explain that?" she asked.

"When did he call?" Greg asked.

"Tuesday afternoon, about the time the bracelet was stolen," Thomas said.

Hopefully Greg wouldn't ask how they learned of the call.

"Maybe Ingram saw something that he dismissed from his mind," Greg said. "I've ended more than one call as soon as I dialed. Maybe he just doesn't remember making it."

"The bracelet is at Carmichael House," Thomas said. He turned to Greg. "You can get it from Lawrence, and we can turn it into the police and end this right now."

"We have to try DI Franklin-Ross again," Stefanie told him.

"I'll do it." Thomas went back to the bedroom to make the call.

Stefanie picked up glasses and cups and set them on the counter near the sink. "Lawrence didn't have to take it this far," she lamented.

"It all comes down to money," Greg said.

"Don't they have enough?" She thought of their beautiful house, the big-name designer Marlene had brought in. Those took money.

"No one ever has enough," Greg replied. "Lawrence has sunk a small fortune into different race models."

Stefanie looked up at that, then at Thomas, who had returned from making his call.

"I don't think their financial situation is all that solid," she said. Both Nathaniel Dimon and Marlene had avoided mentioning that the designer showed up on Tuesday to get paid. Surely that wasn't just a matter of polite societal norms.

"Lawrence might have sunk their entire fortune into his hobby," Thomas said.

"It's more than a hobby," Greg agreed. "It's a bit of an obsession. Ever since he retired, Lawrence has been on a quest to recapture his glory days."

"That bracelet won't go for your collateral or be sold to anyone else if Marlene has a say in it," Stefanie said. "She wants to donate it to the museum and enjoy a little glory herself."

"With the bracelet believed to be stolen," Thomas said, "Marlene doesn't have a say."

Fear tightened Stefanie's chest. There'd already been one murder at Carmichael House. Marlene hadn't been pleased with Lawrence's fixation on building a better boat. Or at least not on financing it.

Thomas's eyes had darkened, and she knew he was worried about the same thing.

"Lawrence killed Beryl and faked one break-in to cover the theft," Stefanie said. "He can fake another."

"One in which Marlene will meet a tragic end," Greg said.

"The garden makeover would be canceled if Marlene was out of the way, and the sale of the bracelet would be back on," Thomas said. "If not to you, Greg, then Lawrence would find another buyer."

She was still trying to put all the pieces together to make everything fit neatly. Not everything did.

"Fabiola," she said. "Why did she go to Carmichael House looking for Beryl Thursday afternoon?"

"Because Beryl knew where the bracelet was," Thomas said.

Finally, she saw how events had played out. "Beryl wasn't scheduled to be there in the afternoon. Beryl knew that, and the office at NMB did as well. So, who did Fabiola call?"

"Lawrence," Thomas said. "She was there to meet him."

Stefanie nodded. "Fabiola needed to cover her visit because the police were there." The Spanish woman knew more about the theft than she had shared. It didn't surprise her, not really. "We don't know to what lengths Fabiola will go to get that bracelet."

She gave Thomas a meaningful look.

He consulted his phone. "Fabiola has left the center of Hamilton. Heading toward St. George's. Let's get to Carmichael House. Now."

"I'll drive," Greg said, flicking a glance at Thomas's cell phone. "This wind will blow your little kiddie car off the road."

Grabbing the house key and her yellow gauze scarf for her shoulders, Stefanie locked up. Outside, the wind blew so strongly, they leaned into it to keep from being blown over on their short dash through the rain to Greg's Jaguar.

A huge gust flung the passenger door wide as she opened it. Thomas was at her back, sheltering her in as he held the door. He slammed it, then got in front with Greg.

Stefanie settled into the soft cream leather. Lawrence would be tricky. Any man that could fake his own accident had an eye out for opportunity. Marlene, on the other hand, was a practical woman. When faced with a problem, she took steps to right it. Lawrence was a dreamer. One who hoped for things to improve, rather than searched for solutions. Unless something fell into his lap. The emerald bracelet had been too much to resist.

She hated loose ends. Almost as much as Thomas hated coincidences.

"Why didn't Lawrence give you the bracelet Thursday morning?" Stefanie asked Greg.

"He said it had been stolen, but I wondered if he was angling for a bigger loan. I was prepared to wait him out. It's a game that I'm very good at."

"Hope you're not waiting for Stefanie," Thomas said.

"I don't see a ring on her finger," Greg shot back, grinning at her.

"Play your little games," she said, glad that Greg was joking. Then she considered. What some thought of as games, others saw as problems.

Stefanie leaned forward, between the front seats. "She didn't call him. We have to get to the Carmichaels' before someone gets hurt."

The words Marlene spoke that first time Stefanie was in the house came back to her. Lawrence was on the phone. *I'm good for it,* he'd said. And Marlene's harsh response. *What are you good for, Lawrence?* The Carmichaels were in financial trouble. Deep financial trouble. And Marlene already knew it. From her tone, she'd been aware of it for some time. As always, Marlene had quietly taken care of the problem.

Chapter Thirty-Five

Thomas turned in his seat to meet Stefanie's gaze. "Marlene," he said.

"Marlene," she agreed.

"Once we get there, we check on Marlene, make sure she's okay," Greg said as he drove through the dark streets. "We keep Lawrence in our sights."

"Fabiola didn't call Lawrence," Stefanie said. "She called Marlene."

"It isn't Marlene who's in danger, it's Lawrence," Thomas said.

"We were wrong," Stefanie said. "I figured out what bothered me about the break-in. The vase was on the table to the right of the front door. There is no way Lawrence could have grabbed it and then pushed Marlene into the same table without it being obvious."

Thomas's eyes shone with pride as he looked at her. "But Marlene could snatch the vase, immediately hit Lawrence with it, and throw herself against the table with no one the wiser."

"I see," Greg said in a low voice.

"These crimes took planning and forethought," Stefanie said. Without mentioning the blackmail note that had been planted, she couldn't go into as much detail as she'd like. "You know Marlene and Lawrence better than we do. Which one sounds like the more meticulous planner to you?"

"Marlene," he said. "But why would she?"

"Beryl told us Marlene came from humble beginnings, so I can see that she would value a priceless historical donation to the National Museum of Bermuda. But Lawrence. He wanted to fund the chance at a fleeting trophy. One that would change hands before long."

"Not so fleeting," Greg said. "Bermuda is sailing country. People here eat, sleep, and drink sailing. And remember, Lawrence is a retired boatbuilder. If he had a part in an America's Cup win, his name would be remembered forever by the people that matter most to him."

"And that's why we need to get to Carmichael House as quickly as possible," Stefanie said. "He wants that bracelet as badly as she does, and Marlene has already killed once to keep it. But at least, the police should get there shortly after we do."

"That might be a problem." Greg glanced at Thomas. "Check the Bermuda weather website. They might have already closed the causeway."

"Is the storm that bad already?" Stefanie asked, peering out the window. Between the grey clouds so dark that afternoon looked like night and the constant rain, she couldn't see much more than the green of tree branches and palm fronds being pummeled by the rain. The white stone roofs of the houses were the only bright spots in the gloom.

Thomas checked on his phone. "The causeway is closed," he said. "High seas due to the storm. DI Franklin-Ross isn't going to make it to Carmichael House."

Stefanie leaned forward between the seats again. "Surely there are police closer than Hamilton."

"I don't know," Greg said.

"She'll send someone else," Stefanie said. "She won't leave it until tomorrow. The hurricane is supposed to hit then."

"Knowing that Marlene is guilty isn't enough," Thomas said. "She's set up others to take the blame. First Beryl, then Jeffrey, and now Lawrence."

"She's made plenty of accusations against Hunter and Ingram, as well. When a powerful woman speaks, people listen," Stefanie said.

"Her word will carry weight." Greg frowned as he drove. "I'm sorry I put you in a situation that involved you in this."

She expected a sharp comment from Thomas agreeing to that, but he didn't have a comeback.

"We'll need to trap Marlene into giving herself away," Thomas said. "Even catching her with the bracelet might not be enough, since she can shift suspicion on to Lawrence, who she's set up nicely."

"So nicely I fell for it," Greg said, angling around a huge swath of water that covered most of the roadway.

On the side of the narrow road, rivers of water gushed past. Stefanie shifted in her seat and felt a weight in the pocket of her trousers. Her lockpick was still in her pocket from the morning's search. It might come in handy.

"We'll need Marlene to believe that we think Lawrence is the one with the bracelet, that he killed Beryl, and get her to let her guard down and give something away," Stefanie said. "I have my lockpick with me. If I get half a chance, I can check in his desk drawer and get caught. She'll believe we think he's the guilty one."

Thomas looked expectantly at Greg. "Someone will have to keep an eye on Lawrence in case Marlene has plans for him. Will Lawrence be willing to conduct a deal with you, if we're in the next room?"

"I think he will," Greg said. "He's pretty single-minded."

"You'll have to be smooth," Thomas said. "Not let him know we suspect."

Greg grinned. "I think I'm smooth enough."

Stefanie rolled her eyes when Thomas grumbled under his breath.

Pulling her scarf more tightly around her shoulders, she considered their options. "We need a ruse to explain why we're there."

A flash of lightning lit up the sky, showing that they were almost to Carmichael House. She prayed that they weren't too late, that Lawrence hadn't met with a fatal accident.

"Hunter Renko," Greg suggested. "Lawrence made a big deal out of suspecting him. We can use that in our favor."

Before she realized it, Greg turned into the drive at Carmichael House. No neon yellow and blue police car was inside the iron gate. They were on their own.

The rain hadn't slackened off. It was still pouring down in sheets, and the wind had become so strong that it thrashed branches of the rubber tree and bent palm trees along the fence.

"I'll call Marlene and get her to open the gate," Greg said. "With us there, she won't do anything."

He tried her number, but Marlene's phone went to voice mail.

"We've got to get in," Stefanie said, feeling her adrenaline kick in. Were they too late?

"I've got it." Thomas hopped out of the car, ran to the gate post, and took a device out of his jacket pocket.

Nothing happened.

"He's a different kind of college professor, isn't he?" Greg said over his shoulder to her. "He tries, I'll give him that."

He did more than try, Stefanie thought, picturing the gold Akrotiri Snake Goddess and the bejeweled Borgia Peacock.

Thomas hunched over the gate. Two seconds passed, then the gate slid to the right, wobbling with the force of the wind. He dashed to the front door as Greg drove in. As soon as Greg stopped, Stefanie hopped out and joined Thomas, who banged on the front door with his fist.

She rang the doorbell.

Lawrence opened the door. He looked them over, in shocked surprise. "What in God's name are you doing out in a storm like this?"

"Can we get out of it? We're soaking wet." Thomas shouldered his way in with a genial smile, forcing Lawrence to step back.

"We heard Hunter Renko had stopped by on his way to the airport," Stefanie said.

With a puzzled frown, Lawrence peered out at the open driveway gate. He pushed the remote at the front door, closing it.

Greg swiftly joined them, then Lawrence closed the door.

"Hunter Renko isn't here," Lawrence said. "What made you think that?"

"Ingram told us he wanted to study the gold *reales* one last time," Thomas said. "We know how you feel about him. Weren't sure if you needed help. If you know what I mean."

Lawrence wore the same windbreaker he'd had on that morning.

"You aren't going out, are you?" she asked.

"Loose shutter," Lawrence said. "Need to get it fixed before Lina comes to call."

"Not in this weather," Thomas said.

Stefanie raked her damp hair back. "Is Marlene here? I think she'd probably like us to dry off before we get these gorgeous wooden floors of yours covered with rain."

"Marlene," Lawrence called in the general direction of the bedrooms.

His wife came out of a room at the back carrying a light jacket and gardening gloves. "This is a surprise," Marlene said.

"The wind has picked up," Greg said. "Let the shutter go."

"Yes, you're probably right." Going into the kitchen, Marlene set the gloves on the small kitchen table and folded the jacket over the back of a chair.

"I think we need towels," Stefanie said. It was certainly true of her. Her trousers were wet, and her shoulders were, too. Her scarf had been a little help, but it was damp from the rain.

Marlene went to the bathroom near the kitchen and returned with three folded towels, which she handed out.

"They thought Hunter Renko stopped by," Lawrence said.

His wife glanced toward the front door, then at her visitors, who were toweling off. She accepted the men's towels, but Stefanie took longer.

"He isn't here," Marlene said, draping the towels gracefully over her arm.

"Come on in and have a seat," Lawrence said, heading into the living room.

"Do you mind if I stop in the powder room and comb my hair?" Stefanie asked.

"Of course," Marlene said. "I'll fix tea."

Removing her gauze scarf, Stefanie hung it over the towel bar to dry. She took a moment to finger comb her hair, then quietly opened the bathroom door. She heard the tap running as Marlene filled the tea kettle, and then the tinkle of silverware. Tiptoeing down the short hall, she glimpsed the men in the living room.

Taking her chance, she slipped into Lawrence's den.

The Carmichaels had fastened their shutters against the storm, and the room was dark. With only the light from the living room and kitchen to filter through doorways, Stefanie crept around the desk and took out her lockpick.

She inserted the pick into the lock, then turned it on. The hum of the tiny motor sounded like a swarm of bees. Shielding the sound with her hand, she turned it off after only a second, then pulled open the center desk drawer and peered at its contents. The folded flannel that Lawrence stored the Spanish coins in wasn't there. She quietly tugged the drawer out further. No bracelet, and nothing that looked capable of holding it.

Disappointed, Stefanie realized she'd hoped the bracelet would be there. Marlene might have worked to set up Lawrence to the end, but no, Fabiola was on the way. Marlene would have the bracelet close at hand in order to take advantage of the least opportunity. Still, it had been a thought.

A slight rustle in the hall made her look up.

Marlene stood in the doorway, holding a tray of China cups. Bracing the tray against her ribs with one hand, she turned on the den light with the other.

"What exactly are you doing in here?" Marlene demanded.

Chapter Thirty-Six

Stefanie slipped her lockpick into her pocket, then pushed the desk drawer closed while she straightened up.

Two angry red spots shone on Marlene's cheeks. "Into the living room." She gestured in that direction with the tray.

When Marlene backed out of the doorway so Stefanie could precede her, the Minister's lips pressed together in barely suppressed anger.

First step of the trap accomplished. But they weren't there yet. Marlene had to either confess or get caught in a lie before the police arrived, or Lawrence would surely go to jail.

Stefanie crossed the short hall.

A shutter banged rhythmically against the outer wall as she entered the living room.

"Don't mind that," Lawrence said. "That's the dining room shutter we needed to fix. Too late to take care of it now. You three might want to think about going home before the storm gets worse. Lina has picked up speed. Going to hit sooner than we thought."

Thomas rose from the sofa when he saw Marlene behind Stefanie. Stefanie shook her head, making sure Marlene noticed. With any luck, Marlene would interpret that as a message that Stefanie hoped to find the bracelet in Lawrence's desk.

"I caught her in your office, Lawrence," Marlene said, plonking the tray on an antique sideboard with a rattle of cups on saucers. "Going through your desk."

"That's outrageous." Lawrence rose to his feet.

Thomas moved nearer Stefanie, blocking Marlene's path to the front door when he did.

"What did you think you'd find?" Lawrence demanded.

"No reason to not bring everything out in the open now," Thomas said. "We're here because the bracelet is here." He stared down Lawrence.

"Don't be ridiculous, man," Lawrence said.

Greg stood up then, and took a stance in front of the French doors, which were shuttered against the storm, like the windows. There wouldn't be a quick escape that way. "You offered it to me. That was before I ever knew it had been stolen."

Unpleasant surprise registered on Lawrence's face. "I was certain we'd get it back," he said indignantly.

"There is only one reason you could know that," Thomas said, with a glance at Marlene.

"Lawrence?" Marlene asked.

"The police," he said. "They're looking into it."

"And they'll find it," Marlene said. "They've got a good woman on the case. Better than the two officers who handled our break-in last night. It's insulting that you are accusing us."

"About that break-in," Thomas said. "Nothing was stolen?"

"No, we interrupted him," Lawrence said. "You know that—you got here right after."

"Maybe so," Thomas said, as if he understood the point. "Marlene, what did he look like, the man who shoved you when you came in the door?"

The tea kettle whistled from the kitchen. "I didn't get a good look," she said. "Did you? I asked you to look for him."

Stefanie followed Marlene and waited in the doorway while the Minister poured boiling water into a sunny yellow teapot. Nothing indicated that Marlene was ready to bolt, although her purse sat on the counter near the refrigerator. Stefanie hadn't noticed if it had been in that spot Wednesday, which would have told her if that was its customary location.

Marlene ignored her, passing her without a look when she carried the teapot into the living room and set it on a granite trivet on the sideboard.

Thomas was still questioning Lawrence. "Can you identify the person? I won't say he. Maybe the burglar was female."

Lawrence touched the small gash on his forehead. "I didn't see anyone at all. We walked in, Marlene was pushed, and I was hit on the head. It was dark, raining out, and it was over in two seconds," he said irritably.

"You didn't follow him," Greg said.

Marlene's cold manner thawed a little. "It was raining so hard, I just looked out the door, then went to help Lawrence. Stefanie and Thomas arrived right after that. And then you did. It must have been someone who heard about the discoveries on the news."

Thomas shook his head. "The break-in was staged."

Marlene lifted her hand toward Lawrence. "He's been hit. He's wounded. He might have a concussion, the paramedic said."

"Really?" Stefanie said. "Look closely. It's barely a scratch. He could have done it to himself."

"All it takes is a little preparation," Thomas said. "Before you leave for dinner, open a drawer or two, break a small window, then be ready to make a move at the front door when you return."

"I've had enough of this," Marlene said. "It's time for you to leave."

"Not until we get the bracelet," Thomas said. "The police are on their way."

Marlene looked sharply at him.

"I telephoned DI Franklin-Ross," he continued. "She was very interested in what we had to say and will be here any minute."

With any luck, the Carmichaels were too flustered to consider the causeway.

"Well, Stefanie didn't find the bracelet in Lawrence's desk, did she?" Marlene asked. "I'm glad the police are coming. It saves me from calling them on you."

"We haven't got the bracelet," Lawrence insisted.

"Not we, Lawrence, you," Greg said. "Stefanie told me you came to the house looking for me today."

Lawrence gaped in surprise, and Marlene listened avidly. But was she buying it?

"I...I thought you might have it. You were here the morning Beryl died."

Greg fixed him with a steady gaze. "You were bringing the bracelet to me."

"Did you also offer it to Ingram?" Thomas asked. "Did he know that you took it? Is that why he called you Tuesday, right after the bracelet was stolen?"

"Ingram didn't call me," Lawrence said.

"He did," Stefanie said.

"It's easy enough to prove that Dr. Ingram didn't call," Marlene said self-righteously. "Lawrence, show them your phone." She picked up the teapot to pour, then waited for him.

Lawrence swore under his breath and took out his phone. With hard jabs, he brought up his call list and swiped through the calls angrily. Then the list scrolled too far, and he had to bring it back to Tuesday's calls.

"See," he said, "I don't have Ingram's number." He blinked at the list. "There's one here I don't know, but it was a hang up. I don't know who it was. Didn't leave a message."

Marlene poured out five cups of tea slowly, carefully. "Help yourselves to tea if you want," she said.

She set the pot back on the trivet, stirred sugar into a cup, then brought it to Lawrence. As she handed the cup to him, she looked into his eyes.

"It's nothing," he said. "I don't know who called. You remember how crazy it was here when we discovered the bracelet was lost."

Marlene went back to the sideboard and spooned sugar into another cup. She took a sip. "Our bracelet wasn't lost, Lawrence, it was stolen."

She had bought it. Time to pounce.

Stefanie did while she added milk and sugar to her tea. The teacups had an elegant bird design painted on them. She turned over the saucer. Wedgewood, Kutani Crane.

"Did you offer the bracelet to Fabiola as well?" Stefanie asked Lawrence. "Fabiola made an offer to Greg for his old mine emeralds. Very generous, you said, Greg?"

"Very generous," he confirmed, picking up a cup for himself.

"No, I didn't," Lawrence said.

Marlene sipped her tea, watching him.

"Fabiola came here Thursday afternoon," Stefanie went on. "She told us and the police that she was here to talk to Beryl. I thought it strange that she would want to talk to Jeffrey's assistant about the emerald bracelet and not Jeffrey himself."

"He was the head of the museum archaeological team, after all," Thomas said. "The senior member at the site."

"Beryl was bad news," Marlene said. "She's the one who stole the bracelet. The police told us Jeffrey saw her."

"Bad news for someone," Thomas said. "She saw or heard something about the theft."

Marlene and Lawrence looked at each other. A fine sheen of sweat broke out on Lawrence's forehead.

Watching the unspoken tension passing between the couple, Stefanie said, "What I wonder most about Fabiola's visit is why she came by Thursday afternoon."

"What do you mean?" Lawrence asked. "What does the time matter?"

"Wednesday night, Beryl knew she'd be done with the site here before noon. All they had left to do was fill in the holes, clean up, and gather the rest of their supplies. The office at NMB would know that as well. Fabiola didn't come here to talk to Beryl. She came here to talk to you about the Spanish bracelet."

In the silence after her accusation, wind whined through the crevices of the doors and windows, and pelting rain beat a rhythmic tattoo against the wooden shutters. A crash on the patio startled them all.

"Our ladder to fix the shutter," Lawrence said.

Marlene's plan for Lawrence, Stefanie wondered? An accidental fall from the ladder onto the stone patio?

"We aren't talking about just a theft," Thomas said. "We're talking about murder."

Marlene set her cup down. "Why would you want to sell the bracelet to Greg, Lawrence?"

"You've always been very generous with a loan," Lawrence said to Greg. "I just needed a little more to get in on that new design."

Marlene's cheeks grew red.

"That new experimental hull," Lawrence said, in case anyone had missed his meaning.

Stefanie could see the Minister's chest rising and falling with the deep breaths she was taking, but Marlene didn't reply to her husband's admission. She hadn't said anything they could use against her.

"You couldn't have gotten the money out of savings, your retirement?" Thomas asked.

Lawrence gave his wife an apologetic look. "That was gone long ago. It would have killed Marlene if she knew."

"Beryl had a way of finding out everything," Marlene said.

"She knew you came from humble beginnings and that appearances were important to you," Stefanie said.

Marlene nodded. "She had to share it too. Jeffrey knows how she is. Tell me, Lawrence. Did you kill her? Did Beryl hear you promising the bracelet to Greg, after we'd spent two days searching for it, hoping and praying the thief would have a change of heart and return it?"

Stefanie smiled at the elegant crane on her China teacup. Prey snared.

Chapter Thirty-Seven

"I didn't kill Beryl," Lawrence said in answer to his wife's accusation. His voice was full of anguish. "Marlene, how could you think that? I'm calling the police. We'll go over all this with them. Tell them everything."

Stefanie locked eyes with Marlene. Knowledge shown out of Marlene's gaze. But Stefanie was savvy enough to realize the Minister wouldn't go down without a fight. Her nimble moves in pulling off the crimes were proof of that.

"How does Jeffrey know that Beryl was willing to share his secrets?" Stefanie asked. "What does Beryl know about Jeffrey?"

"I didn't mean anything by it," Marlene said lightly. "In general. He worked with the woman." Her casual tone was belied by the flinty cast of her eyes.

"Beryl knew his professional mistake, and she kept his secret," Stefanie said. "What he didn't know was that you knew it, also."

"Knew what?" Marlene poured herself another cup of tea. There was very little left in the pot, and she ended up with a few drops.

"About his mistake in losing artifacts from an old cottage when new construction went in," Thomas said.

Marlene's lips curled in a derisive smile, as if she were forced to listen for politeness' sake.

"You gave me the clues yourself," Stefanie said. "When you recommended I take a look inside the buttery, you said, 'We save historical elements when we can.' That told me historical places were an interest of yours. When I asked if you knew Greg, who is the CEO of Riverboat Rum, you said if it made money in Bermuda, you knew about it. New construction of any kind makes money. You might not have held your current position with the government at the time of Jeffrey's mistake, but you're ambitious and thorough, so it stood to reason that you would have been in a position fifteen years ago to know of the site and could have checked it out."

Lawrence put his hand on the back of his chair. "Marlene wouldn't hide our bracelet. She would never harm Beryl. Or..." His voice trailed off as his hand went to the cut on his forehead.

"She would," Thomas said. "She took the bracelet and killed Beryl to keep the theft from coming to light."

"Marlene knows how important investing in the new design is to me."

Lawrence was unwilling to believe Marlene would hurt him, or Beryl, or that she would thwart his plans to invest in the next AC catamaran.

He held onto the chair as if it were a rock in a tumultuous sea.

"What about that call Ingram made to Lawrence?" Marlene asked.

"When did you do it?" Thomas asked her. "When Ingram was being searched by Jeffrey? I will guess that Ingram left his phone in the canvas duffle bag that holds his tools, and you took the opportunity to throw suspicion on Ingram and your husband."

Frowning, Lawrence gave Marlene a bewildered stare.

"Lawrence faked the break-in," Marlene insisted. "You said so yourself."

"That was you," Thomas said. He turned and pointed through the doorway, where the table at the front door was just visible. "He was hit with a vase that was on that table. You grabbed the vase when he opened the door, hit him with it, then fell against the table."

Lawrence's eyes bulged at that revelation.

"I didn't," Marlene protested.

"It would be far too awkward for Lawrence to grab the vase off the table and then shove you into it," Thomas said.

"I sat in the car and waited for you," Lawrence said. "Before we went to dinner last night. You said you'd forgotten your wallet in the house." His mouth worked, as if he were searching for more words.

"Give us the bracelet, Marlene, and we'll leave you alone," Thomas said.

They would, but the police wouldn't, Stefanie thought. With Fabiola on the way, the bracelet had to be close by. In Marlene's purse or jacket. In fact, Fabiola should be near as well, if she'd made it across before the causeway closed.

An enormous crack of thunder shook the house.

Stefanie just had a moment to see the look of absolute defiance on Marlene's face before the lights went out.

"*Scheisse*," Thomas muttered.

In the blinding darkness, before her eyes adjusted, Stefanie heard footsteps running across the wooden floor. Marlene was escaping, and they didn't have the bracelet.

Stefanie aimed for the hall, struggling to get her phone, with its flashlight, out of her purse as she ran. Thomas was ahead of her. He turned his on and followed Marlene into the kitchen. Grabbing her purse, Marlene ran out the side door.

Chapter Thirty-Eight

"She's going for her car," Thomas said. "The front is closer. Come on."

She and Thomas ran out the front door with Greg right behind.

Incredibly, Marlene had already made it to the gate. Stefanie blinked back the rain, searching for a sign of Fabiola's vehicle, any vehicle.

"With the power off, she can't open the gate," Thomas shouted over the rain.

But Marlene disengaged the manual latch and pulled the gate open by hand, then slipped through.

Was she hoping to find Fabiola? Stefanie ran after Thomas and Greg to the gate.

A large branch from the majestic rubber tree had broken off. One end stuck through the iron bars of the gate, preventing the gate from opening wide enough to let a car through. Marlene battled the lashing rain as she tried to move it, but the force she'd used to open the gate had wedged the branch firmly in place.

There was no way Marlene could drive anywhere in the storm, she just hadn't realized it yet. The wind whipped her hair straight back as she hunched over. A single trash can bounced along the street, carried from who knew how far away. Marlene seemed oblivious to the danger.

Thomas grabbed her by the arm.

Marlene tried to shake him off. "I've got to move this. I have to meet Fabiola." She turned her head and saw Stefanie and Greg. "It was Lawrence," she shouted. "He stole the bracelet. He blackmailed Jeffrey."

They had it. Marlene's last desperate play to frame her husband gave them

244

the proof they needed.

"It wasn't Lawrence," Stefanie said. "We know it was you." She pulled at Marlene's other arm, but the Minister fought her off.

"I have to see Fabiola."

Thomas grabbed Marlene around the waist. "Fabiola isn't coming."

Marlene finally stopped struggling. "I called her before you came."

Stefanie wanted to believe that Fabiola would have turned Marlene in after she got her hands on the Spanish bracelet.

"She isn't coming," Thomas repeated. "They closed the causeway. She turned around."

Palm trees thrashed with each gust of wind.

Marlene jerked her arm. "You can't know that."

Thomas's grip on Marlene's arm slipped with the lashing rain. He adjusted it.

"It's over, Marlene," Greg said.

A jagged spear of lightning illuminated the frustration and anger on Marlene's face.

"Let me go," she cried. "Let me go." With a furious wrench, she pulled free from both Stefanie and Thomas and ran across the road.

They ran after her, heads down against a wind so strong it forced them backwards. The grass verge on the side of the road was slick with the rain and mud.

At the top of the cliff, Marlene peered down the road in one direction, then the other, but there was no car coming. Fabiola wasn't waiting to pick her up. Marlene looked down the hill toward the harbor, as if considering her chances with that route. It was just enough time.

Thomas leapt at her before she could run again, and Stefanie grabbed her from the other side, stepping carefully to avoid a misstep that could send her tumbling down the hillside.

Stefanie gulped, trying to catch her breath. Struggling on the wet grass and mud, Marlene sank to her knees.

"Where is the bracelet?" Thomas asked, hauling Marlene to her feet by the back of her blouse.

"Oh, what's the use." Her features sagging with defeat, Marlene held out her muddied handbag.

Thomas indicated for Greg to get it, keeping one hand firmly around Marlene's upper arm. Stefanie held tight to the other.

Another flash of lightning lit up the sky. The thunder that followed rolled across the heavens, vibrating through Stefanie's lungs. She helped Thomas hustle Marlene across the road and into the safety of the house. Greg closed and locked the front door behind them.

In the entry hall, Lawrence took in their sorry state, dripping and covered with a good deal of mud. "Kitchen," he said.

"You and your schemes. You left me nothing," Marlene said to him. "Nothing to pay taxes with. Nothing to pay our credit cards with. Which you have maxed out."

Her husband didn't reply. He went to the living room and returned with several candles, which he lit. He'd already set up two bright flashlights on the kitchen counters.

Thomas deposited Marlene in a wooden chair. Stefanie went to the small bathroom and picked up the gauze scarf she'd hung on the towel bar to dry. She gave it to Thomas, and he tied Marlene to the chair with her arms pinned to her sides, then took the handbag from Greg.

Finding the towels they'd dried off with when they arrived, Stefanie passed them out. She wiped the rain from Marlene's face before she dried her own. Thomas grudgingly took one swipe with the towel down his face and wiped the mud and water from his hands. Then he opened Marlene's purse.

While Thomas rummaged, Greg went into the living room and returned with a fine cashmere throw, which he awkwardly draped around Marlene.

Meticulously, Thomas removed the contents of the purse one by one and set them on the counter. Wallet. Keys. Folded papers.

Stefanie waited impatiently but didn't hurry him. He was enjoying the moment.

He took out an assortment of makeup tubes and compacts next. Then a hard sided sunglass case. Thomas considered it, then rummaged around in the purse again. Satisfied that he'd checked all possible hiding places,

Thomas picked up the sunglass case, then looked at Stefanie.

She nodded.

He lifted the lid, removed a white cotton handkerchief, then smiled.

Stefanie went to his side. There it was, stretched out as if it were on display in a jewelry store. Nine large rectangular emeralds on their links of gold. For all it had been through, the bracelet looked in fine condition. The emeralds would benefit from a more thorough cleaning, but their green color was rich, deep, and vibrant, even with a slight haze of dirt still on them. Fine remnants of soil stuck in the gold filigree that the team hadn't removed with their initial cleaning, but a whisper-soft toothbrush and mild solution would take care of that.

Lawrence came to stand in front of them. "May I see it? Our emerald bracelet?"

Thomas turned the case around, but held onto it.

After gazing at the bracelet for a long minute, Lawrence released an enormous sigh and stepped back.

Leaving the bracelet in the sunglass case, Thomas held it out for Greg.

"Where did you hide it?" Lawrence asked quietly. "You didn't put it in the safe. The police looked everywhere."

Stefanie whipped her towel around her shoulders and hugged it close. Towels. She sought out and spied a roll of white paper towels beneath the upper cabinet closest to the sink.

They'd wrapped the memo book in a paper towel. Greg had wiped up spilled rum, then tossed the paper towel in the wastebasket.

"You threw it away," Stefanie said. "Wrapped in a paper towel?"

Marlene darted a sharp glance at her. "You *are* clever. Yes."

The roaring outside quieted, and the rattling of the shutters stopped, but only for a moment before it started again.

"The bracelet couldn't have stayed there long," Thomas said.

Marlene tried to shift within the scarf's tight grip. "After the team had gone, I rescued it and put it in our car. Where Lawrence wouldn't think to look." She looked at her husband with chilling venom. "He'd already poured our savings into one failed boat design after another. I wasn't going to let him squander this as well."

"And when the police searched?" Stefanie asked.

"Wednesday afternoon, when you archaeologists left for the day, I went into Hamilton to the office to take care of some business I couldn't finish at home. You didn't mind, did you, Lawrence? You were on the phone again, promising someone they'd get a return on their money."

"Wednesday afternoon?" Greg asked. "Me again."

"I brought it home yesterday," Marlene said.

Thomas set his phone on the counter. She suspected it was set to record. "What happened to Beryl?" he asked.

Lawrence stepped forward. "Don't say anything, Marlene. I'll call Kirkpatrick as soon as cell service is back on."

Marlene looked at Thomas's phone. She knew he was recording, and still ignored Lawrence's warning. "When I picked up the bracelet, I realized no one had seen me. I waited, and slipped back into the kitchen."

"That's not all," Thomas said.

Marlene returned his stare.

"I was given the Rite in the Rain notebook that you tore a page from," Stefanie said. "The page you used to blackmail Jeffrey."

"Ah." Marlene raised her eyebrows in acknowledgment. She shook her head, trying to get her sodden hair out of her eyes.

"What about Beryl?" Thomas asked again.

Marlene wouldn't meet their eyes. "I didn't think I'd been seen, and she didn't say anything Tuesday. I caught her looking at me Wednesday. I thought at first it was because the two of you joined the team, and she wanted me to insist that you leave. None of us wanted you here." Marlene raised her head to meet their eyes.

"How did you lure her to the far side of the house, where no one could see you?" Thomas asked.

"She kept watching me. Every time our paths crossed, Beryl had her eyes on me. I knew she must have seen me. Leaving the buttery before Hunter went in, I suppose. Or maybe when I dropped the note in Jeffrey's car. I don't know. I didn't have to lure her. From the kitchen window, I saw Beryl leave the buttery. I wanted to be prepared. I left by the kitchen door, and I knew she saw me go out. I knew she'd come talk to me. I was in the side garden, waiting when she took the side path. I joined her, and said, *'I've seen you watching me, did you have something to ask?'* And before she could answer, I hit her, as hard as I could, then went back inside the kitchen."

By the end of her admission, Marlene's face had grown haggard, her mouth drawn, all vitality gone.

"It was Fabiola's story about Don Reynaldo de Cordoba that led me to you," Stefanie said. "The letter in the archives said that two men survived when the *Santa Ana* went down. That Don Reynaldo died from injuries from the shipwreck. But Don Reynaldo lived long enough to bury his valuables. Why do that if there are only two of you on a deserted island, watching for rescue? Why? Because he didn't trust Alfonso Nunez, his ship master and fellow survivor."

"Perhaps someone else broke into the house like you claim," Thomas said. "Perhaps not."

Stefanie crossed her arms. "It's the survivor who tells the story."

Over the howl of the wind and the pelting rain, a forceful knock pounded on the front door.

"The police," Stefanie said with relief.

She noticed then how bedraggled Thomas looked with his hair slicked back, soaked to the skin, mud on his cheek that he'd missed. She knew she looked just as bad. Her hair hung in ropes and her wide beach trousers had soaked up so much water they threatened to fall down.

Thomas smiled at her, a sad, but triumphant smile, then went to the front door.

Chapter Thirty-Nine

Hurricane Lina arrived Saturday night at eight-thirteen p.m., several hours after the police had taken Marlene into custody. Given the weather conditions, witness statements to the arresting officers were brief. As she'd told Stefanie over the phone from Hamilton, DI Franklin-Ross knew how to contact them when she needed them.

Stefanie and Thomas sheltered at Greg's house, mercifully alone. Greg had gone to Jeffrey's place as soon as he dropped them off.

The power was still out, and was expected to remain out until the following day. Without running water, Stefanie cleaned up as best she could using makeup remover wipes. Thankfully she'd brought a large pack, enough that Thomas had used them as well. At least they were clean after wrestling with Marlene in the storm.

In the dark bathroom, by the light of a single candle, she changed into dry clothes. With no way to recharge her phone, she wasn't going to waste battery power on the flashlight. She chose a sleeveless sundress in sage green that she hadn't yet had a chance to wear. With the air conditioning out, the house was warm.

Her hair was still wet, though. Stefanie combed it out in front of the bathroom mirror, then swept it back in a French braid to keep it out of her way. Smiling, she added a touch of cologne to her wrists, then left the bathroom carrying the candle. As she walked down the hall, soft light from the living room beckoned her.

She stopped at the end of the hall.

The room was aglow with the flickering flames of candles. One stood on the end table, two on the buffet in the corner, another on the television credenza, centered in front of the TV screen, which reflected its light, and one on the kitchen counter. Their flickering flames created an ambiance of romance in the darkness.

Thomas walked out of the shadows in the kitchen, offering her a glass of pinot grigio.

She took it, and he picked up his bottle of beer from the counter.

"Cheers," he said.

"Cheers."

They clinked, drank, then, by mutual accord, went to the couch, where she cuddled close against his ribs.

Outside, the wind battered the house, screaming to get through crevices at doors and windows and rattling the shutters.

"It's only a Category 1," Thomas said.

"That's what, seventy-five mile-an-hour winds?" she asked.

"At least seventy-four," he said, tightening his arm around her. "Stone walls, stone roof, we'll be fine."

She was fine, and so was he. More than fine. Their legs were entwined, stretched out on the leather ottoman. She rested her head on his shoulder and breathed in his clean, familiar scent. Freshly laundered shirt and hops. A scent she wanted to enjoy every single day.

She looked into his eyes. It was almost the end of their vacation.

Thomas set his beer on the end table. He took her glass from her and set that down, too. Then he shifted toward her and held her hands in his.

"Stefanie," he said.

"Yes?" Her heart pounded in her chest.

"Come with me."

"To Munich?"

The corner of his mouth lifted in a hint of a smile, and his eyes glittered in the candlelight. "And whereve René sends us."

Had she expected a more life-changing question? Hoped for that proposal?

The wind howled outside, rattling the shutters with a vehemence that threatened to tear them from the walls. Inside, it was serene and calm, a sanctuary in flickering candlelight.

Stefanie threaded her fingers through his.

"I'll go anywhere you want," she said. "Anywhere you go."

He brought their joined hands to his lips and kissed her knuckle. His gaze held her captive.

Her breath caught in her throat while she waited for him to speak.

"When I give you jewels," he said, "they won't be old mine emeralds."

Stefanie pressed her lips together in a little smile. One point to Thomas.

Acknowledgements

Thank you Verena, Shawn, Deb and the rest of crew at Level Best Books for all you've done to help bring this book into the world. I'm so glad to be on this journey with you.

Bermuda is a fascinating place with a fascinating history, and I hope to go back again soon. My heartfelt thanks go to Dr. Deborah Atwood and Zoe Brady of the National Museum of Bermuda for their enthusiastic help and guidance on archaeology in Bermuda. Any mistakes are wholly mine, not theirs.

Thanks also to Gail, Mary, Melissa, Gina, Heidi, Sally, Jim, Jim, John, and all the others in the Kansas City Archaeological Society, as well as Virginia Wulfkuhle, who have generously shared their knowledge with me on KCAS or Project Archaeology projects.

Thanks also to William and Kathleen Monnin, Pat and Jane Alley, Angi Blue, and Linda Moore for their help, and to the entire Happy Hour crew for their support.

As always, I'm eternally grateful for the love and support of my husband Bob, and the rest of my family: daughters Alie, Heidi and Joy and their husbands Kyle, Brandon and Shawn, my brothers Ernest and Scott and their wives Kristin and Sara, grandkids Katelyn, Kimber, Kennedy and Quinn, and nieces and nephews Cathy, Rosie, Xander and Max. Thank you so very much!

About the Author

M. A. Monnin is the Agatha Award-nominated author of the Intrepid Traveler Mystery series and numerous short stories.

Like her heroine, Stefanie Adams, Mary loves the adventure of foreign travel. If there's the chance to check out an archaeological site, so much the better for this avocational archaeologist and trustee of the Kansas City Archaeological Society. An Air Force veteran, Mary is a member of Mystery Writers of America, International Thriller Writers, Sisters in Crime, and the Short Mystery Fiction Society. She lives in Kansas City, Missouri, with her husband, Bob, and Siberian huskies.

SOCIAL MEDIA HANDLES:
  FB: MA Monnin
  TwiX: @mamonnin1
  IG: m.a.monnin

AUTHOR WEBSITE:
  https://www.mamonnin.com

Also by M. A. Monnin

Death In the Aegean

Death On the Grand Canal

SHORT STORIES: Mary writes the St. Killian, PI and the Hawk Hathaway, Time Traveling Troubleshooter short stories, as well as standalones. Her short stories have appeared in *Black Cat Mystery Magazine, Black Cat Weekly,* and numerous anthologies.

9 781685 126483